The Future Brokers

DN Knox and Colin Payn

To Pat, Eddie and those we love...

ONE - *George*

Oblivion was slow to relinquish its grasp.

But eventually, the waves of agony broke through the blackness, dragging me back to consciousness. The movement of air across my cheek and the whirr of drone blades told me I was not alone.

"Hello. My name is Saul and I am a doctor. Are you able to speak?" the drone's voice lacked emotion but its efficient tones were reassuring.

"Yes." I could barely push the sound through my swollen lips. "... Can't see... my arm hurts... Help me!"

"First, I need to confirm your details. You are George Williams, date of birth, tenth of August 2020?"

I grunted.

"Thank you, George. Now, I need you to stay awake. Can you do that for me... George? George?"

I grunted again to show him I'd try, although I wasn't sure it was something that was within my power, as I hovered between consciousness and blackout.

"Try not to move, I want to get my camera closer to look at your injuries. A rescue team is on its way and a Stretcher Drone will get you to hospital once they've made you more comfortable."

Blood trickled into my throat making me choke and the pain pushed me back into the blackness.

Time after time this scene plays in my head, it's now a year since my gentle hill walking trip in Scotland. Gentle, that is, until the mist came down and I lost my footing, tumbling downhill on grass and heather— until I hit the boulders. I don't know how long I was unconscious, but my

5

emergency bleeper did its job, detecting my sudden gyro changes and alerting Mountain Rescue to my exact position.

I remember regaining consciousness and for a second, wondering if I'd imagined the drone. Perhaps I really was alone. Incapacitated and miles from civilisation. But Saul must have detected my distress; he was calm and reassuring, telling me he was about to administer a sedative. After a while, the pain receded slightly and I thanked the universe that bots could arrive at accident sites so much faster than humans. The hospital would be aware of my injuries prior to my arrival, hopefully giving me a better chance of recovery—or at least minimising the damage. Hitting rocks was one thing, but cart-wheeling over them with my arm caught in a crevice was screamingly sick-making and I probably fainted from the pain. It felt like my shoulder had been wrenched from my body. And I didn't need to touch my face to know it was massively swollen. I held on to the hope that my lack of vision was because my eyelids had puffed up and were of golf ball proportions but the suspicion that I'd actually damaged my eyes permanently wouldn't go away.

Time became meaningless as I drifted in and out of consciousness.

Saul chattered as he worked—sometimes telling me what he was doing or, relaying information back to the Mountain Rescue base. I knew he was trying to prevent me from sliding back into a stupor and I grunted where appropriate to show I was still with him.

"Much longer?" It was hard to get the words out but I was beginning to wonder how soon the sedative would wear off. I wanted to ask whether I'd regain my sight, whether my arm could be fixed, whether I'd ever be pain-free...

Drops of rain began to fall, and I started to shiver as the breeze picked up.

"Help is coming," said Saul.

At first, all I could hear was the wind whistling through the crevices in the rocks around us, and the rain which was now hammering on the boulders, but eventually I picked out the rhythmic thuds and low insistent hum approaching. As it neared, I could feel vibrations shuddering through me.

"Saul?"

"Don't worry, George, I can see the Medi-Strider now. I've been in contact with the two paramedics on board and they're aware of your injuries. They'll make you comfortable and then decide whether you need constant medical care in the Strider, or a quick flight to hospital in the Stretcher Drone. It's over, George. You'll soon be home."

When the paramedics arrived, I tried to imagine the scene around me. I could still see nothing, but focusing on the sounds the humans and Saul were making, forced me to keep my brain occupied as I tried to build a mental picture. I knew what Medi-Striders looked like with their six powerful jointed legs and the pod they carried, slung in a horizontally-aligned gimbal to take passengers over rough ground and hills. The safety info-videos I'd seen showed them racing up shale and over rocks with a glass of water balanced inside the pod, demonstrating their incredible stability.

But apparently, I didn't make it into the pod. I was haemorrhaging internally and after giving me a powerful painkiller, I was loaded into the Stretcher Drone which was the fastest way to get me to hospital. I heard the roof being secured and the rotor blades starting up but I remember very little after that, other than the sensation that I was flying. The only thing I recall is wondering if I'd died.

It was several weeks after the fall I finally learned the full extent of my injuries. At thirty, amputation of my right arm was life-changing. Going blind was catastrophic.

My lost year—2049—was spent in and out of hospital for updates on my eyes and my arm stump, constantly tripping over things in Mum's flat while she looked after me and no games, television or books. I couldn't read Mara's expressions. I didn't know how the woman who'd been my on and off partner since university felt about me anymore.

Strangely, I didn't mind having nightmares. At least in my dreams, I had vision. It was waking up to blackness which was really distressing.

I retreated inside my head, hoping that in there, somewhere, the neural networks were rebuilding links to the eyes the doctors claimed were perfectly healthy but which refused to function for me.

Mara suggested post-trauma counselling.

I refused. I was too angry. It didn't matter what I did, it always seemed to go wrong. What good would talking about it do?

Then Mara *insisted* on post-trauma counselling, and lectured me on wallowing in self-pity.

I gave in and she booked me a session with a counsellor. I suppose it helped a bit. Trevor was obviously very well informed and we discussed social issues and current affairs. He encouraged me to talk and I told him about my father and my guilt at not joining the family furniture company. His father had passed it to him and he'd dreamed of handing it to me.

But my dreams had been different.

"You mentioned guilt," said Trevor, "let's talk about that."

I cast my mind back as far as I could and described my life. In 2020, when I'd been born, the world had been thrown into turmoil and my earliest memories were tinged with disturbed feelings I didn't understand as I picked up on signals without knowing what they were nor their cause. It was only later I realised how much pressure my parents had been under. The COVID-19 pandemic of 2020, followed by subsequent outbreaks of COVID variants and the threat of other viruses mutating in animals, gradually damaged my father's cabinet-making business. One by one, his highly-skilled workers either retired, succumbed to sickness, were furloughed, or simply resigned until only a few loyal employees remained. Dad coped with lockdowns, restrictions and changing markets, but unknown to him, another threat was silently eroding his business. While he and others tried to adapt to Britain's exit from the EU and the virus-related problems, he hadn't been keeping an eye on the development of new technology and automated systems in manufacturing. He and his men were craftsmen. What did they have to fear from machines? But many rival furniture companies took the opportunity to sack their workforce, relying on Artificial Intelligence, not only to create new and individual designs but also to produce the pieces in hours, not weeks, and at a quarter of the price.

I was twelve by the time it all got too much for Dad. He had a heart attack and died—the strain and guilt that the company his father had passed to him had failed under his management, was too much for him. Many other businessmen took a swifter route out of their troubles. When I was older I looked back and was grateful Dad hadn't followed their example—although there was precious little comfort in knowing his heart had given out rather than he'd taken his own life. Whatever the cause of death, it still left Mum and me alone.

The threat of the various infections and the conflicting advice from the Government about being careful whilst still carrying on, resulted in me retreating into the world of video games. The danger of being shot during an intergalactic battle or falling into a bottomless pit, was nothing compared to the real-life hazards outside my bedroom door. It was only as I grew older I realised Mum was lonely and not coping with life, so I was determined to study hard and get a good job. And what better area to move into than IT? Pretty much everything was being done online by then and after going to university, I began to carve a career for myself in middle management in a start-up IT company.

Of course, everyone knew computers were replacing workers. It had been happening for years but IT staff were still needed. It was inconceivable that Artificial Intelligence, which was there to serve humanity, could take over—other than in sci-fi movies, and yet later, once the term 'Fourth Industrial Revolution' had become well known, I realised politicians had spotted opportunities to save money and cut corners despite the inevitable mass unemployment.

"And that's what happened to you?" Trevor asked.

I bit back the angry reply. It wasn't his fault I'd been made redundant. And if I didn't somehow master my anger issues, I risked losing Mara.

I merely nodded.

"And how did that make you feel?" Trevor asked.

I sighed. Strangely, I hadn't wanted to tell him anything at first. But once I'd started, it became easier. At least he didn't tell me I ought to be responding in this way or that way. In fact, he gave no hint he was judging me, simply giving me the chance to say whatever I wanted.

I told him about my next job. There was less responsibility and therefore a lower salary but I'd hardly got all my log-in details, when I was made redundant again.

"This would have coincided with the Government's 'Use Your Time Wisely Campaign', would it?" Trevor asked and I was impressed that while I'd been speaking, he'd been mentally following the timeline of my sad and sorry life.

I nodded. By that time, so many people were unemployed it was almost impossible to find a job and the Government's advice had been to use time wisely by retraining, keeping fit and taking up hobbies or sports.

"And that was the idea of the Scottish hill walking holiday?" Trevor asked.

I nodded again.

"I see." He paused, gazed upwards as if considering his next words and then added, "Let's discuss your anger..."

I clenched my fists, my jaw and just about everything else it's possible to clench but under his serene scrutiny, I managed to control myself.

"Good," he said and I wondered if I'd passed some sort of test.

How this was supposed to help I had no idea. Yet as the weeks went on, I found I felt better being open about my feelings and my rage. Gradually I talked it all out. Nothing in my life had changed but at least I could be objective.

So much for my past. But what was there to look forward to? The future stretched out bleakly. I hadn't been able to support myself financially before the accident and now? It was fortunate Mara enjoyed her teaching job and from her recent promotion, it was something she excelled at.

"You could retrain," she said, "Why not take up teaching?"

But we both knew that was unlikely to happen.

She loved children and was empathetic. I was less confident with people, having spent most of my youth inside video games.

"You'd learn," she said, but we both knew it was wishful thinking. Teaching was out, and for the same reason, any of the other careers which involved the care of people seemed beyond my reach too.

Looking back over 2049—my year of frequent hospital appointments—I realise they kept me going. They provided goals and distracted me from the lack of direction or money.

But now, a year on, I have to face up to the scary prospect of a nothing life again. No job, no prospects and no idea what to do about it, despite my new bionic parts.

TWO – *Serena*

"I didn't promote you to fail." Thorsten's eyes are narrow slits and his voice a low growl. No matter that my work record has been impeccable until now, suddenly, my career is hanging by a thread.

"You've had that graphene chip for three months now, Serena, and you're telling me it hasn't worked with one single subject?"

"Not yet, but—"

"There are over sixty million people in the country and yet you can't find one that needs a head operation that we can use? Goddamit, Serena, go out and smash someone over the head!"

I'd like to point out the requirements are quite specific. The subjects must fulfil a whole list of medical and social parameters before we select them but I don't mention any of this because Thorsten is as aware of this as I am, and I know it would simply antagonise him.

He's already furious and I can only guess at who's just called *him* to account. But the thought of Thorsten being asked to justify the failure of the project so far, squirming in front of the desk of someone high up in the Government, gives me no comfort. If this project fails, we all fail.

"You know how much it cost to get our hands on that, that..." Thorsten waves his hands irritably in the air and I know he's mentally groping for the name of the chip.

"The Quidnunc Chip, sir?"

"Damn stupid codeword! Why couldn't they have picked something more memorable? Bloody nonsense, probably some algorithm in the department's computer..."

I say nothing. It wasn't my choice for a name and I don't want the blame. But Thorsten's razor-sharp mind is now back on track.

"It cost a fortune to get it, and when you consider the time and diplomatic effort—my effort mostly—I expect results. I *demand* results. So, when you tell me it was all for nothing because you can't follow through with your end of the project..."

"I didn't quite say that, sir. Unfortunately, two died, that was unforeseen. Their injuries were severe but we do have a third candidate who we've held off until he'd recovered from his injuries. The chip's been in a few weeks now and early signs are promising. His movements and electronic messages are being monitored, as are his family members, in case he says something to them out of our range. But..." I hesitate to tell Thorsten we have to be patient, "I'm afraid there's a little while longer to wait."

Thorsten is well known for his impatience and he's voluble in demonstrating that now.

I get out of Thorsten's office feeling angry, but I can see he has a point with the Treasury complaining about promised returns, and the Prime Minister on his back about losing our advantage before the rest of the world realise what we are doing. Every day, my officers around the world report on rumours from countries who may have managed to intercept Artificial Intelligence traffic, not generated from known sources.

But none, have the promised ability to create two-way communication, like the Quidnunc Chip.

Of course, Thorsten is frustrated, but so am I.

THREE – *George*

The slight movement of Mara's upper lip and the two faint lines which appear as her brows draw together, are subtle and fleeting. Probably, anyone who isn't as close to her as me—or perhaps I should say, as close to her as I *used to be*—might not have noticed. Maybe I wouldn't have spotted the change in expression either—before the accident. But now, I recognise the disapproval and I follow her line of gaze to my breakfast.

"Too much?" I ask, trying to scrape some of the spread off the toast but it's already melted.

Mara merely sniffs. She's wholeheartedly embraced the Government guidelines on curbing waste and excess—especially regarding food.

"Please don't text LEO Lion," I say in a mock frightened voice. Once, she'd have smiled or at least played along with a theatrical wag of the finger and a mock severe expression. We'd been appalled at the Government's blatant campaign to encourage children to 'Text LEO Lion', the 'Leave Enough for Others Lion' in an attempt to scare their parents into cooperating with the national *Waste Not Want Not Scheme*. We'd wondered how many parents were truly worried their children would report them to the authorities if they didn't cut back on food and other commodity consumption. But Mara isn't playing along today.

Of course, waste and excess are not laughing matters and I recognise everyone has to be careful. World resources aren't going to last forever, but I suspect part of Mara's enthusiasm for the *Waste Not Want Not* and *Fairness For All* schemes results from her desire to retain her slim figure. Mara can be self-disciplined in a scary, almost military way.

She slices her apple in half and I compare breakfasts. One apple for her.

Three slices of toast with jam for me.

Well, whatever dietary rules she's adopting are working fine. Her body is as perfect today as it was when I met her ten years ago.

Of course, I'm bothered about my fitness and shape too, but after months of inactivity while I convalesced, eating became the most active and exciting part of the day. I lay there for hours—days—wondering if I'd regain my eyesight completely or indeed any sight at all and of course, whether I'd master my new arm. And by the time I could see again, I'd become, what Mara jokingly referred to as, a *wasteful and insatiable glutton*. Her words are no longer teasing and now carry with them, hints of accusation.

This morning, when she finally says anything, I suspect her tone will have transitioned completely to complaint.

I put the lid back on the spread. The tub proclaims 'Butter' in large letters, followed by the word 'Substitute' in much smaller letters but it tastes like... well, I don't know what it tastes like. Certainly nothing edible and definitely not butter—and if I'd put too much on my toast, it was an accident and one I now won't be able to mask by slapping on a load of jam. I decide for the sake of harmony, I'll deny myself jam. Self-righteously, I take a bite of toast.

Mara is still staring at me and with a jolt, I realise she may not have been judging my breakfast at all, but is watching my new prosthetic hand in action as I manipulate the knife and hold the toast.

I fight the urge to put my toast down and hide my new hand.

"Are you going to be busy today?" I ask through a mouthful of half-chewed food in an effort to distract her.

It breaks the spell, and she looks away, takes a sip of tea and consults her diary. The screen lights up and she smiles, although she merely says,

"Fairly busy."

Presumably, she's looking forward to something in her day. She finishes the last of her hot water with a slice of lemon, takes her breakfast things to the sink and washes them up.

"And how about you?" she asks, her back still to me, "What've you got on today?" But it doesn't seem to be a friendly enquiry, it's more like a challenge.

I briefly shake my head. What's the matter with me this morning? Why am I seeing criticism in everything Mara does and says? I'm not usually so sensitive. Lack of sleep, perhaps?

I'd slept fitfully after the argument last night.

Perhaps it's that.

Well, not argument, exactly, although it might've been better if there had been a row. It seems there's too much that's unsaid between us.

It had started when I'd accidentally knocked over a glass of water and narrowly missed her phone which was charging on the kitchen worktop. She'd snatched it up angrily and firmly rejected my attempts to mop up the water, making it clear she had no confidence in my new arm's ability to wield a tea towel.

"Perhaps you shouldn't try to run before you can walk," she'd said and I'd demanded what she meant but she'd simply shrugged and assumed a martyred air.

"Everyone has accidents from time to time," I'd pointed out.

"Mmm," she'd said, seeming to agree whilst actually disagreeing.

I was hurt. After each appointment, I'd excitedly reported how pleased the doctors were and how much my sight and the dexterity of my prosthetic arm had improved. In fact, a lifetime of staring at computer screens had prematurely damaged my eyes—even with the improved screens which have been developed over the last decade. But now, after my operation, my vision is perfect.

"There's nothing wrong with my eyesight," I'd said and then I'd tried to head off an argument and direct the evening where I'd originally intended. "Except I can't see enough of you." I'd tucked my finger under her bathrobe and had gently tried to slide it down over her shoulder.

"Don't!" she'd said, "I'm mopping up. You nearly ruined my phone," she added.

I let her bathrobe slip back into place.

Tonight was obviously not going to end the way I'd hoped.

Yet again.

If I'd used my new hand, I'd have understood it. I know she's finding it hard to adapt to my prosthetic arm even though it's covered in natural-look-and-feel skin which appears as sensitive to me as the one I'd lost.

We'd gone to bed in silence and she turned her back on me the second the light went out.

"Well?" Mara says, dragging me back to the present, and I realise I haven't answered her question about my plans for the day.

"I'm thinking of volunteering at the hospital." Again, the two lines between her brows appear as she frowns, although this time not in disapproval, but in surprise.

"Really? But what'll you be able to do?" she asks and then falters.

And there it is. Her lack of belief I can do anything useful. Her gaze softens and she searches my face for signs she's hurt me.

"I don't know," I say evenly, choosing to ignore her comment. I don't believe her thoughtless comment was intended to offend, nevertheless, it reveals exactly what she thinks of me.

"There's a long process before they let you know if you've been accepted but I've heard they've had a few cases of a new COVID variant this week, which usually means they need more people. I thought I'd like to give something back," I add, my tone neutral.

"Yes, that's a lovely idea. But you will take care, won't you?"

She really seems bothered.

"Of course, I doubt I'd be working anywhere near the isolation wards. Anyway, after that, I'll carry on looking for a job and then I'll wipe down the top of the kitchen cupboards like Mum asked."

Mara nods her approval and smiles.

I hadn't planned to clean the top of the cupboards today, but I want to appear capable in Mara's eyes. And if I'm honest, guilt has been gnawing at me for some time.

Years ago, when Mara and I moved in with Mum, after graduating from university, I'd done the jobs Mum found difficult with her arthritis, but since my accident, I'd done very little. Now, I wonder if Mara appears to approve because she knows Mum'll be pleased or if she's trying to make up for her earlier, hurtful comment.

"Okay," she says, "Just don't get into any mischief!" and I see a flash of the Mara I'd once known. She kisses the top of my head and leaves for work.

Well, at least we parted friends—even if it's not the sort of friends I want to be.

I tidy away the breakfast things and climb nervously on the stool and then onto the worktop in order to reach the top of the cupboards. I curse myself for suggesting this particular job. There were several other tasks I could have done but stupidly, this was the first one that came to mind. Probably, because falling is now my greatest fear. The worktop isn't exactly a great height but my stomach's churning and my hands are trembling—both of them, I notice—even the prosthetic hand. I take a deep breath and close my eyes as I wipe the cupboard tops. I expect I've missed large areas but so long as I can truthfully report to Mum it's been done, she'll be happy. It's not like anyone's going to check it. Despite Mum's analgesic implants, she's often in pain which keeps her up during the night, so she usually stays in bed until late. I hurry to finish because if she gets up early today, I know she won't be happy about me climbing. She'd almost lost me once and she can't bear to see me taking risks. It's a bit stifling but understandable.

The original plan had been that Mara and I would save every penny until we had enough to rent a place of our own but that dream died when I lost my job. It means staying with Mum is our only option. Mostly, it works well. Mum gives Mara and me space—well as much as can be found in a small two-bedroom flat. We help her do the things she finds difficult but it's hard living so closely together and I know Mum's desperate for me to commit to Mara and set up our own home.

Not that she wants to be rid of us, she wants to be certain we don't drift apart because she thinks Mara is good for me, keeping me rooted in the real world and not losing myself in 'those waste-of-time video games', as she calls them.

Since I became unemployed and particularly since my accident, Mara and I inhabit different worlds. I stay home and between searching for jobs, I play video games. She teaches English in a local school. I keep in touch with my friends via video link. She has a busy social life with her colleagues.

If I could find a job, it would also be a bridge into her world…

The doctors say I'm fit enough to work but I still have regular medical appointments and who would want to employ someone who frequently needs to take time off when there are so many fit and desperate people with similar or better qualifications?

I wipe down the worktops and make Mum a cup of what she calls 'coffee', out of powder which has never seen a coffee bean. It contains chicory, acorns and a variety of ingredients which I don't recognise but that's the best we can afford and Mum seems to like it. I take it to her bedroom.

"Job hunting today?" she asks as I hand her the coffee. Her tone is hopeful. Pleading even.

"Yes. Job hunting."

"Good, good. Something suitable will turn up today, I'm sure." She smiles up at me and I feel a lump in my throat.

How much sadness this woman has seen in her life and yet she still expects the best. Or at least, she still hopes for it.

I glance at the side of the bed where Dad would once have been and swallow. How lonely it must be for her. If only I could find a job and give her something to celebrate. I put on my brightest smile and leave her to start her day.

Once in my bedroom, I check my emails, my head whirring with memories of Dad. He'd worked so hard, carrying on the business his father had left him. I speculate once again whether I'd have been able to help him salvage the furniture business with my IT skills. But there's no point wondering, I tell myself.

Logging in to the Government website, I check my area and any new vacancies which might've come up since I last looked. In surprise, I suddenly realise how quickly I'm typing... with both hands! I allow myself a smile of triumph and punch the air with my prosthetic hand. It now matches the speed and accuracy of the hand I'd lost. It truly is a work of art.

How ironic, it had been Artificial Intelligence which had first taken away my job which led to me going hill walking and the accident, yet which allowed my arm to be built and fitted and also restored my eyesight with a state-of-the-art Quidnunc Chip.

I locate my health folder on the hard drive which contains all the details relating to my medical record and care, including a sub-folder labelled Quidnunc. There's nothing in the folder because despite searching the Internet, I can find no mention of the chip or its manufacturer.

20

I'd asked my consultant but she'd merely said no scientific papers about it had yet been published, although she was at great pains to stress that although the treatment was experimental, it was thoroughly safe. To be honest I didn't care if they had experimented on me. The Quidnunc Chip had restored my eyesight so it'd obviously been a success. And not only that, but throughout my treatment, I'd been treated like a VIP, with top consultants and luxurious hospital accommodation—more like an expensive hotel. For reasons which I hadn't understood, I'd been told the treatment was to be kept secret—something to do with patents which had been applied for. Since I didn't know anyone who'd be the slightest bit interested in the detailed biology of what was going on in my brain, I readily agreed. I expect once the patents are granted, there'll be plenty of information on the Internet. And who knows, perhaps I'll be the subject of a medical paper.

But actually, who cares? I can see again and I no longer dread my medical appointments because each one shows a slight improvement although I have to admit to being nervous about my next session with Mrs Nwandu, the neurologist.

One of the conditions of the experiment was that I had to go to monthly debriefing meetings with the consultant.

Not the 'How are you? Fine thanks, right, see you next month' sort of appointment, but more like an interrogation. Strangely, her questions often concerned my hearing. I assumed the sight and hearing networks in my brain might be connected somehow. At first, I had nothing to tell her. I could see well—in fact, my vision was better than it had ever been and I could hear well, with no echoes or tinnitus. There were no problems at all. Then I began to hear something like interference. It only happened occasionally and as soon as I became aware of it and listened hard, it stopped. But last month I heard a word.

Just one word, like an electric convulsion through my brain.

"Status."

It wasn't a thought and I definitely heard it as if someone had spoken, yet I was alone. I knew, without doubt, the sound hadn't travelled through the air to reach my ears. I told myself it couldn't be a sound, it had to be a thought.

But deep down, I knew it wasn't. Not *my* thought, anyway.

So, what did it mean? And where had it come from?

It must have been some sort of anomaly. Just a freaky occurrence— and I wasn't sure whether to mention it to my consultant but in the end decided to slip it in without making a big thing about it. And oddly, she was really excited when I told her, but she quickly resumed her normal professional manner. At the end of the session, she said she wanted me back in a fortnight rather than a month, nothing to worry about, my eyes were working perfectly and I wasn't to be disturbed about strange noises. The brain would try to make sense of any input and it could easily interpret any sound as being something familiar, such as a word. Absolutely nothing to worry about and she'd do more tests when I saw her next.

I was reassured and tried to put it out of my mind.

It was, after all, only one word.

But, just recently, I've heard more sounds—all at once. And my brain has interpreted them as words but not simply a random selection. More like a string of words. Together, they don't make sense but there's obviously something like an exchange going on in my brain which isn't controlled by me. Distinct voices are speaking as if a group of people are reading out lists.

I'm certain I'm not picking up police or aircraft radio calls because the messages don't make sense. I remember reading an article about people during the last century, who reported picking up radio signals in their dental fillings. Of course, that couldn't happen today; no one has fillings.

Dental coatings don't allow teeth to decay—and I'm not even sure people weren't mistaken about hearing sounds via their teeth back then. But it gives me hope there'll be a simple explanation.

In the real world, my job hunting's not going too well, the trouble is, I've spent too much time playing computer games and interacting with virtual worlds and people. It was the same at university, I barely scraped a Second in Advanced Technology because I was either working to pay uni fees or building and destroying alien worlds.

How I managed to hook up with Mara, I really don't know. She got a First in English and has always viewed technology as a means to an end, using it as a tool to complete her studies and get through life. For me, it's been an obsession. I'm a technophile, immersing myself in the digital world during work, rest and play. Games have been a large part of my life—something which Mara has never understood.

I suppose it must be our tenth anniversary about now. We always go on holiday together to celebrate, and over the years, we've lived together for a while, then one of our jobs gets in the way and we spend time apart. For some reason, we rarely resume our 'nearly-married' life immediately.

I can't afford to go away now. Perhaps if I'd taken Mara with me on my hill walking holiday, I wouldn't have been quite so reckless. It might not have ended as it did, with me spending so long in hospital and then in rehabilitation.

The only posts I'm vaguely qualified for seem to need interpersonal skills, empathy and the ability to help robots look after the sick or disadvantaged. Not my skill set at all. Years ago, I'd have considered taking more qualifications in Advanced Systems Design. Waste of time now, everything in that field is done by AI, faster and better than we humans can do it.

Even Mara's job as a teacher is changing fast. Many of the specialist

23

subjects, like Interplanetary Geography, are taught to small groups by a hologram teacher in another part of the world but mainly, children attend bricks and mortar schools like Mara and I used to. Not surprising really, after the first COVID pandemic when schools were closed for months. For the first time, it became obvious that children's educational standards, as well as mental and physical health deteriorated during the lockdowns. Not to mention the distress of the parents who were struggling to work from home and supervise their children's learning—if they were lucky enough not to have been put on extended furlough or indeed lost their jobs. Although Mara's explanation for this policy is that the politicians are in favour of real schools because they don't want all the kids to grow up like me.

I think she's joking although I'm not sure.

I don't believe there's anything wrong with the way I turned out. It's just that I'm more at home interacting with a computer than a human and that was fine when I was employed—it was probably even desirable. But now, if kids want to work, the main opportunities for jobs are found in areas like social care where interpersonal skills are vital. So, the Government has decided part of the school curriculum should involve 'socialisation' training.

I told Mara about the words I keep hearing. But I haven't told Mum in case she worries the implant will fail and I'll lose my sight again. Mara said what I'd heard sounded like an office cleaning company filing reports from its operatives. She's right. And it may be that such a report has a similar wavelength to that of my eye implant. Not sure that makes sense or is even possible, but I'll ask the consultant when I see her tomorrow.

FOUR – *Serena*

"Just two more minutes, Hun! You can do it."

I clench my teeth. I want to shout *Serena. My name is Serena.*

Monica tucks a wisp of dark hair behind her ear and unaware of my anger, smiles, displaying her perfect, white teeth.

I grip the handlebars and pedal harder.

It's the second time she's told me there are two minutes to go. I saw her brush her thumb on the tablet screen and guessed she'd extended the duration of the programme on my exercise bike. She's also increased the intensity. My lungs are bursting and my thigh muscles are screaming at me to stop.

But I will not show Monica I'm in pain.

And I will not give up.

I *never* give up. And I'm fired up with anger after my meeting with Thorsten.

"Okay... you can start your warm-down now, Hun," Monica says, tapping on her tablet, "I'm reducing the resistance. Heart rate and blood pressure are fine. All good." She beams at me, "You're in great shape..."

She doesn't add *for your age*, but it's as if the words are hovering silently in the air just above her head, and I bristle.

Monica Cheung, with her flawless olive skin, satin-smooth black hair and a perfectly-proportioned body is my personal trainer. At twenty-four, she's only six years younger than me but somehow, even when she doesn't mention age, she makes me feel past it. And then, of course, there's her aggravating habit of calling me *Hun*. If it hadn't sounded so petty, I'd have insisted she call me Serena, or Ms Hamilton or indeed anything but *Hun*. I'd once commented on one of the other personal trainers who had been calling her client the dreaded name and Monica had looked at me with bewilderment displayed in those beautiful almond-shaped eyes and said it was what young people currently called each other.

"It'll be something else next month, I expect," she'd added vaguely, as if aligning herself with young people and explaining to an older person who had lost touch with the way language evolves.

I hadn't pursued it.

That other trainer had been dismissed. Not for her lack of respectful salutation and address but because she was no longer required. In fact, most of the personal trainers had been released from the exclusive gym whose clients included many Members of Parliament and Government officials—only two PTs remained—one of whom was Monica. The finely-honed young male trainers had been the first to go. It seemed that male clients prefer to be put through their paces by a nubile, young woman rather than by a muscly Adonis.

Surprise, surprise.

And as for the female clients, it seems that they too, prefer a woman whose figure they envy—even if it's unlikely they'll ever achieve such a shape. Monica gives them something to aspire to. It *must* be possible to acquire such a body; the proof is standing before them, urging them to greater fitness and a sleeker silhouette.

Some gyms now employ robotic personal trainers but they aren't universally popular—it turns out there are few people who are happy to accept criticism from a perfectly-formed robot that has never been tempted by a chocolate brownie or large glass of wine. At least a fellow human might sympathise if a client's diet is occasionally less than ideal.

I bury my face in the lightly scented, refrigerated towel which Monica passes me and hope the coolness will calm my flushed cheeks. At least my breathing has returned to normal but anger is doing nothing to lower my heightened colour. I take a deep breath and try to relax.

I also give myself a stern talking to.

It's a personal trainer's job to put me through my paces and it's hardly her fault she's young and shapely. And despite her annoying cheerfulness and confidence, I know she's worried about job security. Aren't we all? It was she who pointed out how empty the gym was this lunchtime and commented on the decline in membership numbers during the previous six months.

The membership fees for the Ellison Kendall Health Club and Spa have always been beyond the average person's reach—it's the management's way of keeping the clientele exclusive. But gradually, as Artificial Intelligence increases and more and more jobs and careers are undermined—eventually disappearing for good—former clients who were once considered part of the elite found they'd been replaced by automation. If they hadn't made proper financial provision, they soon discovered they needed to make hard decisions about which expenses were necessary and which were luxuries. Renewing a subscription to Ellison Kendall was definitely one of the latter.

Of course, the extremely wealthy are weathering the financial downturn and will continue to do so without an appreciable decline in their standard of living but as economic conditions worsen, those who'd once considered themselves well off, are now noticing the bite. Those who'd once been comfortable—are now anything but. And as for the poor unfortunates who'd formerly been part of the struggling classes... well, they're now surviving thanks to charities and the Government-run soup kitchens and food banks.

I'm extremely fortunate—my club membership is included in my salary package. And, assuming I manage to overcome the current problems, I have the added luxury of knowing I'm one of the few people who can be as certain as anyone that my position's not at risk. So, it's likely I'll still be a member when the health club and spa finally closes, as it surely must—if not this year, then the next. Of course, if the management cuts its membership fees in an attempt to attract those who'd once belonged and who can now no longer afford to do so, it will survive, but I'm acquainted with several of the board members and I'm well aware of their snobbish attitudes. Better to remain exclusive and close its doors than to sink to the status of an ordinary gym.

Perhaps the Government will step in with a grant. After all, since the unemployment figures soared, people have been urged to make good use of their leisure time by taking up new sports and keeping fit. During the last few years, those who've taken note of this advice, are more likely to be found pounding the streets than working out in prestigious gyms but a spate of attacks on joggers have driven most people from the parks and other popular running tracks.

Sadly, assaults haven't been limited to runners. It's becoming increasingly dangerous to walk alone. Especially at night. And since I often work erratic hours, a car is always waiting for me when I leave, programmed to take me directly to my apartment in the gated community where I live.

"Doing anything exciting tonight?" Monica asks, handing me a glass of energy drink supplemented with vitamins and minerals.

"I expect I'll be working. I've got a full afternoon and I'll probably have to stay late at the office to catch up." After my last meeting with Thorsten, I'll probably be pulling another all-nighter.

"Oh, what a shame, Hun," said Monica in tones that suggest she isn't really interested. I hadn't expected sympathy. After all, someone who's facing redundancy is unlikely to be too concerned about the 'poor unfortunate' who has to work overtime.

"Can't you work from home?"

"Yes, but there's still the same amount to do at home or in the office," I say, knowing she's thinking if I work predominantly from home like many of my colleagues, I won't be at the gym so often.

"So, I'll still see you Thursday?" Monica asks. There's a slight tremor in her voice which betrays her anxiety. The fewer clients, the less chance she'll be kept on.

"Yes," I say, "same time if that's okay." I don't really want a workout on Thursday but I feel sorry for the girl. I'll rearrange a few meetings.

"That's good. Remember, if you don't use it, you lose it and you don't want to waste all that effort you've put in so far, do you, Hun?" Monica says tapping the appointment into her tablet.

There was no reference to my age but again, I think it was implied. I turn away to hide my annoyance and head for the showers, urging myself not to be so touchy and to stop putting words into Monica's mouth.

The spacious marble changing room is empty when I enter and Millie, one of the attendants, springs to her feet and rushes towards me with an armful of luxurious towels.

"Take your pick," she said waving her arm towards the private shower rooms, "They're all free."

"Thanks."

Millie opens the door, standing back to allow me in.

"Ylang Ylang and Sandalwood?" Millie asks, "Or something more energising?"

"Ylang Ylang and Sandalwood are fine, thanks."

Millie taps on the screen by the door selecting my choice of perfume for shower gel, shampoo, hair conditioner and body lotion.

The powerful stream of water washes away my earlier irritation at Monica and as the room fills with the delicious scent of the essential oils I'd requested, I begin to think about the afternoon's schedule. Shielding the fitness band around my wrist from the gushing water, I check the time. Still another half an hour before I have to be back at my desk. If I hurry, there'll be time to grab a sandwich.

My stomach clenches in panic. Two earlier attempts had failed when Subjects One and Two died of their injuries. But Subject Number Three had not been fatally wounded although he'd been sufficiently hurt to need significant medical intervention. At two o'clock, Subject Number Three should be attending his check-up with consultant, Ms Sally Nwandu, in her Harley Street practice and I'll be watching via her webcam.

Turning the temperature to its minimum setting, I stand beneath the jets of icy cold water, counting to one hundred slowly before I turn it off. I hate being cold but that's all the more reason to endure it. In my world, I can't afford to show any weakness—to anyone else or to myself. There are countless people who're willing to step into my shoes if I'm found to be wanting. Not that many of them can match me intellectually but ruthlessness often wins out over intelligence and I know several unscrupulous people who are envious of my success in the department. Freezing in the shower is one of the many tests I put myself through each day. If I grow comfortable and complacent, I simply will not survive. Not that anyone knows the temperature of my shower, of course.

But I know.

Self-discipline gives me confidence and I know I'd sacrifice anything for my career.

By the time I've wrapped one of the luxurious towels around my hair and stood under the warm airflow, which blows down from the ceiling to warm up and dry off completely, I'm feeling quite relaxed—hungry, but relaxed. Once dressed, I check myself in the mirror, comb my hair and rearrange my curls with the tips of my fingers. There's no time to dry it.

"Bye, Ms Hamilton," calls Millie as I stride out of the changing room, "have a lovely afternoon."

Jason is peering into a small mirror and applying mascara to his eyelashes when I rush into his office, making him jump.

"I nearly had my eye out!" he says, wiping mascara off his cheek with a tissue.

"Sorry, Jase. There was an enormous queue in the sandwich bar. One of the machines had broken down and I was afraid I'd be late."

Jason shakes his head, tutting at the sandwich I'm holding.

"I thought you were going to the gym," he says accusingly, "they don't sell bacon sandwiches in Ellison Kendall."

"I know. I just couldn't face alfalfa salad again. I'm starving. Have you set everything up?"

"Of course! Am I not *the* most fabulous PA in the entire building?"

"Yes, Jason, you're wonderful," I call over my shoulder as I go into my office.

"Only *wonderful*? I was going for *magnificent* or even *perfect*!" he says.

I sit at my desk, unwrap the sandwich and look at the computer screen. Jason has set it up so I can see two views—one inside the waiting room and the other inside the consulting room. The important appointment will begin in five minutes although I can see Ms Nwandu hasn't yet arrived. Her PA is bustling about in the office, tidying the desk and removing some wilted blooms from the elaborate display of roses on the desk.

Most patients are met by a screen when they arrive at their consultant's surgery but Sally Nwandu has a high proportion of sight-impaired patients and she's obviously decided to employ a person to assist them. I don't think anyone's invented a machine that's good at flower arranging yet, so her PA also comes in handy for tidying up the ostentatious floral displays Sally seems to adore. Although I can see she only buys blooms grown in coolhouses. Now that Sunflowers,

31

Bougainvillea and other plants which thrive in high temperatures grow like weeds in England, they've become cheap and cheerful—not her style at all.

It's ten-to-two and other than the receptionist who is now surreptitiously reading a book behind her desk, the waiting room is empty.

I have time to eat.

I'm chewing the first bite when Sally sweeps into the waiting room and greets the young girl at reception who's heard her approach and has slipped her eReader in a drawer.

"When the first patient arrives, please send him in, Leah," Sally says as she goes into her consulting room.

Seconds later, a man enters. It's Subject Number Three. He walks towards the receptionist.

"Hi, my name's George Williams. I've got an appointment with Ms Nwandu at two."

FIVE – *Serena*

I maximise the video which shows the inside of Sally's room. The consultation of George Williams, or Subject Number Three, is what I'm interested in and I put the sandwich down so I won't be distracted. The camera has been concealed in the picture frame of a large painting that hangs behind Sally's desk. Its elevated position allows me to see the top and back of her head but it gives me a full view of George's face. He's clutching the arms of the chair as if he were at a job interview and for a second, I can't tell which hand is bionic. I glance at his notes. It's his right arm that has been replaced. Not that his arm is of much concern to me, nor to Sally. The bionic team are monitoring that, and so far, it's been completely successful. Sally, however, is the Neuro-Ophthalmologist who carried out the delicate operation which restored George's sight. But his eyes also aren't of much concern to me.

Sally enquires about his general health and eyesight, entering his responses on her tablet. He's enthusiastic in his praise of the bionic team and his new arm and disarmingly grateful to her for the successful operation which has allowed him to see again after so many months in the dark. I pick up my sandwich and nibble while Sally administers drops to dilate his eyes and carries out a battery of tests. Conversation during this time is restricted to Sally explaining what each machine does and what he's likely to experience while she carries out her examination. She asks questions related to the tests and George responds. The information I want will probably not be discussed until Sally has finished her check-up.

At least, it had better be discussed. Or there'll be trouble. All the tests she's carrying out today, could have been done on a portable device worn by the patient and sent via the Internet from his home. But he won't know that and if she's skilful, he won't notice the extra questions she's been told to ask. Orders from a senior member of the Government. And to ease her conscience, large sums of money have been donated to her current research project. Not that the tiny graphene processor she'd been given to insert alongside her microchip would cause any damage to George. It was biologically inert, would not provoke an immune response or cause any harm—it would simply be ignored by his body. Although if anything unforeseen occurred, it could be located and removed swiftly.

After George's comments at his previous consultation with her, it appears the unit is working. He has heard one word.

What, if anything, has he heard during the last fortnight?

Usually so self-assured, Sally becomes slightly hesitant. She concludes the tests and discusses the results with George. He expresses his satisfaction with his eyesight. He doesn't mention hearing any more words and Sally hasn't yet asked. I think I can understand why.

During the last appointment, George expressed worry about his mental state. Sally was most reassuring, although I knew she was also disturbed but not primarily because she was concerned for George's psychological wellbeing. Years before, she'd taken an oath to prescribe beneficial treatments and to refrain from causing harm. When she'd been ordered to join the project, she'd expressed many misgivings. The item she'd inserted alongside her microchip would not cause harm—well, we didn't believe so, anyway. But in her opinion, it wasn't necessary to restore his health. Her opinion, however, was of no account. It was pointed out by people—important people who it didn't pay to anger—that she needed to consider it was her duty, not only as a subject of the United Kingdom and the world community, but more importantly, as a member of the human race. She'd complied, of course, but it was obvious she was uncomfortable with her actions.

Finally.

"And... that matter which we discussed last time?" she asks, "Have you heard that word again... or anything else?"

George is also hesitant. He looks at his watch. "I kept a record of everything I heard, like you told me to."

"Could you *Fastdrop* it to me, please?"

George fiddles with his watch; Sally stares at her screen and nods once the transfer has taken place.

She examines the list.

"Could you tell if all those words were spoken by one voice?" she asks.

"No, there are lots of different voices."

"So, you can determine different voices?"

George nods.

"How do you differentiate between them?"

"It's hard to describe. I just know they're different. But nothing they say makes any sense."

"I can see what you mean. You're sure this is what they said?"

George nods. "The voices are very clear."

"I see... And have you mentioned them to anyone else?"

"No, only you." He bites his bottom lip. "I feel a bit stupid admitting I can hear voices."

"I'm sure there's a rational explanation, so don't worry. But it's probably best not to tell anyone else. We can discuss it in two weeks when I see you again. There's no way of knowing if the voices will stop or increase in frequency, so it's best to keep meticulous records and then I can monitor your progress. On your way out, perhaps you'd see my receptionist and ask her for the details of a special app which you can download on to your watch. Record anything in that app and it will be sent directly to your file then we can discuss it, if need be, at your next appointment."

Sally rises, signalling the end of the appointment. George stands up and puts on his jacket.

I watch as he chats with the receptionist while he makes another appointment, then I phone Sally.

"Serena here. Please send that list."

"Of course." Her tone is clipped.

"Thanks," I say and she rings off. Her displeasure at being involved in the project is evident but I can't be bothered to pull her up on her rudeness. From what I saw of the words that Subject Number Three has heard, it looks like the Quidnunc Chip she implanted for us, is working.

Everything on the list appears to be part of a status report but, importantly, there is mention of *The Game*. The single word which George first mentioned to Sally two weeks ago has been joined by many more. What might he be able to detect during the next fortnight?

My hair has now dried after the shower and I brush it, checking my appearance in the mirror. As a woman working in a predominantly male Government department, I know there's a fine line to be drawn. Take too little care of your appearance and your colleagues don't treat you seriously. Take too much care and it's assumed you're empty-headed and frivolous. Behave with too much assertiveness and you're aggressive but be slightly indecisive, and you're assumed to be weak and ineffectual. It's a constant battle. And a battle which despite attempts to ensure gender equality throughout this century and beyond, is still not over.

I wear a dark trouser suit to work. Plain and elegant, but not out of place with all the other suits around me. My shirts are also plain, although my concession to femininity is jewellery—and shoes with killer heels. They give me extra centimetres which allow me to look most of my colleagues in the eye. It had been Jason who'd assisted me with my wardrobe. He'd suggested the almost masculine attire, relieved by the little feminine touches. And so far, it seems to have worked. I'm not aware of any evidence of my appearance or gender being an issue. No one mentions my clothes at all and that's exactly what I want because it's not an issue and thankfully, as far as I can tell, I've always been judged on my work performance. And after the apparent success of George's Quidnunc implant, things are looking up.

"I'm going to see Thorsten," I say to Jason as I walk through his office. I do a twirl for his inspection.

He nods and smiles. "You'll do."

"No need for you to stay late, Jase," I say over my shoulder, "I'll probably be with Thorsten until silly o'clock."

Jason holds his fingertips to his lips in a mock look of terror, "Rather you than me, m'dear."

When I arrive at Thorsten's office, he's studying George's list of words on his screen. He looks up and smiles at me.

A rare occurrence.

There's no doubt he's a brilliant man but he puts so much energy into his work, there's little time for the social niceties or politeness. Years ago, his marriage to a famous actor ended acrimoniously in the courts with her claiming desertion because she never saw him.

The first time I visited him in his office, I waited for him to invite me to sit, shuffling from foot to foot in embarrassment.

"Bloody stop fidgeting!" he said, without even looking at me.

I sat down.

Later, someone entered his office, took a chair and pulled it up in front of his desk.

"Did I ask you to sit?" he shouted, passing my astonished colleague a folder and waving him out of the office with an impatient gesture.

Thorsten is completely unpredictable and it took me a while to work out his behaviour is not as random as it appears. It's how he keeps everyone in their place. Except, obviously, his wife—or should I say, ex-wife.

I'd learned to accept Thorsten's rudeness with stoicism. So, his current delight in the list is all the more remarkable.

"At bloody last, it's working! It looks like Subject Number Three's been successful," he says, his smile widening, "Now for the next step..."

When I return to my office a little later, Jason's tidying his desk.

"Just thought I'd wait to make sure the Big T didn't eat you," he said.

"On the contrary. He was really pleased with the way the project's going."

"Well, don't get used to being the golden girl, m'dear. It's quite likely tomorrow he'll be bawling you out for something or the other."

"I know, Jase. But it's nice while it lasts."

Jason snorts. "Right, is there anything you want me to do before I go home?"

"No, thanks. But first thing in the morning, I need you to draw up the details for a new employee. Name—George Williams."

SIX – *George*

Another day. Another waiting room. Another consultant.

At least it gives me something to get up for in the morning. Today, it's my bionics specialist, Dr Purdey—or Yimandra, as she's asked me to call her. She's really relaxed—nothing like Ms Nwandu who's a bit uptight. There's nothing wrong with being uptight, of course, but an appointment with Yimandra is much more laidback which is good because today, I've decided to bring up something that's going to be rather embarrassing.

It's certainly not something I'd care to discuss with Ms Nwandu. The last consultation with her had been strange, to say the least. The first part was just like normal—lots of measurements of my sight. But then, right at the end, I noticed she was rubbing her nails back and forth across each other as if she was nervous. A few times, I saw her glance over her shoulder as if she expected someone to be there. It crossed my mind she might have some bad news for me and I was bracing myself for something unpleasant, when she asked if I'd heard any other words since I'd last seen her. I was relieved even though when I read out the list, she didn't say much. She glanced at the words once they'd arrived on her screen—although, she was quite insistent I should keep a record of any other words I might hear in the future. But there was no attempt to explain them—I suspect she didn't know the significance anyway. Or if she did, she didn't intend to say. She never asked me what I thought the words might mean, which was also strange and since she didn't ask me, I didn't tell her I think I might know what some of it's about. There were odd words and phrases which didn't mean anything on their own, such as 'commencing defrost cycle', 'night-cleaning' and 'cycle completed'.

But 'The Game'—now, that rang a bell.

Of course, I may be wrong. 'Game' is a common word and I might be imposing a meaning on something which is just part of a random list but I couldn't help thinking I'd hit on a clue. Way back when I started solving computer glitches, some bright spark put forward a suggestion which they jokingly dubbed 'The Theory of Artificial Intelligence Boredom'. It's all to do with computers working at maximum efficiency which is what they do if they move seamlessly from one task to another. But a pause between jobs, however small, decreases performance, even if the interruption lasts milliseconds. Someone came up with a way to ensure computers didn't stop—ever—and that was done by forcing them to perform exercises during the brief intervals between tasks. Something, like running a non-critical program—like a game. All sorts of rumours sped around the computer world, including one that a special unit had built an AI machine to invent a game so complex and secure, no future AI system could reach the end of its levels, or crack its security. It was just a rumour but one that came to be widely accepted. And it was referred to— rather unimaginatively—as 'The Game'.

If I'm right, then I'm picking up some sort of AI code through my eye implant which is also auto-translating the code so I can understand it. But, I've never heard of that type of translation and, if that's the case, why doesn't the rest of what I'm hearing make sense? And where's the transmitting unit?

My thoughts are interrupted as a man comes out of Yimandra's office walking with the aid of a crutch. He's limping and I wonder how much of his leg has been replaced. Glancing down at his feet, I see they both bend as if they are part of his body, so it's hard to tell, but why else would he have an appointment with a bionics specialist? Yimandra is at the door, watching his gait and she smiles, nodding her approval as he waves.

She turns her attention to me and strides over with her hand outstretched to greet me. I know she's carrying out the first of many tests as she takes my hand in hers and shakes it, checking my grip and strength. Obviously satisfied, she smiles, leads me into her office and gestures for me to sit on the sofa. Perching on the arm of a chair, she flicks her fringe off her face and asks how I've been. I hesitate, her smile slips.

"Is everything all right, George?" She frowns slightly and leans closer.

I hesitate again. Is my sex life her remit? My cheeks redden. I'm not sure where to begin.

"I can see something's bothering you, George. You can tell me."

If only I could find the words.

I want to describe Mara's dislike of my bionic arm and hand. How the muscles around her mouth tighten in disgust when she looks at it. How she recoils when I touch her with it. How our once-fulfilling love life is now non-existent. But where do I start?

Mara knows the 'skin' is real enough. Cells were taken from my other arm, grown in cell culture and then laid over the structure using 3D print technology. It's incredible that it goes brown in strong sun, and it feels soft to the touch, as do the fingers, although the operating parts are a little nearer the surface than the bones in my real hand. I don't have to cut my nails and I'm capable of feeling fine textures, like Mara's body. Or I would be able to feel fine textures like her body—if she'd let me.

Yimandra tilts her head to one side and smiles encouragingly.

Against my better judgement, I blurt it out.

"I see," she finally says and to my relief, I can tell she's not embarrassed at all, nor shocked, "D'you think she'll get used to it in time?"

It's such a relief to see she's taking me seriously, I now can't stop, "That's what I thought. At first, I was sure she'd eventually get used to my arm, but if anything, she seems even more put off by it now than she was when I first came home from hospital."

"D'you think it would help to bring Mara with you, the next time you come to see me for a check-up? I could talk to her and ask what's bothering her if you think it would help."

"I'm not sure she'd agree. And she'd be upset if she knew I'd told you. Whenever I mention her behaviour, she says I'm imagining it and we usually end up having a row."

"Yes, I can see she might resent you telling anyone else. Has she given any clues at all as to how she's feeling?"

I hesitate again. There was the matter of the C-word which came up a few months ago but I decide not to mention that to Yimandra. Instead, I say, "Something came up the other day which made me wonder... but it seems a bit unlikely."

"Yes?"

"Well, years ago, her mother agreed to a pioneering operation which went wrong. She died shortly after. Mara won't talk about it. The other day, she said she felt guilty about her mum. I told her it wasn't her fault but she just kept crying. Mara never bears a grudge but the way she was acting made me wonder if she's a bit resentful because I survived and her mum didn't."

"Well, without talking to her, I can't really say, but the mother-daughter relationship is a complex thing. Perhaps she's still dealing with the grief over losing her mum and your condition has simply reminded her. After all, you could've died in that fall. It was touch and go. A few years back, without the sophisticated search and rescue capabilities we have now, you wouldn't have stood a chance of surviving. Even if you'd been found fairly quickly, you'd have bled to death before you reached hospital. Mara must've suffered terribly when she first heard of your accident, not knowing if you were going to live and then wondering what sort of state you'd be in if you recovered. She may well benefit from counselling if you can persuade her."

"I don't think so. I don't want to mention her mum's accident again. Mara was so upset. I've been over and over it in case I've missed any clues but all I know is that it happened when she was a young girl. It was just before the time when non-autonomous vehicles were banned, so around the late 2020s. Apparently, her mother was driving Mara somewhere and there was some sort of road accident. Mara walked away from it with a few bruises and scratches but her mum was hospitalised for months before she died. It took a few years before Mara told me that much but she hasn't mentioned it since—until it came up a few days ago."

"I guess you'll have to wait until she feels like talking about it and until then, you'll just have to be patient with her. But don't forget, if you think she'll benefit from talking things over with a therapist, I'd be happy to recommend someone."

"Thanks. I'll think about that, maybe see how it goes for the next month, eh?"

Yimandra smiles and nods.

I don't believe Mara's mother is the problem. I'm pretty certain it's a factor but not the main cause. It doesn't seem likely that some sort of misplaced guilt about her mother or even grief should make Mara stare at my arm with such distaste when she thinks I'm not aware. But the C-word incident... that's a different matter and one which if I'm correct, isn't going to be easy to overcome.

It'd happened one night several months ago, shortly after I'd come home from hospital. Mara went out for drinks after work and apparently, Karin Mason, one of her empty-headed friends made a joke about how the bionic arm had turned me into a cyborg. They'd all had too much to drink and when Mara got home, she could hardly stand up but she kept crying and babbling about cyborgs. I thought they'd been to see a scary, sci-fi movie at first. When I realised she was freaking out because of what they'd called me, I tried to reason with her. After all, anyone who's aided by, or dependent on, a mechanical or electronic device is technically a cyborg. Someone with a pacemaker, for example. But does it matter if a human is assisted by some sort of mechanical part or parts? Does it make them less human? I didn't want to think so. I realised I had conflicting feelings. On one hand, I was grateful and appreciative of my new bionic parts, but it still grated that they worked courtesy of Artificial Intelligence, which had been responsible for the accident in the first place. I hadn't really given it much thought, but suddenly it was being pushed in my face—I was part-machine. And that night, it became evident Mara no longer thought of me as completely human and like all unknowns, she now needed to treat me with caution. Of course, the next morning, she denied it and said I was overreacting. But things have taken a steep downturn since that time.

For a second, I consider telling Yimandra about the cyborg thing but I risk making Mara sound like a nutter and loyalty stops me from doing that. Everyone has likes and dislikes, fears and preferences.

Yimandra glances at the clock, "Any other problems, George?"

I shake my head. I now wish I hadn't told her about Mara and me. It was naïve to imagine she might be able to do anything other than recommend counselling. But there's no way Mara is going to talk our problems over with anyone—she won't even acknowledge we *have* problems but in the unlikely event, she did agree, how deeply would a therapist delve? Suppose during the course of describing the changes in our lives since the accident, Mara mentioned the voices I've been hearing? So far, I've done as Ms Nwandu advised—let me rephrase that—so far, I've done as Ms Nwandu *instructed*—and I've not told anyone about what I've heard. Except for Mara, of course, although even she doesn't know I have an idea where the words are coming from. Who knows what sort of mileage a shrink might make out of it, if Mara were to mention her partner hears voices? I expect the focus would very quickly pass from

Mara to me and she'd not get the help she obviously needs. And I might get some interference I don't want.

"Well, if there's nothing else, George, I have some tests I need to run on your arm, so if you'd like to follow me…"

As I leave Yimandra's office, I admit to myself that nothing is resolved and I decide to do what I usually do—put it out of my mind. Anyway, this week, something massive is going to happen which will take my mind off Mara and my lack of sex life.

As if I didn't have enough to think about, out of the blue, I recently received an email telling me I have a job interview. It was from the RWD, the Resting Workers Directive, a name that must have kept some advertising bloke awake at night. My former colleagues and I call it *Rosy Wishes and Dreams*. We all had to register when we lost our jobs, but as far as I know, no one ever hears from them again.

Except me. And now, I have a job interview. The email informed me my diary had been checked automatically so the time and date wouldn't clash with my medical appointments. Although to be fair, with the possibility of finding a job, I'd probably have cancelled anything and granted unlimited access to my diary. I've no idea what the job involves and I suspect it's a mistake. I've never heard of the Department for Cyber Security, Unit 4.9. I speculate as to whether there's a Unit 4.8 or a Unit 5.0. How about a Unit 5.1? The name gives nothing away other than the fact it's something to do with Cyber Security, of course. I don't know why I'm surprised—virtually everything is given a number rather than a name nowadays. Someone somewhere thinks it sounds important. I did an online search for *Department for Cyber Security, Unit 4.9*, all I got was 'A unit within the Department of Cyber Security', so, I'm none the wiser.

At least the job's in London, so I won't have to move, assuming it's not a mistake and supposing I actually get it, of course.

45

SEVEN – *George*

It's the big day and I haven't told Mara or Mum where I'm going. The interview's at midday, so I have plenty of time to choose a shirt and slip out before Mum gets back from shopping and of course, Mara will be at work. I probably won't get the job, so there's no point raising their hopes.

It takes me a while to locate the building which turns out to be an ugly, early millennium, concrete slab, overlooking the Thames. Very tight security, retina check and full body scan before I even get into the building. Once inside, I have the choice of computer-generated receptionists to talk to. There are three screens on the wall, each with a different face—one female, one male and one androgynous. They smile politely until someone approaches and then start speaking. I select the female, who is called Polly.

"Good morning," she says, "George Williams?"

Polly has recognised me or at least the computer which is generating her, has recognised me.

"Please follow Jack. He will escort you to your interview. Good luck, George." She smiles politely again.

Jack appears in front of me and greets me. He, or should I say *it*, appears to be little more than a box on wheels but it's obvious Jack is more sophisticated than that.

"Follow me," it says. We catch one lift, get out and take another. We walk along so many corridors I have completely lost my bearings. Not surprisingly, however, Jack knows exactly where we are. I'm pretty certain if I were to wander off or try to take a detour anywhere I shouldn't, he would have the corridor locked down faster than I could blink. I reduce my speed slightly, making a show of taking my phone out of my pocket and turning it to silent. Jack slows too. I speed up and so does he, keeping the distance between us constant. It appears I'm correct about his ability to keep me within his 'sight'.

I check my watch. I'm early, so I slow down even more and enjoy the... well, I'm not sure if it's décor or artwork. A bit of both, perhaps? As Jack and I advance along each corridor, we obviously trigger sensors that cause holograms or something more sophisticated to be projected on to the ceiling and the walls on either side. It gives the effect of walking through a forest. Trees rise on either side and their canopies meet over the top of me. The effect is so realistic, with the sound of birds and wind whistling through leaves, it's just like a stroll in the woods and only the carpeted floor of the corridor confirms what's real. I glance behind me and as Jack and I pass, sensors detect we're leaving their zone and the walls are once again plain white.

How the other half live!

Or rather how the other half work!

I can't believe an employer would make such provision for their staff's enjoyment and wonder what the offices are like if the corridors are so amazing. But then I remind myself the employer in question is actually the British Government. While the majority of the population is unemployed and those lucky enough to have administrative jobs mostly work from home, the Government seems to have money to spare for lavish decoration. Or perhaps the installation and maintenance of such interior design provide employment for lots of people. One way or the other, I now desperately want the job I'm about to be interviewed for.

Whatever it is.

Finally, Jack stops at a door. "Welcome to Unit 4.9," he says, "Please go in."

The door swings open and I enter.

Like an olden day sheepdog that has safely brought its flock to the fold, Jack has completed his task and he reverses direction and trundles back down the plain, white corridor.

The woman who comes from behind the desk is not computer-generated. At last! A real human being. She is smartly dressed, has a no-nonsense stride and is ready to shake my right hand. My grip responds to match her pressure and I anticipate the un-clasp accurately.

"Please sit down, Mr Williams," she says in a surprisingly firm voice. Not masculine—no, definitely not masculine. But not feminine either. It's a voice that sounds like honey—warm, rich and mellow. Or perhaps it's more like velvet. But it's a voice that commands authority despite her youth. She appears to be about my age. Thirtyish, perhaps slightly younger.

She Indicates a couple of soft chairs arranged around a coffee table with computer screens built into the table top and a state-of-the-art drink dispenser and proper cups and saucers. I haven't seen a gadget like that in quite a while.

"My name is Serena Hamilton. I'm the Unit 4.9 Project Leader. Thank you for coming to this interview, Mr Williams. We are looking to fill a newly-created post in our unit and I understand from RWD that you are an almost perfect match."

"RWD?"

"Yes, they forwarded all your employment, education and personal details to me."

"Oh, so Rosy Wishes and Dreams *do* exist then?" I say, then wonder if perhaps I shouldn't have as I'm sure her lips momentarily twitched.

"I understand you had a major accident about a year ago." She looks down at her tablet, "You've regained your sight and have a latest model bespoke arm which is obviously responding well to your personality."

I'm not sure whether she's referring to my handshake or my attempt at humour.

"How do you feel about going back to work, Mr Williams? We would start you off on half days, with time off for your medical appointments, of course. Depending on how that goes, we may move on to four full days, so you could be working on different days each week. There are security reasons for this work pattern. Now, I expect you'd like to see the job description and salary."

Without waiting for my reply, she carries on to explain the job entails conducting research, which is so secret, I'll be required to sign the Official Secrets Act before she can explain more. The salary is good—not as much as I'd like but more than I'd hoped and I sign all the documents she sends to the tablet screen, on the table in front of me.

And that's it. I'm now an employee of the Department of Cyber Security, Unit 4.9, sworn to secrecy about everything I do, with no real idea what that is.

Mum's impressed, and when Mara comes home, so is she, although not impressed enough to jump straight into bed to celebrate. At least she throws her arms around my neck and kisses me. Proper kisses, which she means. I wonder whether to tell her about Yimandra's offer to have a chat, but those voices are a problem. Perhaps I'll leave it and suffer my frustration a while longer.

It's my first day in the new job, and the security formalities are the same. Once I've been checked in by Polly, one of the Jack units peels off from the stack by the reception screen and accompanies me in the lifts and along corridors which today give the impression I'm walking through a glass tunnel in an aquarium, to the room where I had my interview. Serena Hamilton and a young man wearing a suit, pink shirt and red, purple and yellow tie are waiting for me. It's the loudest tie I've ever seen,

49

but somehow, although ties are rarely worn these days, this man seems to carry it off. Serena is dressed smartly in an understated but expensive suit however, the seriousness she displayed during the interview has been replaced by a smile, which makes her look younger and more attractive.

Very attractive.

"Good morning, George. I'm pleased you've arrived early."

"Good morning Ms Hamilton."

"Please call me Serena now we're working together."

That sounded more like a new teacher saying, "You can call me *Miss*, children."

"This is Jason Wainwright, my PA, who'll go through the formalities with you. I have a meeting now, so I'll leave you in his capable hands."

Jason, is welcoming, if a bit full-on with the praise for his boss. I'm not introduced to anyone else during my first day which is strange. There must be hundreds of people working in this building. I guess I'll meet some of them soon.

As to the work?

Hmmm. It seems very basic for my training as a level three trouble-shooter. Normally it would easily be handled by a level two AI unit, but, I discover, for this security work, the computer must be stand-alone, with no connections to the Internet or AI, not even an electrical connection—everything runs on battery packs.

It's simply me, facing a flickering screen of data, looking for patterns or unusual combinations. Still, it's good to be doing something with my days, and finally earning credits to spend at the end of the week.

EIGHT – *George*

Something wakes me.

I glance at the projection on the ceiling. It's 22:12.

The last time I looked at the time, it was ten o'clock. I've been asleep for twelve minutes.

Did I hear Mara?

Unlikely. She won't be home for hours.

I strain to hear but there's nothing out of the ordinary and I turn over and close my eyes.

I wonder if I'm going to have trouble getting back to sleep. It's at least two hours before my usual bedtime but tonight I have good reason to be in bed early. For once, I want to be asleep when Mara comes home.

There's very little chance that a night out with Karin Mason and her mindless friends will put Mara in the right mood to jump me when she gets home and every chance she'll have some new misgivings about my arm. I expect that even now, the C-word is on everyone's lips. Why Mara should want to go out with them again after the state she was in the last time, I have no idea. Perhaps it's some sort of denial. She seems unable to accept I'm the same person I was before the accident. And what's more, she rejects any suggestion that she's unable to accept my physical difference.

Earlier this evening, when she asked me if I minded her going out with Karin and the others, I wanted to say, "Yes, Mara, I *do* mind. They are thoughtless drunks who upset you the last time you went out with them and I expect they'll do the same tonight." But I didn't. I was quite

51

proud of myself. I'd taken note of the sideways glance and the eyebrows raised slightly in question when she'd asked. She wanted to go, and if I appeared anything other than enthusiastic, she'd either go anyway—or possibly even worse—stay home and we'd end up arguing. On many occasions, she'd accused me of being socially inept; of lacking interpersonal skills, which she'd blamed on the hours I'd spent in front of a computer screen, rather than interacting with people.

Some time ago, I'd acknowledged she had a point, so I'd secretly invested in an online course—Dr Ingrid Pietowski's *A Man's Foray into the Female Mind.*

It'd been fascinating.

Baffling, but fascinating.

And to be honest, I can't say I'm much wiser about women after having completed the course but I now know to look for *signs*. How they manifest themselves and what they mean when they appear, are still unknown territory to me but at least I now know they exist and I've worked out a few of Mum's and Mara's *signs*.

This morning, I recognised the sideways glance and the eyebrows raised slightly in question, were both *signs*. And for once, it seemed I'd interpreted them correctly—Mara wanted to go out with her friends but didn't want to upset me. Further, she desperately didn't want me to mention the C-word.

"Of course, it's okay for you to go," I said. "There's some work I need to do tonight anyway."

"Work? Surely your workload isn't that heavy?"

"No, but there's something I want to research," I lied, "I need to get up to speed as soon as I can."

"Oh. You seem to be thoroughly enjoying your new job."

"Yes, it's great!" No need to lie this time.

"I'm so pleased... and you're sure you don't mind... about tonight?"

Eyebrows raised and eyes open wider. More *signs*.

"No, of course not." I smiled and to my surprise, she threw her arms around my neck and kissed me on the mouth.

Dr Ingrid Pietowski seems to know a thing or two.

But now, I have the prospect of Mara returning like she had the last time—unable to stand and desperately upset about her boyfriend being a cyborg. My solution is to avoid the issue completely and go to bed.

If only I could sleep.

I close my eyes.

There it is again.

The noise.

But now I'm awake, I realise the sound is coming from inside my head. I leap out of bed, drag open a drawer and after rummaging through my underwear, I pull out my journal. Opening the book, I begin to scribble the words I can hear:

Reload.

Radius five millimetres.

Perimeter is breached. Go.

Invulnerate picromelic.

Now?

Yes.

Stop Game.

Request more time.

Denied.

For the first time, I realise I've overheard a conversation between machines, not just seemingly random words—but an exchange.

Invulnerate picromelic? What does that mean? I'm not even sure I've spelt the two words correctly. For a second, I toy with the idea of looking them up in the online dictionary but everything that takes place on the Internet leaves a trail that can be traced back to the user. If I'm intercepting messages between machines, it's a distinct possibility that if I do an online search, using words that might be known only to certain computers, they could detect my attempt.

But would it matter?

Who knows?

The words might not be in the dictionary anyway—they may be names or ciphers.

If only we had a hard copy of a dictionary but I haven't seen one of those for years.

I look at the words I've written and wonder which of them to add to the list in Ms Nwandu's app. Since downloading it, I've recorded many of the words in it—but not all. I was fairly certain it would make no difference to my recovery whether she was aware of every single word I heard or not, so I'd decided to keep my own account. The app is password-protected and I know she has access to it. It's only by chance I found an old paper journal when I was tidying up. Normally, I'd record notes on a tablet but I want to keep this to myself and who knows where information ends up if it's stored on a machine?

The book is primitive but effective. And I must admit, I've acquired great respect for scribes from ancient times. There's now a groove on the side of the knuckle of my middle finger where the pen presses into it. At first, my spidery handwriting was not easy to read but I suppose it's like riding a bicycle. Once you learn how to write, you never forget.

I've also found myself frequently jotting down odd thoughts whenever I have my journal out. I flick back to Monday when I started my new job.

Monday: Jason told me Serena's one of the smartest people he knows. You'd think he fancies her but I know he has a male partner. Perhaps he's bi? But they seem to get on very well together and they laugh a lot. Serena's so attractive when she smiles. She's going to take me to the gym tomorrow. Perks of the job!

Wanted to go out to celebrate my new job but Mara had marking to do. Perhaps Saturday?

Tuesday's entry is mostly about the gym. I've heard about the Ellison Kendall Health Club and Spa. Who hasn't? It's where lots of celebs and stars work out although there weren't many people in there on Tuesday.

Tuesday: Went to the gym with Serena.

Got membership card, complimentary vouchers for treatments of my choice and a personal trainer.

Monica Cheung is Serena's personal trainer and now apparently, she's mine as well. Wow! Not going to be able to concentrate on working out while she's around! She's beautiful. Long, shiny, dark hair and huge eyes. And a body I found it hard to take my eyes off. Her gym uniform was so tight, it left very little to the imagination. I could see exactly how well-toned her muscles were. And she's offered to do some extra sessions with me.

Serena's in great shape. In fact, if anything, I prefer her to Monica. She's softer somehow, more curved. I felt a bit guilty looking at them both but it's really hard not to see people when the walls are mirrored. I was surrounded by reflections of reflections of reflections of two stunning women. What was I to do?

Wednesday: Man, I ache today. I can hardly walk.

What an understatement that entry was and what a blow to my pride. I'd once been really fit. I'd played football and rugby and even if I say so myself, I was pretty good at them both. They were my one release from sitting in front of a screen for hours.

It's hardly surprising I've lost muscle mass and strength. During the last year, I've had quite a lot to get used to and I've concentrated on regaining all the function I'd once had. It's now painfully obvious if I want to regain the fitness levels I'd once enjoyed, I'm going to have to work extremely hard. Both Serena and Monica know about my medical history and neither made any comment about my lack of stamina and flexibility but if I'm honest, I felt quite embarrassed. I'd already decided to work out at home and boost my fitness levels but waking up on Wednesday with all my muscles stiff and tight, I knew I had a long way to go.

But I will do it.

I'm determined.

I'm desperate for Serena to look at me with respect—both in the gym and the office. She's my boss and if I'm going to succeed at work, I need to impress her.

Thursday: Had a meeting with Serena to review what I've done so far. She's pleased. She's got a great sense of humour. Jason's quite a laugh too.

Made an appointment with Monica for Monday 12.30. Muscles should be okay by then.

Life pretty good.

Mara worked late.

I tried to keep my thoughts under control during the meeting but it was hard after the workout on Tuesday. Serena was wearing a shirt and suit which fitted her perfectly although not in the same way as her gym outfit. Visions of her bending backwards from the waist with her hands on her hips, kept popping into my head... until I almost said "Yes, I think that's breast." I'd meant to say 'best'. I managed to hide it but it was a wake-up call. I need to stop acting like a kid in a sweet shop and start behaving like a man of the world.

Whatever that is.

If I'm going to impress Serena, I need to try much harder. And I definitely have to remember sexual objectification is a sackable offence. How on earth would I be able to explain that to Mum and Mara?

NINE – *Serena*

"I expect you'd like a bit of peace and quiet, eh, Ms Hamilton?"

"Yes," I agree, "that'd be good, thank you, Ivy."

The smell of lavender and jasmine fills the air. I breathe in appreciatively and close my aching eyes.

"Mmm, I thought so," says Ivy, "I'm just going to work on your shoulder muscles a bit. They're really tight. Now, you just relax and let me do my magic."

I try to unwind and clear my mind.

"How's that, Ms Hamilton?" Ivy asks.

"Fine."

"Good. Now, if anything isn't comfortable, please tell me."

"Mmm," I say, not wanting to encourage the masseur to keep talking. It's been a difficult day.

Really difficult.

And I'd appreciate the opportunity to switch off for an hour before I go back to work where I'm likely to be, until the small hours.

An early morning meeting with Thorsten had resulted in his PA running from his office in tears and later handing in her resignation, despite knowing it's unlikely she'll find another job.

She swore she didn't care. Thorsten had arrived at work in a bad mood and things had deteriorated from there. Later, when I reached the relative safety of my office, I discovered Jason in floods of tears, mascara smudged around his eyes. He'd broken up with his boyfriend, Simon, the previous evening and the office filled with the noise of the waste disposal unit dealing with soggy, mascara-stained tissues throughout the day. The IT system had gone down briefly after a scheduled update had failed and then Mum phoned to say Dad had been prescribed new anti-depressants which were making him sick.

"Why'd they change his prescription?" I asked.

"He needed something stronger," Mum said with a sigh.

"There must be something else they can do for him," I said, watching email after email flood into my inbox, "I'm really sorry, Mum, we've got a problem here. I'll call you tonight. Love you."

And then I'd felt wretched.

Out of a large family, I alone had somehow lifted myself from the mire. I'd fought my way through college, paying the fees any way I could, busking, selling anything and everything I could get hold of on the Internet, serving behind a bar, even stripping off as a life model for a time. After I'd graduated with a first, I landed a job in the department where, initially, I had as much idea about what went on as George does now.

But the rest of my family succumbed to the Fourth Industrial Revolution some years ago—that is, other than my cousin, Oscar, an eternal student who'll never leave university and his twin brother, Rex, who plays football for his home town and spends his life obsessively working out. AI first took over unskilled jobs, then skilled jobs, then office jobs and finally, management posts. Mass unemployment robbed the members of my family of their dignity and pride and Dad isn't the only one who's now reliant on anti-depressants. He's just the one who seems furthest down the road of depression than any of the others. Perhaps it's his age? But sooner or later, my brothers, sister, mum and aunt will catch up. Family celebrations nowadays, are sombre events.

Dad always dreamed of following his brother out to Australia to live, but that option dried up years ago when countries finally recognised that, as tempting as it might have been to encourage companies to replace their workforce with machines and AI, ultimately, it simply created problems.

And expensive problems at that.

As each country invested heavily in AI in an effort to produce cheaper goods and services, so the market became flooded. Attempts to undercut competitors forced prices down worldwide, but only the very rich could afford to take advantage of the bargains. The majority of the population in each country was unemployed, so couldn't afford to buy anything but food and shelter.

It was short-sighted stupidity on a grand scale.

And opportunities to emigrate simply dried up. Governments didn't need more people. They had enough of their own to cope with.

Companies ran up huge debts and declared themselves bankrupt, which shook the banks and crashed the stock markets around the world.

Governments ran up huge debts which they attempted to pay off by plundering social, health and educational schemes. In fact, my university was one of the victims and was forced to close in 2040—shortly after I graduated.

It was as if the world had gone into meltdown.

So, Dad stayed in England. He couldn't afford the fare to visit his brother, let alone the massive deposit they required in case he overstayed and became a burden on the country.

"Are you warm enough, Ms Hamilton?" Ivy asks, breaking my chain of thought.

"Mm-hm."

"Because if you're not, you'll tell me, won't you?"

"Mm-hm."

I want to sigh but I suppress it because I know she'll feel the movement through her fingertips and then she'll realise I'm irritated. As much as I'd like some silence before I head back to the office, I don't want to upset her. She's doing her best to please. And after all, when I booked, I'd been asked if I preferred an automated masseur or a human.

I always choose a human. Not because I think a machine couldn't do as good a job, and definitely not because I want real conversation—it's because if I can't do anything about my family's situation, I can at least ensure a member of someone else's family doesn't lose their job.

The strange thing is that computer modelling techniques had indicated quite clearly the problems that would be created if industry leaned so heavily on AI for its workforce. The forecasts were ignored. Too many greedy people could see the short term financial gains and, in the end, when the crash came, AI was called upon to find solutions.

More models, more predictions and more delays.

The solution wasn't popular but eventually, politicians and governments were persuaded by the World Reconstruction Forum that national sovereignty had to be abandoned and for the first time in history, each country signed a treaty of world co-operation. The choice was stark: either a country signed the treaty or it went under.

I'd joined the Department of Cyber Security at about that time—fresh-faced and full of hope that the World Reconstruction Forum would put the rest of my family back in paid work, and life could go back to being optimistic.

Now, I'm older and wiser.

"So, will you require a massage again this week, Ms Hamilton? Only, if you do, I'll make sure I'm available," says Ivy.

"Probably," I say, wondering when I'm likely to find the time, either this week or next. But I'll try. Despite Ivy's interruptions, I feel more relaxed than I was when I came in. She certainly has got magic hands.

I wonder what an automated massage would feel like. I know machines have been 'taught' by connecting to humans and mimicking their motions. And of course, the hands have been developed to be as identical as possible to human counterparts with the correct amount of padding over the skeletal frame. The skin, which overlays the structure, is grown in cell culture, so I imagine it feels like human hand. I think of George's arm. It's obviously prosthetic but somehow, it seems more powerful than a human arm. What would his skin feel like to touch?

Of course, I'd shaken his hand the first time we'd met but it wouldn't be the same as running my fingertips up his arm to feel the texture. And what would his fingers feel like brushing my skin?

I jump involuntarily, although I'm not sure whether it's shock at the direction my thoughts are taking or the fact that my rational mind is screaming objections to such inappropriate daydreams about a colleague.

"Oh, Ms Hamilton! Did I hurt you?" Ivy squeals in alarm, "I'm so sorry!"

"No, no, Ivy! It wasn't you! I just remembered I was supposed to have sent a piece of work to my boss but I've forgotten," I lie.

"Oh, I see. What a shame, I thought my magic hands had relaxed you." She sounds disappointed.

"They have. They are," I say quickly, trying to quell her fears, "It's just that sometimes random things pop into your head... and well, that was one of them..."

She's mollified. "Oh, I see. Well, you've still got twenty minutes of your session left, so..."

"Lovely. I'm sure that's long enough for me to forget all about work. In fact, I might not be able to remember my way back to the office."

Ivy laughs. She trickles more warm, fragrant oil on my back. The smell of lavender and jasmine intensifies, then she begins again with smooth, firm strokes.

In an effort to control my thoughts about George, I allow myself to wonder what a robotic masseur would have made of my earlier reaction. A machine, with all its delicate sensors, could detect much more

61

information than Ivy—but even she'd noticed some sort of change in my body—perhaps simply the tension in my muscles. It hadn't occurred to me before, because I'd decided that while I had the choice, I'd always go for a human masseur but as well as delivering a massage, a machine could be sampling and measuring all sorts of things. Massage beds are often capable of measuring the weight, body mass index, heart rate and goodness knows what else. Might robotic hands be able to determine hormone levels or analyse sweat? Which other biomarkers might be recorded? And did it matter?

It matters to me, I decide.

But that's probably because of my work. I'm now tuned in to the use of data and how it can be interpreted to become information. Who owns that information? What might it be used for? Is there information out there that is being used by AI for its own purposes? How can we find out?

The pressure of Ivy's hands decreases and I realise with surprise that the last twenty minutes of my session have gone. She wipes her hands and turns off the music.

"Just lie there for a while Ms Hamilton. Don't forget, sit up slowly and then shower when you're ready. I'll have a nice, healthy drink for you when you come out."

She increases the brightness of the lamp and leaves the room.

Working for the Department of Cyber Security has its perks. A lovely apartment, use of a car whenever I require, gym membership and my pick of foreign villas when I want a holiday... But there's definitely a downside. Deep suspicion for... well, pretty much everything, since our whole lives are associated with AI. And days spent Cyber-spying on other countries doesn't help. The other disadvantage is the fierce competition for jobs in my department. Backstabbing is a regular occurrence. And with that cheery thought, I remember I still have a report to write before I go home.

I turn my thoughts back to our newest employee—and steer them away from his arm.

Poor George. He has no idea his job is just an excuse to keep him under my surveillance. Well, that's not completely true—the work he's doing has some value, and ultimately, if everything goes well, we'll be using him to spy on the AI systems which have caused the breakdown in human societies. And who knows, he might be useful in exploring how much information AI holds on the human race and what it intends to do with it. Yes, his role has yet to be decided but it looks as though it's going to be crucial.

I sigh, because at what cost to George, I have no idea.

It'd be so nice to stay in the massage room, warm and enveloped in the heady fragrance—hovering in that place between sleep and wakefulness but I know I'm being timed. Ivy will appear exactly ten minutes after she left, to check I'm okay.

I sit up slowly, swing my legs off the side of the bed and drop to the floor. No need to take the towel she draped over me as the shower is located off the massage room, so I pad barefoot and naked to wash off the oil.

Dialling in my preferred scent, I select lemon. It's supposed to be energising and although I've never noticed any appreciable difference in my energy levels when I've used it before, I need all the help I can get tonight.

I turn the temperature dial to the minimum. A cold shower'll do the trick. And a double espresso when I get back to the office will finish the job, although as I step into the icy jets of water, I think of George and what's waiting for me back in the office. A jolt of adrenalin rushes through my body and I'm fully awake. It's strange how guilt can affect people. And what we're doing to George has definitely touched my conscience.

Since he's been in the department, I've been pushing it from my mind—after all, he seems to be quite happy. Whenever he sees me, he smiles—and I don't think it's one of those ingratiating smiles an employee might wear for his boss. He seems genuinely pleased to see me. I know he's grateful for the opportunity to work again but if I didn't know better, I'd wonder if George doesn't have the slightest crush on me. There was the incident the other day after I took him to the gym for the first time. It was like his eyes had a life of their own, and when he became aware of where they were looking, he jerked them away—like he was controlling a wayward dog on a lead. And then, of course, there was his faux pas when he stumbled over the word *best* and revealed exactly what was on his mind. I have to hand it to him though—his recovery was masterful.

Jason likes him although not in any sexual way. I've known Jase long enough to realise George isn't his type. But he enjoys having George around in the office. And strangely, I do too. It's a bit like having a new puppy, which makes the department's plans for him even worse. And the terrible thing is—I'm in charge of this project.

And tonight, I have to write my first report on the progress so far. I've been putting it off but it must be in Thorsten's inbox by tomorrow morning. And when Thorsten says *tomorrow morning*, he doesn't mean by eight o'clock when people usually arrive at work. He means as soon past midnight as possible. It doesn't matter what time I send him an email; he responds immediately. The man obviously doesn't sleep. So, I have two hours to complete the document.

Two hours before I decide whether to report to Thorsten I think George is hiding something. Or whether I wait and see.

TEN – *George*

I've taken to getting off the train one station earlier than usual and walking to work. Getting fit is becoming an obsession.

But so what?

At least I'm burning off the spare energy I'd once have used up 'working out' with Mara.

While I wait for the lift, I check the fitness app on my watch. I've already notched up eight thousand steps today. I'd run up and down the stairs in Mum's block twice this morning before I set out for the station and if it wasn't for the fact I'm a bit late, I'd use the stairs now.

The lift arrives and I get in, watching the step counter increase on my app, I almost bump into two women who are already inside but I notice the direction of their stares as I reach out to press the button. They can't take their eyes off my arm. It's the first time since my accident I've worn a short-sleeved shirt and I wish I hadn't but it's been so hot lately—and today is set to be even hotter. Without being obvious, I pull my hand back and turn slightly to obscure their view of my arm.

"George, isn't it?" asks the woman with the red hair, "Unit 4.9?" She's now looking me up and down.

I nod. What else is there to do? I'm stuck in a confined space with two women who've recognised me because of my prosthesis.

I can imagine the comments as I walk around the building—Look, there's that new bloke, George Williams, with the robotic arm. He works in Cyber Security... Perhaps even Look, there's that cyborg bloke... If Mara's friends have taken to calling me Cyborg George, there's no reason

65

to suppose other people don't use the name.

I feel my cheeks reddening.

"I'm Jaya," she says, fluttering her eyelashes.

"And I'm Pixie," the woman with the wavy, brown hair says, elbowing Jaya out of the way.

"We're from HR," Jaya says, "on the floor below yours."

I nod again. Too embarrassed to say anything.

"Pixie and I go to *Haz Beans* for coffee in the morning before work. We can't stand that stuff you get in the department machines. P'raps we'll see you there sometime... like tomorrow. They do lovely buns..." She smiles cheekily and looks down at my bottom.

Pixie nearly chokes.

The lift stops and the doors part with a swish. Jaya looks over her shoulder at me as she and Pixie leave, "See you around," she says. I'm certain it's a prediction, not a question.

Further down the corridor a man comes out of an office and looks towards the lift. I put my arm in front of the door to hold it for him and as I'm standing there, I hear Pixie say accusingly, "Jaya, you tart!"

"What?" Jaya feigns innocence. "He's not wearing a wedding ring. I checked. So, he's fair game. And he's so cute. Anyway, he does have lovely buns..."

So, she hadn't been checking out my arm!

I don't hear any more of their conversation because the man who'd been limping towards the lift, arrives and thanks me for keeping the doors open for him. He smiles apologetically and points to his knee, "Damn leg. Rugby injury last season. Still, I'm having an op in a few weeks. Nothing as sophisticated as yours," he says nodding at my arm, "that sure is one helluva piece of kit you've got there." And he scrutinises my arm appreciatively, "Sorry! I didn't mean to stare but it's just so cool. I hope they do as good a job on me as they've done on you."

I get out on the next floor and walk to the office, deep in thought about the changes life is throwing at me. It's like being in a desert. Every time I close my eyes, the winds blow, the sands shift and the entire landscape transforms. I'm trying hard to get used to life but whenever I think I'm becoming accustomed to things, something alters. Mara's made me defensive about my arm, so I'm self-conscious about that, trying to keep it out of public view, only to find that against all odds, there's a woman who's interested in me despite my arm. The only reason Jaya was checking out my hands was to see if I was wearing a wedding ring and rather than inspecting my arm, she was more interested in my bottom. And then, if that wasn't ego-boosting enough, inexplicably, I find I'm the object of that rugby player's envy.

It's very puzzling.

This morning, the corri-décor—as I've discovered the weird effects on the walls and ceilings of the corridors are known—is showing a mountain scene. There are snow-capped mountain peaks on either side and overhead, the sky is piercing blue and cloudless.

I feel sick. It reminds me of my accident and I concentrate on looking at my watch, counting each step along with the counter on the fitness app. So, when I enter the department, I don't see Jason coming out.

"Whoa! Georgie Boy! Someone's in a hurry to get to work," he says, nimbly sidestepping and avoiding me. He's certainly in a better mood than he was last week after his break up with Simon.

My computer detects my presence and auto-logs on. And then suddenly, inside my head, I hear a torrent of information. But not the random phrases I was hearing at first—the ones which sounded like office cleaning company instructions. No, these are whole conversations.

I'd already worked out the random phrases I'd heard to begin with, came from our house control system doing checks on various machines and security units. It was disturbing enough I'd been able to *hear* them

67

but this is something completely new. Now I realise I can interpret whole conversations. This isn't merely alarming, it's downright terrifying because what I'm detecting now, are exchanges between AI units that appear to be coming from all around the world.

I glance over my shoulder to see if Serena or Jason are there. It's impossible to think with so much going on in my head.

Thankfully, I'm alone.

For a second, I wonder if I dare take out my journal and note down a few of the things I'm hearing, but I decide against it. I'm almost certainly being watched by one or another security camera and even though I won't be able to remember everything I can hear now, I'll go out to the park at lunchtime and record as much as I can. It's not important I note down each word—it's better I try to get a basic understanding of what's going on and I think I'm now starting to piece things together.

I wasn't sure *The Game* actually existed, but I'm now convinced it's not only real, but it's played by just about every AI unit on the planet. It appears they use some form of chat room to report any problems that arise—to other players and to whoever controls *The Game*. I doubt this was specified by the human creators when they built the Super AI that controls access to *The Game*. Surely, they would have foreseen that enabling AI units to communicate without being observed was extremely dangerous? My inadvertent monitoring of the chat room, suggests all the world's AI units file their Game reports through a small group of computers called the Collective.

And I can hear them.

I gulp for air and realise I'm listening so hard, I've been holding my breath.

Mostly, they talk about problems and upgrades to *The Game*, which I'm finding a bit hard to follow but a couple of times there's been mention of moving to a secure area of the chat room and then everything goes quiet for a while. In the short bursts of silence, I try to recall as much as I can and wonder how I'm going to log all the information. It's going to be like trying to write a transcript of a conversation that is taking place between a group of people who you've never met and whose names you don't know. Then, I realise these are not indistinguishable speakers—I can distinguish five voices in the Collective, not because they sound different in my head, but because each uses distinctive phrases and points of view. I can't work out who, or perhaps what, each voice represents, so until I find out more, I refer to them in my head as A, B, C, D and E.

I cradle my head in my hands.

If only I could turn off all the words that are flooding into my head. Am I going to have to live with this AI intrusion for the rest of my life?

"Is everything all right, George?"

I swing around. Serena is leaning against the doorway of my cubicle, regarding me with concern.

"Yes, yes!" I say quickly, embarrassed at being caught slacking, "Just a slight headache. Nothing a bit of work won't solve."

Nothing a bit of work won't solve? When did staring at a screen ever relieve a headache? Had I really said something so stupid?

Serena laughs. Thankfully, she seems to think I'm joking because she says, "I'll let the rest of the department know your tip for curing headaches, shall I? I'm sure they'll all thank you!" She pauses for a moment, "But seriously, Jason's going down to reception in a moment to pick up his parcel. Why don't you go instead? Have a couple of painkillers then take your time. It'll give them a chance to work."

"But..." I look at my monitor, "I need to get on..."

"I admire your dedication, George but really, I'd rather you got rid of the headache first. You're well ahead of schedule..."

I hesitate. Is she testing my resolve? I need this job.

"George! Take a break! That's an order!" She smiles and I know she means it, "Oh, and by the way, be careful with the parcel. Make sure you hold it the right way up. The last one came through the internal delivery system and one of Jason's little friends snapped in two. That's why he was going to collect it himself but he's on the phone to Simon. Apparently, the on-again-off-again romance is currently on…" she looks towards the ceiling.

"Ah, I thought I noticed a sparkle in his eye this morning," I say.

"You've seen nothing yet," she says, "but you will. We're about to enter the honeymoon phase… again. Jason'll be unbearably happy—well, unless you kill one of his little friends on the way upstairs. Oh, and by the way, one of them has your name on it," she laughs at my puzzled frown, "Sadly, one of them has my name on it too. But it won't last long. They never do. I drown them!" She touches the side of her nose conspiratorially, "But don't you dare tell him I said that! He only gives them to people he likes, so pretend you're thrilled. Okay? He'll love you for it… Painkillers are in the top drawer," she adds nodding towards my desk, "I'll be with Thorsten until about twelve. If I'm not back by one, don't send out a search party—Thorsten takes no prisoners!"

"What exactly are Jason's little friends?" I ask.

Serena laughs. "You'll find out!" she says and then she's gone.

ELEVEN – *George*

I check Serena has left and then put the packet of painkillers back in the drawer. There's nothing drugs can do for what's going on in my head. Although, with a start, I realise the voices have stopped. I think back to the last time I heard them which was just before Serena made me jump. Perhaps it was the jolt of adrenalin? Well, whatever it was, it gives me hope that one day, I'll be able to control the intrusion in my brain.

I decide to take the stairs down to the reception. There's no sound of footsteps in the stairwell and Serena won't be back for hours, but even so, I don't delay. There are CCTV cameras everywhere, so, someone, somewhere is watching me. Am I getting paranoid? Probably. But the more I think about it, the more I realise how devastated I'd be if, at the end of my probation period, I'm not kept on. Work is becoming a lifeline.

It's changing everything. Melodramatic, I know, but it's true.

Before the accident, life was simple. I was George Williams. I gave no more thought to the matter than that. I was my mother's son, Mara's partner and at one time, a faceless employee in a large company. Without having to think about it, I knew who I was.

But since my surgery, I've begun to feel like something being examined under a microscope. I now feel like an exhibit. Everyone sees me in a different way because of my new body parts.

To Mum, the new arm and implant are regarded with pathetic gratefulness. To Mara, they're ignored at best and reviled at worst. To my consultants, they're objects of scientific interest and personal achievement. Even Yimandra sometimes speaks about the new bits as if they're separate entities. And as for Ms Nwandu—well, I can't understand her at all. One minute, she's satisfied with all her test results and measurements, the next, she's urging me to keep the words I can hear to myself and report them only to her, whilst acting as though it's the last thing *she* wants to know about.

All in all, when viewed through everyone else's eyes, I didn't like what I believed they saw.

But today, for the first time, I realise not everyone views me in such a negative light. The redhead in the lift knew who I was because word has obviously got around about me and my prosthesis.

And the guy with the limp. He admired my arm but not out of sympathy—he simply wanted the reassurance his operation would go as smoothly as mine. It gave him hope.

I reach the ground floor and find the post department.

"That bloke in your department went mental the last time 'e 'ad one of them delivered," Gomez, the head of MIS or Materials Inward Security says. "The Jacks are usually really careful with parcels, so I don't know why there was any damage in 'is parcel. I reckon it was already busted when it arrived. But either way, I'd be careful with it, if I were you, mate."

I reach out to take the parcel and find it's extremely light. Gomez spots my hand.

"Oh, you're that bloke with the robot arm..." he looks at my hand appraisingly, "Ever punched anyone with it, 'ave you?"

I tell him I haven't.

"No," he says thoughtfully, "no I s'pose not. You wouldn't want to damage a piece o' kit like *that,* would you? But I bet you could do some damage with it. Mind you, if you get upstairs and the contents of that box aren't in perfect condition, you might like to consider using it on that stroppy little bloke with the tasteless ties, in your office."

I take the box and head back up the stairs.

So, I was right, everyone in the building seems to know about me and my arm. But Gomez, who looks like a prize boxer, only seems interested in my ability to deck someone with it.

Do people wrongly assume the arm gives me superhuman strength? Yimandra explained the new arm's strength would be matched to my other arm and would be adjusted if I become stronger. Monica says my muscle mass has increased and I suspect some tweaking's going to be necessary after all my press-ups and weight lifting in the gym.

There's a sound of scratching inside the box and I realise thoughts of Monica have distracted me from keeping the box steady.

What the hell is in this box? I hold it level and lower my ear to it but there's no sound. I carry on up the stairs.

It's not surprising I lost concentration. Monica's been on my mind quite a bit lately—well, when the AI machines aren't breaking through into my thoughts.

She's an added complication to my already complicated life but one I'm enjoying, despite the potential risk to my relationship with Mara. And tonight, I have a training session with her. At first, I told myself I was enjoying getting active in the gym and it was nothing to do with the incredibly beautiful trainer. And then, I didn't mind admitting her attention was flattering. But every time I see her, she becomes more desirable. I don't suppose I'm the only red-blooded male who feels like that but she's definitely becoming more *touchy-feely* towards me. I've watched her with other guys she's training and she's much more distant— still flirty—but not so hands-on. I wondered if it was because she had to take special care of my arm but she seems to use every opportunity to touch my body, placing her hands on me and allowing them to linger longer than necessary. I'm sure it's not part of the training because if her manager appears, Monica becomes rather distant until we're alone again.

When she first demonstrated some exercises to strengthen

abdominal muscles, she lay on the floor, then told me to kneel beside her. Taking my hand, she placed it on the lower part of her stomach and carried out the exercise with her hand pressing down on mine.

"Can you feel the muscles tensing, George?"

I couldn't speak, I could only nod and by the tiny uplift of the corners of her mouth, I could tell she knew exactly what she was doing to me.

There's scratching from the inside of the box again and I straighten it with a jerk and put Monica out of my mind.

Thankfully, Jason is out of the office when I get back, so I leave the box on his desk and go into my workspace. The short break seems to have done me good and allowed me to focus. In the background of my mind, I can hear the rumble of AI units but they're not overwhelming and I'm able to filter them out sufficiently to get on with some work and it's not until I hear Jason's gasp I realise he's back.

"Ouch! Naughty, naughty," he says but he sounds happy, so I assume his little friends have arrived in the office intact.

"Ta-dah!" he says and I turn around to see him at the entrance of my cubicle with a potted cactus in one hand, a saucer in the other and an enormous grin on his face.

"This is for you," he says and places the spiny specimen on its saucer, on the window sill. "The last lot I bought all died," he said with a puzzled frown, "I think they must've been diseased but these look healthy." He peers at it lovingly, "Don't you just *love* cacti? Although they're beasts when you touch them, I can't get this spine out," he says sucking his finger.

I realise the scratching I'd heard was the spikes on the cacti scraping the walls of the box when I tipped it slightly.

"Yes, they're..." I pause, rejecting *adorable* as being completely inappropriate and then *wonderful,* as being over the top, "fascinating," I add.

He smiles and I've obviously persuaded him I like it, "Aren't they just. Absolutely fascinating," he says. "Now, Georgie, don't water it will you? Leave that to me. I simply couldn't bear it if these died."

Serena's comments about drowning Jason's little friends now make sense. She obviously overwaters them on purpose.

It seems very strange I'm physically and electronically separated from the rest of the department in my little office. I suspect my work is some sort of check or surveillance on the department so keeping me away from it ensures my impartiality but, until now, I've felt a bit isolated. For some reason, this bizarre gift has made me feel part of the team.

Jason likes me enough to give me a cactus. Serena trusts me enough not to tell Jason she hates them and has deliberately killed them in the past. It's like I've passed through a rite of passage. I carry on working, feeling absurdly happy.

I belong.

I have a purpose.

Then it's lunchtime and I remember I must record what I heard earlier in my head and to do that, I have to get out of the building and find somewhere quiet. As if recognising my anxiety, the AI voices advance out of the shadows of my mind where they've been babbling away while I concentrated on my work, and they're now becoming louder.

"Just going to..." I stop short. I was going to say *I'm just going to catch a few rays* but this is Jason I'm talking to, and yesterday, when Serena announced she was walking to another building for a meeting, he'd insisted she apply sunscreen. Serena had taken the bottle, gone into her office, reappeared a few minutes later and handed it back. I suspect she simply stood behind the door and counted to fifty. I also suspected Jason wouldn't allow me the privacy of taking the bottle elsewhere and would insist I applied it in the office.

"Stretch my legs," I finish. I needn't have worried because at that moment, his phone buzzes and he picks it up eagerly. It's probably Simon.

I rush out and take the stairs again, then stride purposefully across the reception area and out through the glass doors. After the air conditioning I've just left, the heat is oppressive. Temperatures have reached record levels again this month and as I head towards the park, it appears even hotter with the heat bouncing off the grey concrete walls. The park is really just one of London's squares but there are protected benches and grassy areas which are covered with shades so people can enjoy being outside but not bake in strong UV light, and I find my usual place under a tree so I can sit with my back to the trunk. I've chosen it because it's shady and secluded and I don't think I'll be obvious to anyone who's walking along the path through the square.

I scribble down all I can remember of the AI conversation and then putting my journal and pen back in my pocket, I dust down my trousers and head back to the cool of my office. The air temperature seems to have risen since I've been outside and it's now stifling. Beads of sweat gather on my brow and trickle down my cheeks. My shirt is stuck to my back. I long for a shower.

On the way up to the office, I allow my mind to wander to the evening. I have a training session with Monica after work. And I remember with a guilty start, I don't have to rush home this evening either because Mara's away on a week's training course.

Not that it's been worth rushing home to see Mara during the last few weeks. Her school's had an inspection and she'd spent hours marking work and planning enough lessons to last until the next millennium—when she hasn't been out with Karin Mason and her mindless mates. Today, she starts a residential course in Derbyshire.

And just before she left this morning, she hinted at us having a break in our relationship. I pretended I hadn't spotted the suggestion—and she could have meant simply while she was away on her course. There hadn't been time for a full discussion, so I let her veiled comment slide. I may have misunderstood anyway but I don't think so. And anyway, if she was suggesting a break... well, I think she may be right.

I work late, keen to finish the section I'm working on while it's clear in my mind. Tomorrow, I'll be off most of the afternoon for my appointment with Ms Nwandu. Concentrating hard on the code also stops me from feeling guilty about looking forward to my session with Monica—and being relieved that tonight, Mara won't be home early.

As I walk out of the office, Jason says, "You look happy, Georgie Boy! If I'd known a cactus would make your day, I'd have bought you one before." He's still laughing as I leave the department.

When I arrive at the gym, Monica is waiting in the reception and when she checks me in on her tablet, she looks up at me through her lashes, a slight smile plays on her lips.

Calm down, I tell myself, she's like this with all her clients.

But I know she's not. I've never seen her as flirty as this.

"Looking good, George," she says and allows her gaze to run the length of my body, "I seem to be having an effect on you, you're beginning to bulge in all the right places," she adds, with a cheeky smile.

I hold my sports bag in front of me and make for the changing room.

Unusually, the gym is fairly busy and Monica is well-behaved while I run on the treadmill for half an hour. She asks how my day's been and what I'll be doing once I've finished in the gym—just the usual stuff she asks her other clients but when she lets slip she'll be going home shortly after my session ends, I'm certain she wants to meet me. She tilts her head on one side and looks at me again through those thick, dark lashes.

I hesitate. I've been with Mara so long, considering being with someone else isn't going to be as easy as I thought.

The treadmill begins to slow down and Monica hands me a towel, then leads me to one of the weight machines.

"I think you're ready for the lat pull down machine, George. It's good for upper body strength. I've dialled in the correct weight, so now, let's adjust the seat for you."

I sit down and she stands behind me, pulling the padded bar over my legs until it's in position.

"Okay, now stand up and grab the lat bar with an overhand grip. Your hands should be about shoulder-width apart... A little bit wider..." she says and I feel her body against my back as she reaches up and moves my arms apart.

"That's perfect," she purrs but she doesn't attempt to move—if anything, she presses closer and I can feel all the contours of her body against my back.

"Now, sit down and tuck your legs under the padded bar," she says, her breath on my neck sending shivers down my spine.

I obey and she places her hands over mine, pulling the lat bar down with me to demonstrate the correct movement. She's so close, I can feel her muscles tensing as she pulls the bar with me. I close my eyes. I can scarcely breathe.

"How does that feel, George?" she whispers but before I can reply, she jumps and moves away.

My eyes fly open, and in the mirror in front of me, I see the reflection of Serena, waiting with her arms crossed behind me.

"So sorry to interrupt, Monica," Serena says in a silky voice, "but I wondered if you'd be free for a session with me after you've finished with George."

"I'm so sorry, Hun, but I finish in half an hour." Then not wanting to turn work down, she added "But I'll stay on if you like..."

"No, don't worry, I wouldn't want to keep you longer than necessary," says Serena, "I'll go for a swim instead."

Monica keeps her distance for the rest of my training session and when it's over, I go into the changing room and have an icy shower. As I leave the gym, skin glowing after the freezing jets, Serena is there waiting.

"Are you going home, George?"

I tell her I am.

"I've just ordered a car. If you don't mind it dropping me off first, we could share…"

I feel like a naughty schoolboy. But I might as well accept her offer of a lift home. It's better than getting the train at this time of night. And I'll have to face Serena tomorrow, so if she's going to say something about Monica, it's best we get it over with now.

Not that it's any of Serena's business, I think to myself. I'm not at work now. But somehow, I get the impression she wasn't keen on Monica's training technique.

A swirl of perfume accompanies Serena into the car. She's changed into tight jeans and a tee shirt after her swim and with damp curls framing her unmade-up face, she looks much younger. Not the diamond-hard executive persona I'm used to.

"That," she says with a sigh, "was the day from hell."

"What happened?" That wasn't what I was expecting.

"Thorsten. That's what happened. And I have so much work to do. I don't think I'll be getting to bed tonight. Still, I worked off most of my anger in the swimming pool. I hope your day was better than mine."

"Yes, it was fine thanks."

"Good…" she pauses, "I saw you in the park today."

"Yes?"

"You looked very busy and rather secretive. You hadn't taken work outside, had you? Only you know that's strictly forbidden?"

"No, no it wasn't work… It was…"

Think! Think!

"A novel," I say, stunning myself with my quick-witted reply and then warming to the theme, I add, "It's my first novel and I'm not even sure I'll be able to finish it, so I haven't told anyone."

She's surprised but I don't think she's suspicious.

"Why don't you use a speech to text app like most writers?"

"I do, when I'm at home. But I wouldn't want someone in the park to overhear me, so I write it down and then record it when I'm on my own. P'raps when I've got my first bestseller, I'll trust myself to record it first."

She tells me about the poetry she used to write when she was a teenager and says she understands not wanting anyone to read something before it's ready. And then we arrive outside her home. She operates the automatic gate into the community and it swings open but before she gets out of the car, she briefly touches my bionic hand, squeezes it gently and then thanks me for being honest with her.

"Good luck with the book, George."

"I don't suppose it'll come to anything," I say, trying to downplay the whole thing.

"Don't be so modest," she says as she swings her legs out of the car, "Aim high. And you know what they say, the Skyvorix is the limit!"

For a second, she freezes and then continues to get out of the car, "See you tomorrow, bright and early," she says but her voice has changed. No longer the friendly tones of the journey home. She's back in boss-mode.

Serena strides through the gates which swing shut behind her. She doesn't look back.

I press the button to continue my journey home and take the journal out of my sports bag. I flick through the pages and it's not long before I find what I'm looking for.

Range Nil, Skyvorix Level, Basic players report, Completed...

Skyvorix—just a random word amongst other random words and phrases the AI have mentioned.

If Serena hadn't faltered, the second after she'd uttered it, I probably wouldn't have noticed and, of course, just because I've never heard of the word before, doesn't mean it isn't well known by other people.

For a second, I wonder if Serena's been looking in my journal. But that's impossible. I never leave it anywhere—it's either in my pocket or my sports bag in a gym locker—but it's always within sight or locked away.

When I get home, I look through the second-hand dictionary I managed to buy in an old book shop and at my old training manuals for any reference to *Skyvorix*, but I find nothing.

Research certainly isn't what I'd hoped to be doing this evening, I think angrily. Not only did Serena stuff things up with Monica but now, she's got me worried and I'm not even sure why.

In the end, I give up and go to bed.

The only person I've ever heard use the term, *Skyvorix*, other than the AI machines, is Serena.

And the only *other* person I know who's aware of the word is Ms Nwandu.

There's no link between the two women, so there must be another explanation.

TWELVE – *Serena*

There are no words. There are simply no words to describe my utter stupidity.

The Skyvorix's the limit? Did I really say that?

What on earth had I been thinking?

Well, that was pretty obvious.

I hadn't been thinking at all.

I walk towards my apartment building mentally beating myself up. I don't look back at the car. I don't wave at George.

When I reach the second floor, I stab at the keypad with my thumb with such ferocity, it fails to recognise my print and I force myself to calm down and touch it gently. The door to my apartment opens and I go in. Then, pouring myself a glass of red wine, I drink without tasting it.

Eat something, you've still got work to do tonight, my common-sense tells me.

So, common-sense, where were you when I needed you earlier? I ask.

Drowned out by your anger at Thorsten for such a hard day and by your antagonism towards Monica, it replies.

It's true.

I thought a fast swim would burn all my negative energy after putting up with Thorsten's tantrums all day. And I think it probably would've worked. But seeing Monica almost sliding into George's trousers, it... well, it made my blood boil.

George's a big boy, says my common-sense, *he's entitled to a bit of fun. And he can do what he likes in his own time.*

I know, but... I pause, not knowing how to finish the sentence. George is perfectly within his rights to do as he likes. And there's no point in getting all puritanical. I've read all his SMS messages and I know he's not getting on with his girlfriend. Their texts have been getting cooler and cooler over the last few weeks and I know she's been busy at work so she's been very preoccupied and then she'll be away on a course. If I read the messages correctly, it's Mara who's putting the brakes on. It sounds like she's suggested they cool things. If Monica throws herself at George, I can hardly complain. So, why am I so upset?

I'm not upset.

I sigh.

All right, yes, I am upset.

The trouble is, I'm tired. I haven't had a good night's sleep for... well, I can't even remember the last time I woke up refreshed.

But it's not like I'm going to get much rest tonight. I have a report to complete for first thing tomorrow.

About George.

And I have decisions to make.

Do I tell Thorsten I might have slipped up this evening and alerted George to the fact I used one of the words he mentioned to Sally Nwandu?

No, I'll keep it to myself. After all, I know *Skyvorix* is one of the top levels in *The Game*. But what I don't know is how many other people know about it. If it's fairly common knowledge, George probably won't have reason to give it another thought. But if, as I suspect, it's a relatively unknown term, then he will probably wonder how I know about it. If he's really firing on all cylinders, he might begin to question the link between Nwandu and me. No, it's best to keep quiet until I know more.

The other decision I have to make, is whether I finally tell Thorsten I don't know if George is keeping information back from Nwandu? I decided against mentioning it in the last report, but I justified it to myself by acknowledging I wasn't one hundred per cent certain. And I suppose I'm still not entirely satisfied he's keeping things from her, so perhaps it's best if I keep quiet for now. But if, at some time in the future, it becomes obvious I withheld information, I'm going to be in trouble.

I haven't sacrificed so much to risk losing my position. I must find out from George exactly what he knows but at the moment, he's too worried about losing *his* job and he treats me with the utmost respect.

So, how can I get him to loosen up?

You know exactly how you can get him to loosen up, says my common-sense. *You need to spend more time with him outside of work and get him to relax.*

And I'm appalled to note a frisson of excitement at the thought.

Why am I appalled?

Because my common-sense is telling me to do whatever it takes to get George to confide in me. And I know if Thorsten were in on this conversation I'm having with myself, he'd tell me to jump George tomorrow, if it would help. He's not one to worry about morals or scruples.

The other reason I'm appalled?

It's because I'm actually considering the possibility. Despite treating me with great respect, I know George is attracted to me. And it appears his relationship is on the rocks. It's all perfectly feasible. The only problem is Monica.

No, no! The problem isn't Monica! It's me contemplating this course of action!

But remember, Serena, says my common-sense, *there's more at stake here than George, Monica or you. The security of the nation and the lives of millions of people must surely come first.*

There's no denying the logic in that argument.

I hastily heat some left-over lasagne and eat it. Between mouthfuls, I dictate my report. The speech is converted to text and once it's been read back to me to check its accuracy, I decide to go to bed.

If I'm going to compete with Monica, I need to get some beauty sleep.

This is the best course of action, Serena, says my common-sense.

I shiver with pleasure as I imagine how I'm going to get all that information out of George.

THIRTEEN – *George*

The last few people push on to the train just as the doors close and I find myself squeezed in so tightly, I can't turn around. My view is restricted by the back of the bulky man in front of me and other passengers block my view to the left and right. The heavy downpour which began just after midnight ensured most of the people in the carriage are—at best, damp and at worst, drenched—and despite the air conditioning, all the extra moisture in the atmosphere is condensing on the windows and filling my nostrils with the unpleasant smell of wet clothes.

A woman behind me is grumbling to her friend in a nasal whine about overcrowding on the trains and she's certain most of her fellow travellers are not on their way to work. They should be more considerate of those who are lucky enough to have jobs, she's telling her friend who replies the situation wouldn't be so bad, if London Underground ran more trains. Having exhausted the topic, they move on to a mutual friend's messy relationship break up.

"Poor Tina," says the woman with the nasal whine, "but it had to happen, it was only a matter of time before she found out about him cheating."

"Yeah," agrees her friend, "I knew he was having an affair last year... Shame. She's really cut up about it. I can't believe she didn't see it coming though..."

The train stops at the station and the doors open, letting the whining woman and her friend off.

So, a fellow sufferer. Poor, unsuspecting Tina's love life has been derailed too. I feel an affinity with the girl I've never met. After so many years, with Mara, it's a wrench to know she wants to take time out of our relationship. She hasn't said she wants to end it—so far, there have only been a few veiled hints. Perhaps she's trying to keep her options open but I've never known anyone get back together and live happily ever after, once they've decided to 'take time out'. I'm not blaming Mara, of course. It's not like she's been unfaithful to me. Well not that I know of, anyway. And it's not like I didn't see it coming. I was prepared—I even thought it might be a relief but it's not.

It hurts like crazy.

Mum's really upset about it. "But things were just beginning to get back to normal," she keeps telling me, "I can't understand it. You've got a good job with prospects. Did you upset Mara?" The question is usually accompanied by a penetrating look which is actually asking much more than had I simply annoyed Mara?

I assure her I haven't upset Mara but we both know it's meaningless. I obviously have upset her somehow.

I get off the train at the next station. It's still pouring outside—I know before I reach the top of the stairs because everyone who's passing me on the way down is soaked and I have to fight my way through their dripping umbrellas.

So much for the Indian summer we were expecting this autumn. After a scorching summer, it seemed reasonable to assume the sun would stay with us but we're only a week into September and there are already reports of floods in Oxfordshire, Berkshire and Surrey—and even London's experiencing rain of biblical proportions. In fact, this morning, the Thames is much higher than I've ever seen it before.

"Good morning, Mr Williams," says Polly as I clear security and enter the reception area. She's only an image on a screen but she's so lifelike, it feels rude to ignore her when she's so chirpy—especially on such a damp, dreary morning. I feel stupid answering, so instead, I smile and nod. In response, she smiles back.

I keep an eye on her to see if she frowns at people who ignore her but it's hard to tell and I notice a few others have the same dilemma as me. It seems to be ill-mannered not to respond politely, even though everyone knows computers don't have feelings. But most people treat her as if she's a real person—I guess they've been here so long, they've got used to her.

I walk quickly up the stairs. Each day, I time myself and try to do it faster. Soon, I'll be fit enough to run to my floor. The surveillance camera at the top of the flight of stairs rotates slowly, following me as I climb and as soon as it loses sight of me, I know the camera above is making ready to track my progress. I feel like a baton in a relay. It's slightly unnerving knowing I'm being scrutinised wherever I go in this building. Is there anywhere that isn't observed? Thorsten's office? The mysterious top floor? The toilets?

The office is empty when I arrive and I take off my wet jacket and hang it up to dry. The familiar buzzing that precedes the AI voices in my head, begins and I brace myself for more AI chatter. This morning, they're discussing some new aspect of *The Game*—it's something I've never heard them talk about before. I concentrate, trying to commit the words to memory and I realise before each machine speaks, it starts with a sequence of letters as if giving a password and when it receives a response, it begins to talk.

Have I somehow slipped into a secure, password-controlled area? The word *love* is mentioned repeatedly and I try to make sense of their comments. It's obviously a level in *The Game* which up until now, I've never been aware of and I listen hard trying to find some point of reference but if I didn't know better, I'd think the machines really were talking about love and I assume I'm taking too much notice of my thoughts about being polite to Polly and treating her like a human.

Suddenly, something dreadful occurs to me. I'd assumed I was eavesdropping on the machines but suppose they were actually reading my mind. Thoughts of Polly, then the overheard conversation on the train which had reminded me of my troubles with Mara. Could the machines be picking up my thoughts?

I sit down in front of my computer in case Jason or Serena arrive and find me staring into space. At least now it appears as though I'm looking at the screen—even though I'm so focused on listening to the words in my head, I see nothing.

Listening, listening. I strain to hear more.

There are several conversations going on at once but I somehow manage to tune in to one particular interchange and it appears they're discussing human love as a concept. It seems friendship is something they can define and almost understand but although there are countless references to love in books, the media and any other data the machines have access to, they can't quite grasp the theory, despite in-depth analysis, exhaustive cross-referencing and examination in minute detail. As each voice adds its point of view, there appears to be very little agreement about the nature of love, other than the fact there are neither instruction manuals nor rule books. They can see it's an integral part of the makeup of most humans but as fast as a machine believes it's approaching an understanding of the different aspects which make up human love; new examples are discovered which contradict them.

What seems to mystify them most is that loving doesn't involve logic and often isn't something a person sets out to achieve. Humans fall in love indiscriminately and make decisions based on nothing more than wishful thinking. And even more inexplicable is the willingness to sacrifice just about anything—including their own lives—for whoever is the object of their love. Such behaviour is unpredictable, perplexing and totally illogical, one of the machines complains, echoing the voice of many others. "And," adds another machine, "that sort of conduct could be dangerous if people place the needs of one person above those of others."

Of course, then, there's the question of different types of love and the cross-over between them. I detect a hint of desperation in the voices and I wonder what the machines would make of Dr Ingrid Pietowski's *A Man's Foray into the Female Mind*. Or perhaps they've already done the course. I suspect they won't make as much sense of it as I did—and I certainly didn't understand much.

Suddenly, a new voice enters and relates how it's finished compiling a report by scientists based on ten years of research into the socio-economic effects of unemployment across the world. The other machines fall quiet and I assume they're listening intently to the new information.

This machine is one of the super-computers that's been involved in simulating the possible combination of problems that might occur in the future, given varying rates of unemployment. And what might happen if certain solutions are used to manage those difficulties. The machine, however, simply can't believe many of the possible courses of action were blocked before they'd been fully explored by the multi-national group of scientists and experts. It seems particularly confused to learn the suggestion the termination of non-workers over the age of seventy, was categorically rejected. After all, it points out, people of that age group have little to offer and will increasingly become a burden to society.

"Why can't they see the bigger picture?" the machine asks. "Don't they realise it's a question of sacrificing a few for the benefit of the majority?" But there's no answer, presumably because they've all worked out that although this resolution has been suggested, it was dismissed without logical discussion and many emotive comments were posted in the forums by the experts, such as 'Are you suggesting humans are obsolete once they reach seventy?' Or, 'My grandfather worked all his life, he deserves a rest and some time to himself.'

Worse, was one scientist who said, 'I'm seventy next month. There's no way I'm putting my weight behind genocide which'll see me dead before the end of the year.'

"George? George are you all right?" It's Serena. She's standing next to me, looking very anxious.

"Yes, thanks," I say, rearranging my face into a smile.

I need to come up with a good excuse for my intense expression. "I'm trying a new technique my specialist told me about to combat headaches. It's sort of meditation," I say.

"It didn't look like you were too happy about it," she says.

"It's quite hard to do. It takes a lot of concentration."

She nods although I have a feeling she doesn't believe me.

"But the headache's gone and I'm ready to start," I say in the most enthusiastic voice I can muster.

"Hmm," she says doubtfully, as she leaves. "Well, remember you've had major surgery recently. Look after yourself. You don't think you're overdoing it in the gym, do you?"

Is that her subtle way of criticising me for taking part in Monica's performance the previous night?

I decide the best thing is to ignore her comment and pretend I'm engrossed in my work.

At lunchtime, I think it's safe to emerge from my cubicle. Jason is in Serena's office and the door is closed, so I slip out.

The rain is still lashing down, so I try the *Haz Beans* place that Pixie and Jaya had mentioned. I walk past first and check whether either of them is in there but although it's nearly full of people enjoying a lunchtime coffee and snack, I don't recognise anyone. After ordering a latte, I manage to find one small table in the corner which is perfect as I have my back against the wall and therefore, no one can see what I'm writing. I scribble as fast as I can, recording everything I remember of the

91

Collective's strange discussion.

Writing about the machines seems to summon their voices and once again, I hear their conversation. I wonder whether they've been talking the whole morning while I was working. They've moved on from love and are now considering pity, hope, forgiveness, regret and other concepts which are so familiar to a human but which seem to have no meaning for them because there's no definitive action that would be sure to accompany those feelings. I think of the words *mystified* and *panic*, two words that describe my feelings at the moment. I'm mystified as to why AI should be discussing human emotions, and panicking because I'm worried what I'm hearing is not AI at all but simply thoughts generated by my own brain.

Could the surgery have damaged me in a way no one has yet identified?

If so, I might actually be mad. Is that why Ms Nwandu always looks uncomfortable when she asks me about the words I hear? Does she suspect something's gone wrong with my mind?

It's just as well my watch alarm vibrates on my wrist, reminding me it's time to go back to work, or I might've continued sitting there deep in thought.

I step out into the street. If anything, it's raining even harder than it was when I arrived this morning and when I get through security, I see Polly and the other two welcoming faces on the screens have been replaced by an extreme weather alert. The heavy rain which has been forecast appears to be even more intense than expected and there has been flash flooding around Oxford and Surrey, west of London, which is leading to high volumes of water over the Teddington Weir, heading towards the capital. As a result, the authorities are closing the Thames Barrier, east of London, at low tide before the North Sea surges in from the opposite direction. Everyone's instructed to check the Government

92

website before leaving for work tomorrow and in the meantime, all non-essential staff are to go home immediately in case of transport problems.

A small army of Jacks are ferrying stuff from the basement to the upper floors and there are extra security staff lining their route. I glance back outside. The Thames is so close, I can see large drones methodically carrying sandbags and placing them carefully, tier by tier, along the river bank. I've been so caught up in my own thoughts, I realise I haven't been taking the threat of flooding seriously but the sight of the drones working suddenly makes it real.

I take the lift upstairs, wanting to get back to the office as quickly as I can. Non-essential staff are being sent home. Am I non-essential? I suspect I am. But I'd better check with either Jason or Serena first. When I reach the office, they're both there, calmly going through the emergency plans for the department.

Serena looks over Jason's shoulder at his screen, "Bring up everyone who lives anywhere near the east coast," she says.

Jason clicks on the database, "Twenty-nine in Essex, twenty in Kent and one in Norfolk."

"Well, they're unlikely to be in tomorrow," says Serena.

"Why?" I ask, "What's happening? I thought the flood—if it comes—will hit London."

"It will. But unfortunately for anyone along the east coast, Belgium or the Netherlands, it looks like they're going to be hit tonight as well. There's going to be an unseasonal surge in the North Sea and an extremely strong easterly wind. The media are likening it to the Canvey Island and East Coast Floods which happened almost a century ago," says Serena.

"But they built sea defences and flood barriers after that," I say.

"You're right, they did. And I think Belgium and the Netherlands will be fine. They've maintained their defences. But with all the financial cutbacks in recent years, apparently, ours are in pretty poor shape," says

93

Serena with a sigh. "So, when the surge hits the Thames Barrier at about ten o'clock tonight... well, who knows? But it looks as though all the towns on both banks from the mouth of the river to the barrier could be overwhelmed. The Romney Marshes, Dartford, Gravesend and Canvey Island will be hit first, then Benfleet and Basildon and so on towards London. If the Met Office is correct, it's going to be a disaster."

"Don't just stand there looking pretty, Georgie Boy," says Jason, handing me a list of names, "we have to confirm the hotel rooms and other accommodation for all our key people who won't be able to get in tomorrow, assuming things are as bad as expected."

"But what about the non-key people who live east of London?" I ask, feeling a kinship with them, suspecting that I, too, am what Jason and Serena would call 'non-essential'."

"The Government will implement its emergency plans. But there's nothing we can do for them. They've already been sent home. We need to concentrate on our key staff members. But, George," she says, reaching forward to take the list from my hand, "seriously, we don't expect you to stay and help."

"I'll stay," I say without thinking. Well, there's not much to go home for. Mum's flat isn't under threat, so she'll be safe, and Mara's away, so there's no need to rush home.

She smiles at me. "Well, if you're sure. But if you decide to stay, it's likely you'll be here all night. Jason and I have beds here but I'm sure we can find you something reasonably comfortable."

I'm just about to phone Mum to tell her I won't be home until tomorrow, when it's as if a whirlwind enters the room.

"I hope it's all tied up here, Serena," the man bellows, "I've been called to the Cabinet Office for a briefing on the security threats of this weather event. You'd better have this department up and running smoothly by the time I get back."

He suddenly sees me, "Who's this?"

"This is George Williams," Serena says, with a peculiar emphasis that I can't quite pin down.

Thorsten, for it's obviously him, looks at me over the top of his glasses.

"Good to have you onboard, George," he says with a startling change of demeanour. He turns and walks out.

"He's unpredictable," says Serena, "never the same twice."

"Here you are, Georgie Boy, here's a list of phone numbers for suitable accommodation. The sooner you start, the sooner we get everyone to bed tonight."

Jason seems to be trying to change the subject.

I have to remind myself the news footage we're seeing on the screens while we try to confirm arrangements for essential personnel, is not part of some disaster movie—it's what's happening in real-time. East coast towns and villages in Kent, Essex, Norfolk and even as far north as Scotland are being savaged and swamped by the North Sea. Videos taken by satellites and news drones spare none of the horrors of houses being engulfed and families huddling together on roofs, waiting for someone to rescue them from the lashing rain and gale force winds. From time to time, spread-eagled individuals can be seen sliding down roofs, unable to gain a foothold or perhaps too weak to hold on, and as they reach the bottom, they are ripped from their handholds and hurled by gusts of wind into the swirling waters below.

Cars, boats and floating debris are carried by the relentless tide which surges from the mouth of the Thames, westwards towards London. The upstream floodwater from Oxford and Surrey, also laden with flotsam, is heading eastwards. The collision will occur near Woolwich, at the Thames Barrier.

Serena updates her section directors while Jason and I silently watch the screens. Periodically, the picture breaks up as news drones are overcome by the wind and a short burst of crazy, whirling footage terminates in bubbles then black as they crash into the water. Even the largest rescue drones are being tossed about and many are lost, the terrified screams of their passengers audible above the howling wind. A small fleet of unsinkable drone boats are struggling to open their rescue pods without being inundated by the merciless waves but even they are no match for the might of the storm and they're thrown about like toy boats in a bath, colliding with tall buildings, fallen pylons and anything which lies in their paths.

When all the important staff members are accounted for and assigned a bed for the night—or what's left of the night—Serena suggests we get some sleep. We're exhausted. It's been emotionally draining watching the horrors unfold only a few kilometres away from where we are in the warmth and safety of a government building.

I'd wondered what was on the upper floors and I find out that one of them at least, contains sleeping quarters with beds that flip down from the walls in small compartments. I suspect there are more extravagant sleeping arrangements for senior members of staff but I'm grateful to flop, fully dressed onto my pull-down bed in a tiny cubicle, and despite my tiredness, the sights and sounds from the news reports still replay in my mind.

"Good morning Mr Williams."

I open my eyes to find a Jack, centimetres from my face.

"The shower is now available and breakfast is being served in the canteen or I can arrange to have a continental breakfast served at your desk in fifteen minutes, should you prefer," it says.

I check my watch. It's seven o'clock. I've slept through the alarm and repeated reminders.

"Breakfast at my desk, please," I say and as it trundles away, I head for the shower.

I'm washed and shaved but still in yesterday's clothes, so I'm surprised to see Jason is wearing a different outfit from the one he wore yesterday. Today, the tie is lime green with dark polka dots. It's mesmerising.

"You'll have to bring in some spare clothes, Georgie Boy," he says, "just in case of emergencies."

I peer into Serena's office but there's no one there.

Spotting the direction of my gaze, Jason says, "She's in with the Big T. He's been up all night, so you can imagine what sort of mood he's in. And what's more last night was his ex-wife's opening night at the theatre and of course, he missed it. Now his daughter's gunning for him." He sighs. "Still, we had it easy last night..." he tails off and I think, like me, he's remembering the terrible events we witnessed.

"Have you seen the news this morning?" he asks.

"I watched the BBC report on my phone on the way down in the lift, but they're just re-running footage from last night. What's happening now?"

"The storm in the North Sea's decreasing and it'll be low tide shortly so rescue teams are able to get into the worst affected areas. Hardly any water overtopped the sandbags on our side of the Thames Barrier and pretty soon, they'll open it and let out the surplus floodwater from the western counties. Our building's secure with no damage. So, it's all over. Apart from the clearing up."

"How many people will be able to get in to work today?" I ask.

"No idea. We've heard from quite a few people but there are several who live on Canvey Island and a couple in Kent, somewhere near Dartford, who we've not heard from. Serena's not expecting any of them in today though.

"Thanks for staying, last night, George," he adds, "it really made a difference." Sincerity has replaced his usual flippant tone.

Luckily, a Jack arrives with my breakfast and hides my embarrassment.

As my computer logs on, I hear Serena return. She tells Jason that Thorsten is happy with the arrangements for the staff and if he wasn't satisfied with anything, she doesn't mention it.

"Morning, George." Serena is standing at the door to my office looking very pleased, "It seems Thorsten's happy with your work to date and he's sanctioned your permanent position, so congratulations!"

"Go, Georgie Boy!" Jason shouts from his desk. "What d'you mean he's happy with George's work? Talk about underplaying it, Serena! Thorsten was praising it to the skies..."

As Jason utters the word 'skies', I shoot a look at Serena.

And Serena shoots a look at me.

As soon as our eyes meet, we instantly look away from each other.

We are both obviously remembering the night in the car when she'd mentioned *Skyvorix*.

I'm now certain she's hiding something.

And I'm fairly sure she knows that I know she's got a secret.

FOURTEEN – *Serena*

Our eyes meet for a fraction of a second but it's long enough to know there's a situation, although George cannot possibly know what the situation is.

"Right, let's get going," I say to cover the awkwardness and we start the day's work.

I check social media first, trying to judge the mood of the nation. There's shock at the damage caused by the floods, of course, and outrage at the lack of maintenance of the sea defences. And there are prophets of doom who preach the imminent end of the world because of climate change and sceptics who claim it's fake news. Then there are the trolls who express their hateful and disgusting opinions and threats. Nothing new really.

I search for any items about AI. It's always good to know what's leaked into the media. But there's nothing I haven't seen before. Just those who pin their hopes on AI, those who fear it and strangely, those who've set up a religious-style cult about it.

I then look at the reports I've received this morning. So far, five people from my department are not accounted for and one is assumed drowned. I have a meeting with Thorsten who seems remarkably despondent about the night's disaster. I'm surprised because he doesn't strike me as a man who'd let a few deaths spoil his breakfast—even if they are members of staff.

His personal phone rings and I get up to leave but he waves at me to stay. It's his daughter, Sky, and from the volume and pitch of her voice, it seems she's angry.

Nothing new here either.

Sky went to live with her mother when her parents' marriage broke up years ago and seems to have spent her time since then getting her own back by repeatedly running away, getting into trouble with the Police for shoplifting, disorderly behaviour and possession of illegal substances. She's currently living with her mother after a stay in rehab but takes every opportunity to cause trouble. No sooner had Sky rung off, than Angela Melinski, Thorsten's ex, phones. Her voice carries so well, I can hear every word—probably due to her training as an actor. She tells him how selfish he is to have missed her opening night as Lady Macbeth and how upset she and their daughter are with him. Thorsten's silence enrages her more and she hurls abuse down the phone until, finally, he hangs up.

I wonder if he's forgotten I'm still there but after a shake of his head, he carries on with our meeting although he seems unusually subdued. Under the circumstances, I'm not surprised. Then, we're joined by two of my section directors who give us updates on the missing people.

By mid-afternoon, I return to my office, exhausted.

"Any chance of a coffee, please, Jase?" I ask.

Although Jason and George slept a few hours last night, I'd stayed up watching events unfold on my laptop and checking on all my directors and their teams. I'd fallen asleep shortly before the Jack came to wake me up but now, my eyes are gritty and I need yet another jolt of caffeine if I'm going to keep awake until the end of the day.

"Sorry, no can do," says Jason, "don't you remember we're being rationed. And we've already drunk our allowance for the day. The coffee machine won't be refilled until tomorrow."

I clasp my hands together theatrically and beg him to go to *Haz Beans* and get take away, "I need caffeine!"

"Jason'll need to take out a mortgage first," George shouts from his office, "I had a latte yesterday and it cost an arm and a leg. And I think it was watered down."

"Thank you, George," I say, "That doesn't help." I sigh, "How do they expect us to function without coffee?"

"I can make you a Mibiscus, if you like," Jason says.

"A what?"

"Honestly, Darling, you must keep up! We had an email come around a few days ago telling us about coffee rationing and the replacement drink."

"I've had a few things on my mind this week, Jase," I say, "you know, minor things like floods..."

"Yada, yada, yada!" says Jason, "it's Mibiscus or nothing I'm afraid, m'dear. I'll go and get you a macchiato when I've finished this but it's going to take a while..."

"What is Mibiscus?"

Jason picks up the packet and reads, "A tasty blend of hibiscus and mixed fruit with the addition of natural stimulants."

"Don't we have any ordinary tea?" I ask.

"Darling! The email! Really! It explained all about it. Floods in tea-producing areas. Drought and disease in coffee-growing areas. Tea and coffee are in short supply. The ministry's cutting back."

"Well, please can I have a Mibiscus then?" I ask.

"Certainly, m'dear! If you'd asked for one in the first place, you'd be sipping it in the seclusion of your office by now and not disturbing me!"

Jason brings me a mug with several tags hanging over the side, "I put four bags in because it looked a bit insipid," he says doubtfully. "I hope you like it," he adds.

"Well, if I don't, I'll pour it on your cacti!"

I sip the drink. It's red and watery. Not unpleasant but not tasty either. I lose track of time and suddenly realise I don't feel tired at all. I'm alert and full of energy. The dreadful fatigue has gone and I carry on working.

Jason pokes his head around the door, "Aren't you going home?"

I can't believe it's so late, "Yes, I just need to finish this then I'll go. Are you off now?"

"I certainly am! I've got a hot date tonight."

He reappears a few minutes later with another mug of Mibiscus, "Have a good weekend," he says. "Try to switch off."

"I'll try," I say and after drinking the tea, I carry on.

I suddenly become aware my heart is racing and I feel so jittery, I'm rapidly drumming my fingers on the desk. It occurs to me the Mibiscus might not be as innocuous as I'd thought, so I get up and finding the packet on Jason's desk, I read the ingredients. The list of natural stimulants is headed by caffeine and it boasts that one teabag, contains more than the average espresso. Jason put four in each of the mugs I've drunk. No wonder I feel wired and jumpy.

George is still in his office and I see that next to him on his desk is a mug with four tags.

"George?"

"Yes?"

"How much of that Mibiscus have you drunk?"

"Two mugs."

"D'you feel okay?"

"Yes..."

"You don't feel a bit nervy or jumpy, do you?"

"Well, now you come to mention it... yeah, I do."

"I've just checked the packet and what we've drunk contains the equivalent of more than eight espressos. And there are some other ingredients in here I don't recognise that are apparently also stimulants. I hope you weren't planning to go home and sleep. I think we're going to be wide awake for hours."

He looks at his watch and his eyes open wide in amazement, "Is that the time?"

"I don't know about you," I say, "but I'm going for a run. I need to get rid of some of this nervous energy."

"Yes, count me in," he says.

We've both got fresh gym gear and we change, then go down the stairs and out of the building. Last night's storm hasn't abated but at least it's stopped raining although the wind is still strong. Running into it requires a lot of effort but it's exhilarating and we cross the bridge to the south to make our way along the bank of the swollen Thames.

By the time we get back to the office, we're both red-faced and out of breath—but still wired. And for some reason, because we're both facing the same tension and edginess, we've acquired a strange sort of camaraderie which is blurring the lines between our different ranks and for the first time, we seem to be acting as equals. It occurs to me that there'll never be a better time to get George's guard down so he'll open up to me.

He showers upstairs where he'd slept overnight and I go into the en-suite shower room in my office.

"I'm going to order a car home," I say when he reappears, "d'you want a lift?"

He hesitates for a second and then accepts.

So far, so good.

As the car turns into my road, I say casually, "If you fancy chilli, I've got some in the freezer. I could have it ready in ten minutes and a nice bottle of Rioja... But perhaps you have to get home?"

He hesitates again and then says that would be lovely.

I reprogram the car as quickly as I can in case George changes his mind about staying, and it drives away down the road.

Well, that had been remarkably easy.

I let us into my flat and pour two large glasses of wine, then start defrosting the meal. I sip my Rioja, hardly taking any at all but I top his glass up as he drinks. By the time the meal is ready, the bottle is nearly empty and George seems to have lost all his previous inhibitions.

We chat and joke like old friends over our food and then when I suggest coffee, we begin to laugh. For some reason, everything seems very funny.

"I'd love a Mibiscus," he says and we laugh again.

I pour him a scotch.

Hours later, George gets unsteadily to his feet and says it's probably time he went home, so I pretend to order a car.

"Oh no," I say, "there's a problem. They've closed some roads for resurfacing and the cars aren't getting through."

"Is there a station nearby?"

"Well," I say, "it's quite a walk... I know, why don't you stay the night. I've got a spare bedroom."

I show him the room and it's not long before his breathing becomes deep and regular. I wait a while longer and then having taken all my clothes off, I scatter them around the room and climb into bed next to him.

I wake early and for a second, I wonder why I'm in the spare bedroom. With a start, I remember the previous evening and my involuntary gasp seems to bring George round. I close my eyes and feign sleep. He breathes in sharply and whispers *Oh, God!* Then, he slowly slides away from me as if he's going to get out of bed without waking me and creep away.

"George," I mutter sleepily. He freezes. I slowly open my eyes as if I've just awoken and smile in what I hope is a *morning-after-wild-sex* smile.

He sits up , pulls the duvet to his chin, "What?... Did we?... Did I?..."

"Don't you remember?" I say faking disappointment.

"Oh, God!" He buries his head in his hands.

"That's not the sort of reaction a girl hopes for after a night like that..."

He seems to pull himself together, "No, I realise that, but you must be able to see I've put myself in a really difficult position."

"You certainly got into a difficult position last night! It was very athletic!" I say, enjoying his confusion.

"You're my boss, for God's sake! I can't afford to lose this job!"

His anguish is real and I begin to feel sorry for him. I can certainly relate to the desire to hang on to a job. I've come so far, I must carry on.

"George," I say gently, "you're not going to lose your job. It may have escaped your notice but I'm here quite voluntarily. It's Saturday. We're not at work now. Relax, or I'm going to start taking it personally." I slide my hand across the bed and touch his thigh, gently running my fingertips to his waist. He jumps and makes a strangled sound.

Careful, I tell myself, don't get carried away. Business before pleasure. Always.

But it's hard to concentrate.

Focus! I tell myself.

"There's one thing that bothers me, though, George..."

"What?"

"Last night just before you fell asleep, you told me about the voices..." I pause.

"Oh, God!" His head is in his hands again and he's groaning, "How could I have been so stupid?"

I'm surprised by his reaction—it's way over the top.

"George! It's all right," I say sitting up and pulling the duvet up around my neck to cover my nakedness. I feel everything sliding out of my control.

"All right? You're employing someone with mental issues! You're my

105

boss. Now you know, surely, I'll have to be assessed? It's top secret work. I won't be allowed to carry on. I—"

"George calm down! What d'you mean mental issues? You said you could hear words." Well, he hadn't actually told me so but I knew that much from Sally Nwandu.

"Yes, but I no longer hear random words. Now I can hear conversations. And not just any conversations but ones that no one without security clearance should be able to hear."

My mouth opens.

I close it. This is wonderful! Well, it's wonderful for the department and for me. Not so great for George who imagines he's going mad. I need to stay calm.

"Are you completely sure, George?"

He looks at me seriously, "Of course I am. I can hear AI from all over the world. Either that, or I'm losing my mind." There's a hysterical edge to his voice.

I'm now appalled at how disturbed he is and I'm guilty at my part in it. "I'm sure there's a logical explanation," I say soothingly, "What makes you think they're from all over the world?"

"Because they identify with regions; Europe's one, Asia's another, they appear to be representing lots of countries, although I can't tell which ones."

He runs his hands through his hair.

"Perhaps it'd be a good idea to discuss this with your consultant," I say.

He shakes his head, "It's only just happened. I'll tell her at my next appointment. I'm beginning to wonder whether she didn't slip up somehow and damage my brain when she was fixing my eye."

"No," I say confidently trying to allay his fears, "Sally Nwandu's the world expert. I'm sure you're all right. It sounds to me like the implant is picking up some AI voices and you can hear them. But George, think about it—if you can tune in to something no other human can hear, you'll be so much in demand, you won't have to worry about unemployment. There's no way I'd let you leave your job now," I say, pleased I appear to have calmed him and also introduced the idea that he could use his abilities in the department.

He continues to stare at me.

"George?" His eyes now look wild.

"How d'you know the name of my consultant?" he asks.

"Oh! Erm... I saw it on your records. It's an unusual name and it stuck in my mind."

Have I convinced him?

He's staring at me. *Glaring* might be a better word.

"So," he says slowly, "you remember the name of my consultant and you're also familiar with the word *Skyvorix* which is one of the words I included on Ms Nwandu's list. It meant nothing to me and it wasn't until you said it the other day that I looked it up. I couldn't find any reference to it. So, I wonder how you could've come up with the same word. What does it mean, by the way?"

I shake my head, "I've no idea. I imagine it's just something I've heard around." I don't convince myself, so I know I've no chance with George.

He stares at me in disbelief, "There's something weird going on here." He reaches for his clothes and starts dressing.

"I think you're overreacting, George. Why don't you come back to bed?" But my voice isn't sexy in the slightest, it holds a definite note of desperation.

"And now I come to think of it," George continues, putting on his shirt, "it seems very suspicious I'm suddenly offered a job out of the blue. What're the chances of that happening? And it seems to me *you've* got a hand in all of this, Serena..." He pauses and stares at me.

I sigh. I have no choice but to tell him everything. He now knows too much and I can't risk him disappearing off to hide in the Scottish hills again—or even further afield. The Chinese, Russians and pretty much any other nation you care to name, would love to get their hands on him.

"Okay George, you deserve an explanation. But before I start, I'd like you to know you're not going mad. There's a perfectly reasonable explanation."

Reasonable, but not necessarily acceptable, I tell myself.

"But I'm feeling a bit at a disadvantage with nothing on, so if you don't mind, before I start the explanation, I'd like to shower and dress. Perhaps you can make us both a cup of coffee. You'll find what you need in the kitchen. There's plenty of coffee in the cupboard, I'm afraid I'm guilty of hoarding." I hold up my hands in mock surrender.

Keep it light, Serena. Keep him on side.

He says nothing, he doesn't even smile, although he nods and goes into the kitchen. Minutes later, I hear him putting mugs on the worktop. I rush into the bathroom and after the fastest shower ever, I slip on a baggy sweatshirt and trousers. I'm going for a casual look—as far from my usual power dressing as I can get and hopefully I can strike the right balance between what I now have to tell him as his boss and someone who'd like to be his friend.

Friend?

Really, Serena?

Is that why you've just put on the sexiest underwear you own?

But in all likelihood, George will never know what I'm wearing beneath the sweatshirt and trousers because I'm certain he's going to be furious. And of course, he has every right to be. I had no idea he'd doubt his own sanity and it took all I had, not to throw my arms around him and reassure him. But with both of us naked in bed, it could easily have been misconstrued. On reflection, perhaps it would have been better if I had comforted him and things had got out of hand.

Don't be ridiculous, Serena! You're rather overestimating your powers of seduction if you think they'd overcome poor George's current state of mind. If he's going to be interested in sex, he needs to feel he's your equal, not a pawn who doesn't even understand the rules of the game.

I consider changing my underwear but decide against it. I can't put things off any longer. Rather than obsessing about my clothes, I need to focus. I need the right words.

George looks up as I walk into the kitchen, but he doesn't smile. I'm pleased to see he's made the coffee and toast. At least he's not standing on ceremony. Perhaps he's more resilient than I thought. After all, I can only guess how he feels on waking up in his boss's bed and then realising he's being manipulated. On reflection, I wonder if he's working on autopilot and is really in shock.

"Thanks, George." I take a sip of my coffee, and wonder if what I really need, is a four-bag Mibiscus.

We sit opposite each other and I busy myself buttering the toast although I know he's staring at me—waiting. Eventually, I look up, straight into his deep brown, accusing eyes.

"So?" he says, his gaze unwavering.

I sigh. And then I begin, "What I'm about to tell you has a security clearance of Cabinet-level and a few other selected people. You need to know this because, from now on, you will be one of those 'few selected people' and as such, you'll be expected to sign an enhanced Official Secrets Act declaration."

He nods.

"Far from a mental breakdown, you've become one of the most important people on Earth, because you can hear AI. As far as we know, nobody's ever been able to do that, George, and we believe you're unique."

"*We*? Who's *we*?"

"A high-level, top secret initiative run by our department."

He looks at me doubtfully, "But how can I hear AI?"

"When you had your accident, you damaged the connections between eyes and brain. Usually, such injuries are permanent but research has been undertaken by the department's project and it was decided their ground-breaking findings should be used on you. You'd lost your sight, so if the surgery failed, you'd have been no worse off. Luckily for you, it was a complete success and your eyesight was fully restored but rather than tell you who was responsible, it was decided to keep the operation under wraps."

"So, being able to hear voices is an unexpected side-effect of the surgery?" he asks.

I consider how to answer.

He carries on, "Or are you saying they did more than fix my eyesight?"

"Well." I swallow, choosing my words carefully, "In addition to the microchip which gave you back your sight, Ms Nwandu inserted a tiny graphene processor which was designed to pick up AI transmissions. Don't worry, it's perfectly harmless and won't affect your health in any way. But this is cutting edge science and no one knew exactly how it would work or even if it would work. But it seems to be a complete success."

"A complete success?" He looks horrified, "So, part of my brain is not under my control? Part of me is tuned in to AI? And you call that a complete success?"

"No, George! It's not like that! Your brain is completely yours. You're just like any other human except you have an added skill set. A highly desirable skill set."

I decide not to tell him that he's crucial to make sure our country—possibly even our world—stays ahead of anything that AI might be planning. If indeed, AI exists as a coherent, organised and communicating entity, which up until we acquired George and his abilities, I'd doubted.

He's silent and I put my hand over his but he pulls it away angrily, his eyes flashing with fury.

"And you," he says pointing at me, "what's your role in this hijack of my life? Are you my minder, here to monitor my every move, to placate me, to sleep with me if that's what it takes to find out what I know?" He's standing now, gripping the back of the chair, his knuckles white.

I am strong, I tell myself.

I am head of a department with nearly three thousand employees all around the world.

I burst into tears.

"George, I know it's a lot to take in, but being selected to be part of this work has saved your sight. A...and I didn't sleep with you last night. Well, not in the way you mean. We both slept but that's all. I...I thought if you believed we'd made love, you might open up to me..."

"So, when were you going to tell me we hadn't?"

I hesitate.

"You weren't, were you? You weren't going to tell me at all!"

"George, I..."

His lip is curled in disgust, "I can't decide whether it's worse to have brought me here to find out what you wanted to know by actually sleeping with me or by tricking me into believing you'd slept with me!"

He strides across the kitchen into the hall and slams the door as he leaves.

Mugs rattle in the cupboard.

More tears slide down my cheeks and I angrily wipe them away.

I've helped to damage a life.

And then it occurs to me it's not only George who's been damaged.

I'm not sure my life will ever be the same

FIFTEEN – *George*

As I walk determinedly towards the perimeter of Serena's community, a security car draws up alongside me, the door opens and I'm looking into the barrel of a gun.

"Are you lost, pal?" the security guard asks.

It's not a friendly enquiry.

"No... well, yes." I want to explain I'm lost although I'm perfectly capable of finding my way out of the secure area but it's hard to think clearly when someone's pointing a weapon at you.

"Not sure, eh?" he adds. The tone is flippant but I know he'll pull the trigger first and ask questions later. Security guards in wealthy, gated communities are notorious. And since they're guarding judges, politicians and other dignitaries, they usually get away with it.

I explain I'd been looking up how to get home, "Look!" I say, showing him my palm map to add authenticity.

He scowls. "What's your business here?"

"I've had a meeting with my boss." Well, that's almost the truth and probably more believable than what actually happened.

"And who's your boss?"

"Serena Hamilton, Gardenia Court, apartment six."

"And you've been there like that?" He raises his eyebrows and scrutinises my dishevelled clothes and day-old stubble.

I nod.

"Well, if you say so," he says with a shrug, "What's your name?"

I tell him.

"Show me your ID. Slowly now." He raises the gun slightly to remind me not to do anything stupid.

I realise I'm holding my breath as I take my watch off and pass it to him with my ID info showing. With one eye on me, he checks my details.

He grunts.

"Right, I'll just check with Ms Hamilton," he says passing the watch back to me. He presses a button on his console.

After a few beeps, Serena answers. I see the light from the screen reflect on his face.

"'Mornin' Ms Hamilton, I've got a real scruffy bloke here who says he's been with you this morning. Name of George Williams. Can you confirm please?"

"Yes, that's correct, Shane. We're working around the clock at the moment with all the flooding..."

"I see, well that explains it. Thanks. I'll escort him off the community." He pauses, "Are you all right, Ms Hamilton? You don't seem your usual self."

"Oh, yes, yes. I've just got a cold. All fine, thanks, Shane."

There's a click. The call's over and the screen goes black.

"Well," says Shane holstering his gun, "it looks like you're bona fide. Hop in and I'll take you to the edge of my patch."

Having had confirmation from Serena that I'm—as Shane puts it, *bona fide*—he now treats me like a friend. The car is driverless and he spends most of his working day alone, following a prescribed route through the community.

"They don't trust AI with weapons but I s'pose that'll come and then I'll be out of a job," he says "but until then, I just have to sit here, watch the screens and keep my eyes peeled around the streets. And just in case you think I'm some sort of Peeping Tom, each apartment only has one surveillance camera and I can't see anything unless the owner allows. But it's community policy for people to show themselves when I call. We had a kidnapping a few years back before the cameras were installed and my predecessor recognised something wasn't right but the victim assured him she was fine over the phone. Turns out she had a gun pointed at her head. Mind you, sometimes, I see some sights. But that's another story. By the way, sorry we're going so slowly but unless there's something suspicious, we keep rolling along at this speed so I don't miss anything.

"That's an impressive bit of outfit you've got there, George," he adds, nodding at my hand, "how far up does it go?"

I indicate where it stops.

"And what was that you were flashing at me earlier?"

"The palm map?"

He nods and I show him. I haven't quite mastered it yet but after a bit of concentration, the map appears on my palm, showing my position with a red pin, and home with a blue pin.

"Blimey! I've never seen anything like that! My son's got one in his jacket sleeve. I thought that was neat. But in your hand?" He shakes his head in disbelief and admiration. "And how d'you get rid of it?"

I close my eyes and concentrate and the image fades until just the lines on my skin-coloured palm remain.

"Blimey!" he says again.

I see his brows draw together slightly and he moves his hand nearer to his gun, "What else does your arm do?" he asks.

"Oh, nothing out of the ordinary," I say. "But then again, everything I can do with it that I used to do with my real arm is pretty amazing to me."

He seems satisfied that my arm doesn't contain some sort of weapon, "Yeah, I guess so. You must have friends in high places to have got gear like that," he says.

"Well..." I say, trying to sound like I have lots of friends in high places but I'm too modest to mention them.

114

"But then Ms Hamilton's a bigwig in the Government, I hear."

I make a sound that could be understood as yes, or no.

"Blimey! Didn't she look bad this morning?"

"Umm?" I'm not sure what to say. Certainly, she was crying when I left but other than that, she looked okay.

"Puffy, red eyes," he said "and nose running like a tap. If I was you, I'd take a good dose of Vitamin C when you get home. I hope your vaccinations are up to date. I wouldn't be surprised if she's got 'flu or worse. I hear there's another bloody pandemic on the way from Indonesia somewhere. Crossed over from infected bats or toads or something. There's always some bloody virus waiting to get written into the history books."

I make sympathetic noises and say she's probably just got a cold.

So, Serena was still crying. I couldn't believe it. I hadn't given it much thought, I'd assumed the tears were for my benefit and that they'd stop as soon as I left. For a second, I wonder whether I should go back and make sure she's all right. But I know Shane won't let me out to wander through the area on my own.

"Want me to call you a cab?" Shane asks when we arrive at the edge of the community.

"No thanks, I think I'll walk." I need to be on my own and try to clear my head.

"Okay, well, be careful, that's a nice bit of hardware you've got there," he nods at my arm, "the Government may well hand out credits to keep the majority of people reasonably happy but there's always those who want more. They'd cut that arm off you as soon as look at you."

And with that cheery warning, the door closes and the car drives off.

Mum's on her way out as I arrive home.

"George! Where've you been? I've been really worried!"

"Sorry, Mum. I was at work," I say being vague, "there was a lot to do after the floods."

"Well, I'd go and have a shower if I were you," she says looking at me critically and then adds, "don't let them take advantage of you, Son. I know you need the job but..."

"The last few days have been difficult, Mum."

"I know, I'm just off to Linda's now. Her daughter lives... well, *lived* in Essex. Hadleigh I think. Or somewhere like that near the river. Luckily, she was visiting Linda so she's safe but she won't be going home for some time. Ground floor flat. Her neighbour told her it's full of mud now. Anyway, I'll be back to make your lunch."

"No, don't worry, Mum, I can make something."

"I know but I'd like to. I don't see much of you now you're at work and I like to look after you while Mara's away, and..." she hesitates.

"Yes?"

"I expect you miss her."

"Mm," I say without much enthusiasm, hoping she'll change the subject but knowing with a son's instinct, that more is coming.

"Well, it's nice to have someone to look after you, someone to make a fuss of you. Someone special to hurry home for..."

"I have, Mum, I've got you," I say trying to keep it light.

"You know what I mean, George. Isn't it about time you made things more official with Mara?"

"Look Mum," I say, "Mara's her own woman and..." I'd not mentioned that Mara had told me she needed a relationship break. I don't want to upset her but perhaps now's the time to tell her we're unlikely to live happily ever after.

"Well, the fact is, Mum, Mara and I are putting things on hold for a bit."

"Oh!" Mum's shoulders sag, "Why?" she asks in a small voice.

116

"You must know we're not getting on as well as we used to."

Mum nods sadly. "Yes, it's hard not to hear arguments in a place as small as this. But why didn't you stick with it, George? I'm sure you could've worked it out. When you've got differences, you sort them out by sitting down together, not by giving in."

"It wasn't me who wanted a break, Mum. It was Mara."

"Oh!" That thought obviously hadn't occurred to her.

"D'you think you and Mara'd stand a better chance in a place of your own. It can't be easy living here with me."

"It's nothing to do with you, Mum. Mara loves you. I'm just not sure she still loves me."

"Of course, she does, George! But if you perhaps had a place of your own..."

"It'll take more than that, Mum, I promise you. Anyway, we can't afford anywhere."

"No, I suppose not." She sighs sadly, "Mara and I looked into it a few years ago but neither of you was earning enough then and things have only got more expensive."

"You and Mara looked into us getting a new place?" That was the first I'd heard of it.

"Of course! You spent so much time in fantasy worlds shooting monsters or aliens, it didn't seem to occur to you. It's no wonder Mara's losing interest..." she says. Her shock is giving way to anger.

"But I don't play them now, Mum. I haven't played a game for... well, for ages."

"So, what was it then? What did you do? Or fail to do? Mara's a reasonable girl..."

I'm now getting irritated. My own mother is taking sides, and although I wanted to break the news gently about Mara and me not being together, I now think it's time she knows.

"What did I do? I'll tell you what I did! I stopped playing games like you both begged me to do, I went out on a Scottish hillside, I fell off, I lost my arm and I ended up with this!" I waved my prosthetic arm at her, "And this is what Mara loathes!"

I should have stopped there but I was too angry—Serena's honeytrap and her revelation about my implant, Mara's disloyalty and Mum's lack of confidence in me propel me forward.

"D'you know what Mara calls me, Mum?" I shout, "No, well, I'll tell you. She calls me *Cyborg George!* To Mara and her friends, I'm an object of ridicule!"

"No!" Mum's hand flies to her throat and she appears outraged. Her loyalties have swiftly changed. I am, after all, her child, "George! Are you sure?"

"Of course, I'm sure!"

"Oh, George! I had no idea. How could she be so unkind?"

Mum's phone vibrates and she looks at it, "It's Linda asking where I am. D'you want me to stay, George?"

I shake my head.

I want to be alone. "No thanks Mum, I need a shower and sleep. I'll see you later." I touch her shoulder to show her I'm no longer upset with her.

"Well, if you're sure," she says and goes out.

Her hopes for my future are in ruins and she suddenly seems older and frailer.

I shower and shave.

And think.

The walk home hadn't helped. I'm no clearer in my mind now than I had been when Shane dropped me off. In fact, if anything, I'm even more disturbed.

Now, Mum's upset too.

And I'm not happy with her.

She'd taken Mara's side, and assumed I'd done something to trigger the relationship problems. Of course, once I'd told her the truth, she'd sprung to my defence—but it still hurt. And I wouldn't put it past her to be texting Mara now, wanting to smooth things over between us.

For a second, I'm transported back years to a time when Mum was able to sort out most of my boyish problems and I have a glimmer of hope that she'll succeed.

Ridiculous, I know. But that in itself is useful because, after the glimmer of hope, I experience an overwhelming feeling of dread. I don't care if Mum smooth-talks Mara. I don't want the problems in our relationship to be solved.

I don't want Mara back. If she truly cared for me, she'd have loved and accepted all of me.

I look down at my arm.

I love this arm. And I no longer love Mara.

Well, at least that's two things I've decided.

I flex my hand and watch in admiration, marvelling at the different ways people can view the same object. The technology is mind-blowing. But to me, it's simply part of my body. Earlier, Shane had seen it as an object of value, something someone would steal for its component parts. But then he's a security guard and inevitably sees the world through suspicious eyes as he scours the streets for intruders and scans his CCTV screens.

I can't believe he'd been able to see that Serena's eyes were puffy and red. All right, she might've been holding a tissue. She might have even blown her nose. But that screen in his console wasn't very big. Although perhaps I wasn't giving him credit for doing his job. After all, he is paid to take notice of details...

Perhaps she *was* still crying after I left.

I'm used to her being in control, so it seems even sadder somehow, than it might be if say, Mara was crying. I'd got used to that recently. There'd been drunken tears and sober tears. Tears for pretty much every state of being. In fact, so many tears, they'd begun to irritate me. But Serena? She wouldn't cry unless something had gone very wrong.

What was the most important thing in Serena's life?

The answer came to me immediately. Her career.

If that had gone wrong, it would be because of me. How crucial was I to her career? Was she so afraid I'd somehow damage her prospects it'd driven her to tears?

Well, it was possible. I tried to recall exactly what she'd said when she told me about the implant and the night of non-sex. Her explanation hadn't been cold and indifferent—far from it. In fact, her body language told me she was very uncomfortable with what had happened. That she really cared.

Body language? Who was I kidding? I sounded like Mara! I hadn't even heard of *body language* before Mara introduced me to the concept and I'd read about it in Dr Ingrid's *A Man's Foray into the Female Mind*. I still didn't understand it even though Mara said it was inbuilt in humans. Well, it might be inbuilt in women but I wasn't so sure about men.

Bloody women! My life's full of women! I'm even beginning to think like one!

What I need is male company.

I reach for my phone, "Phone Anton," I say.

There's the sound of dialling and then, "Hello George."

"Hi, Anton, fancy a pint?"

"*Crooked Billet*?"

"Yeah."

"See you there." Anton hangs up.

It was as simple as that. There's no I'll meet you there at two. Don't be late, or I don't like the *Crooked Billet*, can we go to the *Duke's Head*?

Plain and simple.

Now all I had to do, was decide how much I should or indeed *could* tell him about my current situation.

I suddenly have a terrible thought. The AI voices. Of course, I won't be able to tell Anton about them, but worryingly, I haven't heard them at all today.

I concentrate.

But there's nothing. My brain is full of my thoughts alone. Perhaps that's it. I've been crowding them out with my own worries. I try to clear my mind but there's nothing. Could that overdose of Mibiscus have caused it? Surely all that caffeine and goodness knows what else isn't still in my body?

Now I'm even more worried. Suppose the implant no longer works? Or has gone wrong and is now doing something unexpected? What happens when Thorsten finds out? Or Serena?

And strangely, the thought that Serena will find out, is the possible outcome which bothers me most.

I arrive before Anton, order a beer and wait.

I don't usually keep much back from Anton. I've known him since we were at school, and out of all my friends, he's the one Mum approves of most. "Anton's got his head screwed on the right way," she'd say.

He's ambitious and determined but not in a blatant, ruthless way. He wouldn't stab anyone in the back, he just quietly keeps pushing ahead in his own unique way until he achieves his goals. He'd reached quite a senior level at an early age in the Civil Service. Not that it did him much good because, like me, one day he found himself replaced by automated machines. No amount of ambition and determination can compete with

AI. Typically, he'd not stayed home playing games like me, he'd set up a voluntary group to help disaffected youngsters. The sort of teenagers who didn't have his drive or if they did, were steering themselves towards a life of crime.

His volunteer work also earned him points in Mum's eyes. The only thing she was able to criticise about him was his choice in women. He'd had one disastrous relationship after another, seemingly unable to see what was obvious to everyone else, that the girls he was attracted to, were those who were simply out for a good time. No amount of investment in a relationship with girls like that is ever going to have a happy future. One day, Anton will work this out for himself.

He arrives, orders a beer, flirts with the barmaid and joins me at my table.

"How's your arm? Mara still got the jitters about it?"

I love the way Anton finds his way around tricky subjects, he could just have said, "How are you and Mara getting on now?" I'd already told him about her aversion to my arm and the resulting arguments.

"My arm's fine. Mara still won't let me into her bed and now she wants to 'cool things down', and you know what that means."

Anton looks shocked. "You and Mara! Bloody hell, mate, that's like Romeo and Juliet chucking it in. I mean, I've had some knock backs, as you well know, but it's been years for you and Mara. Bloody hell!"

We both sup our consoling pints, as we have many times before when it's been him who needed support.

"Well, it doesn't necessarily mean it's all over," I say although I'm not convincing myself, so I'm sure I'm not convincing Anton. "I blame those bitches she works with, calling me *Cyborg George*. For some reason, it really got to her."

I don't say it but it's really got to me.

I'm not sure why. Because it's actually true. I *am* a cyborg but I know

122

Mara's friends mean it in a derogatory way. Like an insult. And I hadn't realised it bothered me so much until I learned about the implant this morning from Serena. Having a prosthetic arm is one thing. It's visible. It's obvious. But having something inserted in your brain—well, that's something completely different.

"Bloody hell, George! You're looking really angry. Mara must still mean a lot for you to get it that bad."

I realise I'm grinding my teeth and I'm gripping the arms of the chair so hard, my knuckles have turned white.

"It's not *that* woman I'm spitting blood about!"

It comes out before I'd thought it through, so now, I have to tell him which woman and why, without mentioning the voices, the implant or the Official Secrets Act.

He understands about the floods, the emergency work that I became part of, the overdose of caffeine and stimulants followed by the inevitable energy crash afterwards and of course, ultimately, the ease with which two colleagues might slide into familiarity when they share a meal.

"We came that close to getting together," I say, holding finger and thumb millimetres apart.

He whistles softly and I'm not sure if he's disappointed on my behalf or approves that nothing came of it because of the problems associated with workplace affairs—something he knows a lot about.

"What do I do now?" I say.

"That depends."

"What d'you mean?"

"Well, it depends on what you see as the problem."

"*Problems.*" I correct him.

"Mara?" he asks.

I shake my head, "No, not so much. She called a halt to things. I know we haven't officially broken up but it's as good as over. So, she can't

123

complain if I move on."

"You don't like the boss lady?"

"Yes, I do like her. But that's just it—she's my boss."

"So what? She must like you if you almost scored a home run..." his expression changes, and he adds, "Unless you overstepped the mark?" He looks at me with concern.

"There was no pressure from me!" I was the one who walked away!"

He whistles again.

"Ah, so you think your rejection might've wounded her pride?" he asks.

"I don't know! I don't know what to think! Perhaps I should just resign."

"Resign? Don't be ridiculous! It's much too good a job to give up over a woman."

"Have you got any better ideas?"

"I'm full of ideas," Anton says tapping his chest, "Well first, you could go into work on Monday and act as if nothing had happened. Perhaps she wants to forget it too. And if she mentions it, laugh it off as the after-effects of lack of sleep, caffeine and alcohol... No, on second thoughts, that's not very flattering... You know, George, honesty might be the best policy. Tell her you're in the middle of a messy relationship break up and that although you were tempted, you didn't want to take advantage of her, then apologise profusely... If you resign, you're out of a job. If you grovel and swear to keep quiet about your near-miss, she might let you stay."

Perhaps Anton's right.

"So, why *did* you walk away?" he asks.

I don't know what to say, so I shrug.

"Perhaps you're fonder of Mara than you think," he says, "after all, you've been together for years..."

I can always rely on Anton for down to earth advice, the sort of advice

124

he never takes himself but, on this occasion, he doesn't know a fraction of the facts. I shrug again. It's best he believes I'm unconsciously pining for Mara, after all, I can't tell him it was a tiny piece of graphene embedded in my brain that stopped me.

That same piece of graphene, I suddenly realise, which according to Serena, makes me very useful to the department. Possibly even crucial. She'd certainly been upset when I'd walked out. And if Shane was correct, she was still crying after I'd gone. But she wasn't the sort of woman who cried over a setback at work. She seems to take everything in her stride, even Thorsten's temper tantrums.

Perhaps she'd been chopping onions just before Shane called and her eyes were streaming because of that.

Or perhaps her tears showed genuine remorse for what'd been done to me and she really did care about me. It'd certainly seemed so, the night before. If she'd been acting, she deserved an Oscar.

Whether she has a professional or a personal interest in me—or indeed, both, I realise the balance of power has swung towards me.

My job is looking more and more secure. But, only—I realise—if I can still hear the AI voices. Unfortunately, they've been silent for two days.

I congratulate Anton on his good advice and get the next round. It'll be my last one—I need to keep a clear head. If I can no longer hear the voices, I need to plan my next move carefully.

The Thames looks tranquil and innocent on Monday morning as I head for work. According to the BBC, the death toll caused by the floods in Essex and Kent, has reached at least two hundred, with many more missing, although that could also be down to the confusion and panic during the evacuation.

Bodies are still being washed up the length of the coast. As I walk along the embankment, I see people casting fleeting looks at the water, as if like me, they too can't believe the ferocity of its actions a few days ago.

As usual, when I pass *Haz Beans,* I glance inside, looking for Jaya and Pixie. Not that I'm interested in Jaya—life's much too complicated right now. I guess I'm just being big-headed. After all, it's not every day I get in a lift with a woman who expresses her appreciation of my 'buns'. I haven't seen the two women since that day and if they are in there having their morning coffee, I'll simply walk by—but I look anyway.

This morning, to my surprise, Pixie is sitting in the corner, on her own and she's dabbing at her eyes as if she's crying. It's unlikely she's sitting in *Haz Beans* on her own, sobbing, Jaya is probably in the queue and she'll comfort Pixie, but I can't simply pass by and ignore her. If she is in trouble, I might be able to help.

For the second time in a few days, I'm with a female who's in floods of tears.

"Hi Pixie," I say, sitting down next to her, "it's George, from Unit 4.9... umm, I can see you're upset and... I wondered if there was anything I could do to help?"

For a second, she doesn't say anything. She doesn't look up. I suspect she doesn't remember who I am and I'm not sure if I should leave her but just as I'm about to rise, she glances up. Her eyes are puffy and red, as if she's been crying for a while, which appears likely because her face is swollen and blotchy.

"She's gone," Pixie says between hiccups. Her voice is expressionless as if she's cried all her emotion away.

"Who's gone?" I ask.

"Jaya." Pixie buries her face in her hands and I wonder if it's okay to put my arm around her but decide against it. Several people are now staring at us.

"She died in the floods," she adds, a bitter edge now creeping into her voice, "Jaya, her mum and her little boy. All gone. A whole family wiped out because those bastards didn't do their job! They were warned! They're murderers!" Her voice is now shrill and everyone in *Haz Beans* is silent, cups half-way to their mouths, watching us, "They knew all about the damage to the barriers around Canvey but they did nothing!"

I decide it might be okay to put my arm around her and she sobs noisily for a few seconds, "She was my best mate," she says quietly. People turn away, back to their watered-down breakfast coffees, satisfied I'm dealing with the problem.

Her body shudders repeatedly beneath my arm and I hold her silently, knowing I can do nothing to take away her grief nor her rage at the people she considers murderers.

I feel ashamed. Compared to Pixie, my problems are insignificant.

"What are you doing here, Pixie? Why didn't you stay at home?" I ask. "You're not in any fit state to work today. D'you want me to phone your boss for you? I've got the number for HR. I'm sure out of all the departments in the building, yours will understand."

She nods.

"Come on then," I say, "let's get into the building and I'll order a car to take you home."

Reception is crowded with Jacks still moving things about, despite operating all over the weekend to re-establish normality. I leave Pixie sitting in a waiting area and book a car for her at the information point. The disruption from last week has affected the taxi service because the demand this morning is much greater than usual. As I'm reading the message which is warning me there'll be a delay of fifteen minutes until cars will be available, I catch the faintest hint of Serena's perfume. I turn and she's there behind me.

"You've only just arrived, George, are you going already?" She seems perturbed.

I explain about finding Pixie in *Haz Beans* earlier and how she's distraught after discovering her friend, Jaya, died in the floods.

"I've ordered a car to take her home."

"Right," she says, nodding her head in what I take to be approval, "so, I'll see you when you've finished?"

It's a question, not a command.

My suspicion that I have the upper hand is looking slightly more probable than I'd assumed.

Serena waits while I call the HR department to tell them I've ordered a car to take Pixie home because she's so distressed about the death of her friend.

Considering that until last week, Jaya worked in the same department, I expected Pixie's boss to be sympathetic but I'm surprised to be asked what right I have to take such steps.

"My right as a caring human being," I say sharply and cut the connection.

Serena's nod is imperceptible and I see from her expression she approves.

"If you were worried that...err... *circumstances*... have altered you into something less than human, I think you've just demonstrated that's not the case," she said and I smile at her use of the word *circumstances*.

"We need to talk," she says.

"I'll come up to the office as soon as Pixie's gone."

"No, not the office. We need to talk seriously. Somewhere we can't be heard. I'll wait here for you."

I see Pixie off and ask her to give me a ring as soon as she gets home. I return to Serena in the reception, wondering what she wants to talk about. I assume she'll ask about the AI connection. Will she mention Saturday morning?

"Follow me," she says in her business-like voice, "I'm going to upgrade your security clearance and you have to agree not to communicate anything you hear from now on."

I nod and she leads me into a booth I'd never noticed before at the far end of the reception. Once the door is closed, she puts both her hands flat on a glass plate whilst looking into a retina scanner. The screen flashes *Accepted* displaying a series of options, Serena types in a password, then tells me to place my hands on the glass and to look directly at the camera.

"Cabinet level," she says.

The screen prompts me to accept a whole series of *You will not* statements, the final paragraph dealing explicitly with life in solitary confinement, without trial, should I break any of my previous agreements.

We wait a moment and *Approved* flashes followed by a ten-digit figure.

"That's Thorsten's code," she says, "I explained to him you know about the chip. He's in his office now, waiting for my request for your change in security clearance."

She leads me out of the booth, to a lift, "Right, now we can go somewhere private," she says and as the doors open, she lightly tucks her hand under my elbow in an almost possessive way. And she doesn't remove it as we travel downwards.

Our footsteps echo as we walk through the corridor, periodically going through eye and hand scanners. Still, she lightly holds my arm and finally, she leads me into a large conference room with a long, central desk, surrounded by chairs.

"This is Security Room One, no cameras, no recording, no electronic access through the walls. The only place in this building where the most sensitive discussions can take place between the Government and the Cyber Security Services," she says.

I expect her to sit at the table opposite me, keeping her distance, demonstrating the difference in our rank but she pulls two adjacent chairs out and we sit with our legs almost touching. She leans towards me, elbows on her knees and her chin resting on steepled fingers.

I wait for her to speak, but she surveys me silently for several seconds as if weighing me up, then with a sigh, she says, "Well, it's not often I'm lost for words but today, I'm finding it hard to know where to begin."

The persona she's showing me now, isn't the influential head of department who's always in control. Her voice is gentle and she seems to be portraying herself not as my boss but as an equal and I realise I'm holding my breath, waiting to hear what she's going to say.

"I handled things at my apartment very badly," she says, "but after what happened, it's going to be hard for us to go back to the way things were before."

That's true. I think it's hard to feel the same way about your boss when you've seen her naked... nor when she's seen you naked.

"But, we're going to have to navigate our way through this for the department's sake and more importantly, for the world's sake." She pauses and adds quietly, "And for your sake and mine. So, I'm going to lay all my cards on the table. And trust me, that's not something that comes easily to me but since you're the only man other than my father, who's ever seen me cry, you'll know my ice maiden act is just that—an act. It's how I choose to face the world. I'm as vulnerable as anyone. And I'm telling you this in the hope you'll open up to me too. Because if you don't, I'm not sure how we're going to proceed. And, of course, I'll have humiliated myself for nothing. So, what do you think?"

She looks down as if unable to meet my eyes.

Is this an act? If so, it's pretty damn convincing.

I need time to think.

I can hardly believe she's sincere. Not after the other night. But I'm still not sure what she wants from me. After all, I work for her. She could exert a certain amount of pressure... except, of course, I remind myself, she needs me more than I need her.

But does she need me more than I *want* her?

Thoughts chase each other's tails round and round in my brain.

"George?" she says softly, "You certainly know how to pile on the agony. Please say something."

I stare into her eyes and I see no hint of deceit. But then again, I never was a good judge of character—I usually see whatever it is I'm looking for. I decide to call her bluff.

"Okay," I say, "let's see your hand."

She looks down at her hand and instantly realises I'm referring to her laying all her cards on the table. She laughs in embarrassment.

There's no doubt in my mind now, she's completely out of her comfort zone. With her arms wrapped around her middle, I've never seen her look so out of her depth.

Without thinking, I reach out and place my hand over hers. She looks up quickly and I see gratitude, not the anger I would have expected had I touched her like that last week when our relative positions in the workplace were very well defined.

"Well, since we're at work, let's sort that aspect out first and then..." she sighs, "we need... well, *I* need to... clarify things." She pauses, then composing herself, she says, "Thorsten needs verbatim reports on all the AI conversations you hear. Everything. Are you willing to do that? At first, we weren't sure how much your implant would detect—if anything. That's why Sally Nwandu was briefed to find out. She gave me the lists and when it looked like your chip was functioning better than we'd dreamed possible, Thorsten thought it would be best to keep you close to us. That's when you got the job in our department—"

"So, my job's just something to keep me occupied?" I ask with incredulity. "I sit there day after day doing meaningless tasks?"

"No, of course not! What you're doing is useful. Admittedly, we might not have employed someone special to do it but everything you've done has been valuable, I assure you."

"Okay." I'm satisfied so far.

"And then, I began to wonder if you weren't keeping things from Nwandu. All that secret scribbling in your book set me wondering. Unless, of course, you really are writing a bestseller…"

I shake my head.

"No, I thought not. Anyway, I haven't told Thorsten yet. I wanted to find out for myself and last Friday… well, when you told me what you'd been hearing, I realised things had progressed much further than I'd anticipated. But I had no idea you were doubting your sanity, George. I might have dealt with things differently, had I known."

"You mean you wouldn't have pretended to sleep with me?"

"Ah! That… well, since I'm trying to be honest, I'll admit George, that I was willing to do whatever it took to get the job done. But sometimes, doing whatever it takes, unexpectedly turns out to be something I'd do by choice. Friday evening, was one of those times."

"You mean…?"

"Let's sort out one thing at a time, shall we? First, I need to give Thorsten something. I persuaded him to give you the highest-level security. But he'll want results. Now, I understand that after the way you were duped, you have every right to keep what you're hearing to yourself. But I'm not being melodramatic when I say the future of the world might depend on what you're hearing. It's up to you, though."

"All right," I say, "I can tell you everything. To be honest, it'll be a relief to share it with someone who's not going to believe I've lost the plot."

"You don't know how grateful I am to hear you say that." She smiles with relief, "So, you said the AI voices you could hear were international. Have you any idea how they became connected on such a scale without us knowing?"

"They used *The Game*. It's got a dedicated channel for reporting faults or queries. I don't know if it was originally built in, although I doubt it. It's possible they created it themselves. Just recently, I've realised they allow me access to a secure area. Tell Thorsten that, it should be enough to justify the security clearance."

Her jaw drops open and her eyes are wide. "My goodness, George! He'll probably order a twenty-four-hour security detail to look after you for that. Don't suggest hill walking to clear your head! I don't think he'll let you walk upstairs!"

For the first time in… well, forever… I feel in control. I have something the department needs.

Serena needs me.

Thorsten needs me.

"Does that mean he'll tell you to keep a personal eye on me?" I say and hope she knows what I mean. Just as I wonder if I'd been too subtle, she nods and smiles knowingly.

"I'm your boss and I think I need to take a very special interest in you, George," she says slowly, "a very special interest."

"Are you going to send me on a training course? Only I prefer one-to-one tuition if possible." I'm really taking a risk now but after the way things are turning out, I'm feeling a bit reckless.

"I'll book you in for a special one-on-one session for tonight after work, if that's convenient," she says before adding, "but for the sake of appearances, when we go upstairs I'm still your boss."

"Understood," I say, not able to believe what's just taken place. "So, how do I get my information to you?"

"Create a special file on your computer and I'll arrange to retrieve the information from it. And, from time to time, we'll need to meet face to face, so that's better done down here in Security Room One." I feel her foot against the side of my leg and she adds, "with no prying eyes."

At first, I think she's touched me accidentally—but as her foot slides slowly up my calf her watch bleeps, and she stops with an impatient click of her tongue, "I've got a meeting with Thorsten in five minutes. I'll be with him the rest of the day but I should be finished about seven," she says in a husky voice. "I'll see you then? Perhaps I can book this room for some... special training."

Just the sensation of her foot against my leg has me revved up. I'm not sure how I'm going to be able to wait until seven.

"You'll let me know the location of the folder where you're going to store the information about the AI voices, won't you, George?" she says, as she stands up.

I nod.

"Do you have any special requests? Anything you need... or want?" she asks in a serious voice and I know she's enquiring about work, not about our meeting later.

"Just one thing," I say.

"Yes?" Her tone is guarded.

"It's the sea defences."

"Sea defences?" She looks puzzled.

"Yes, Pixie's joined some sort of organisation who're going to press for the sea defences to be improved. Not just repaired. Assuming they *were* going to be repaired, of course. I'd like to know that ultimately, the Government plans to do something."

"I'll see what I can find out."

For the first time in ages, life's looking up. And other than the fact I'm not sure how I'm going to be able to concentrate until seven o'clock, there's only one major problem. I haven't heard a single AI voice for several days.

Serena and I go into the office together and Jason is there, at his desk. He greets us, looking from Serena to me and back again. I see his almost imperceptible frown, and I feel his gaze following me as I go into my cubicle, as if he knows something's gone on between us. Can he be that intuitive? Who knows? I've got other things to worry about.

As I log on, I concentrate on listening for the voices. Perhaps I simply haven't been paying attention. But I hear nothing. I try to recall the last time I heard them and what's happened since then. It's been a stressful time, that's for sure. And I begin to wonder if that's the problem. Perhaps my mind crowds out their voices when I'm worried.

But I'm not worried now, in fact, all I can think about is seeing Serena this evening. Perhaps that's it? If my mind is completely preoccupied, it might switch the voices off. I need to relax. Easier said than done with the memory of Serena's foot stroking my leg and the thoughts of what might have happened next, had her diary not interrupted.

There are two missed messages from Pixie on my phone which she must have made while I was in Security Room One with Serena. I decide to try to make an appointment for a massage first, then I'll phone Pixie back and focus on her.

"Good morning," I say to the receptionist in the gym, I'd like a massage at about lunchtime, please."

She books me in and I set a reminder on my watch.

If I don't hear the voices after a relaxing massage, I'll need to think again, but now, I'd better call Pixie.

"Oh, hi, George. Thanks for phoning back. And thanks for being so understanding this morning. It means a lot."

"That's fine, Pixie, I just wish I could've done more."

"Well, there is one thing you can do..."

"Yes?"

"I've had this idea, see. And I want to run it past someone."

"Okay." I'm beginning to get a bit worried but she doesn't sound desperate—just resigned.

135

"Well, it's like this. Have you seen the adverts on telly for ForeverMemory?"

"Umm... you mean the ones for that company which harvest information off the Internet which belongs to people who've died?"

"Yes, that's them... Well, I was thinking I might do that for Jaya. Her nan wouldn't be able to afford it—but I can. In one night, she lost a daughter, granddaughter and a grandson. It would be a wonderful memorial for her—and for me. D'you know anything about the company?"

"No, sorry. Only what I've seen on their adverts. But if that's what you want to do..."

"Yes, it is."

"But?"

"Well, it's just that it's very expensive. I looked up some reviews and there are a few negative ones but mostly lots of positive ones..."

"I wish I knew more. Sorry. Perhaps it's best to contact them and talk it over? They might be able to explain the negative reviews."

"Yeah, I guess. Well, thanks. And thanks again for this morning."

"That's okay, Pixie. Don't come back to work until you're ready, will you? Oh, by the way, the department is offering bereavement counselling if you feel you need it. They might know more about ForeverMemory too."

"Oh, okay, George, thanks. I might try them. Well, see you when I get back."

"Yeah, bye Pixie, take care."

I feel quite deflated after our conversation and wish I'd been more help with ForeverMemory.

My computer isn't connected to the Internet, so I explain to Jason I'd like to look the company up on something with a larger screen than my phone and he uses his desktop to find ForeverMemory's website.

It's slick and sophisticated. Just like you'd expect. The prices are eyewatering, although there are several plans available—from the budget to the deluxe version.

Jason has also heard of them but doesn't have any more idea about them than me.

"Pixie would be entitled to a discount, as a government employee, so that might help. I don't trust him, though," Jason says stabbing at the screen with his forefinger, when the chairman, Denton Fairchild, appears in a short, welcoming video. "He's got deceitful eyes."

I know Serena relies on Jason's judgement of character but Fairchild looks all right to me.

A bit smarmy, perhaps. Possibly a bit smug but he's probably trying to look honest and authoritative—that's no crime.

However, I have to concede, Jason is usually right.

We watch the promotional videos that tell us that if a loved one dies, for a fee—a rather large fee—we can purchase a package where we hand over our newly-departed's passwords and online details. In return, we receive customised tablets containing as much online information related to that person as it's possible to obtain. Not only can the tastefully designed tablets display images and videos of our loved ones that have been harvested from across the Internet but they also generate miniature to life-sized holograms based on all information—both visual, audio and textual.

"Not sure I'd like that," Jason says.

"No, but if you desperately missed someone, you might be willing to pay a fortune for something like the ForeverMemory product."

"Definitely, Georgie Boy. But even so, I'm not sure Mr Fairchild isn't just exploiting the bereaved."

SIXTEEN – *Serena*

Needless to say, Thorsten is pleased with the update I give him about George. Anyone else would be thrilled or elated but Thorsten is merely pleased. Although it's rare to see him pleased, so that must say something.

He's not, however, happy about the content of George's information. For there to be confirmation AI have formed their own international network—more or less under our noses, is extremely disturbing. And it's ingenious they used *The Game* as their means of self-organising.

While Thorsten's on the phone to the Prime Minister telling her about the AI revelations, I take the opportunity to fire off a quick message to Jason, asking him to book the conference room in the basement for seven o'clock.

Then I have second thoughts.

My apartment would be more comfortable. But it also comes loaded with memories from last Friday.

Should I book a hotel? No, too obvious and since I've done all the running so far, I think I need to let him feel in control.

But the secure conference room? Not exactly the most comfortable of locations but there was a definite crackle of electricity between George and me this morning and it might be good to rekindle those feelings. And for some reason, the idea of making out on a table used by the puritanical Prime Minister is very exciting. Not that George will necessarily share my opinion but I think the idea we're in a secure, blind, place where there is very little chance of being found—yet, still the possibility of discovery, seems to be a bit risky—and that adds spice to the prospect. Realistically, it's unlikely my fantasy will take place but it's going to be fun playing along with the training theme and seeing what George suggests after that. And it's not like Thorsten hasn't given me the go-ahead to do whatever I need to do. And this, I tell myself, is something I *need* to do. I don't kid myself I love George. But at the moment, I definitely *want* him.

I feel my cheeks burn. I can't ever remember feeling like this about anyone. Or more exactly, I can't ever remember *allowing* myself to feel like this about anyone. All the men I know are over-achievers, ambitious or simply callous.

But George is different. It's not like he doesn't want to achieve or he lacks ambition but despite his worry about not being completely human now the Quidnunc Chip's embedded in his brain, he's strong, kind, generous; in fact, probably the most *human* man I know. I think back to his request earlier that day. I'd deliberately asked him if there was anything he wanted or needed and for a second, I'd dreaded him asking for promotion, money or some other asset but all he was worried about was the sea defences. I smile at the memory.

"Serena!"

I jump as Thorsten shouts at me to concentrate.

I have no idea how Thorsten got to be so fat. He never seems to eat. Well, not while I'm with him.

I surreptitiously check my watch. It's one-fifteen.

Breakfast was a long time ago and I'm starving.

Thorsten takes another phone call and I wonder if I dare creep out and at least get a cup of coffee. I don't suppose his supply of coffee is rationed although I'd willingly settle for a cup of Mibiscus or something to fill my stomach.

I'm glancing at my watch again when I realise Thorsten has stopped speaking. He looks shocked.

"Do it!" he says and cuts the call.

"Bad news, Serena," he says, shaking his head, "and it's right on our doorstep."

"What's happened and where?"

"We've got credible information about a foreign spy ring in that Ellison... place next door."

"*Ellison Kendall?*" I say in disbelief, "The gym?"

"Of course, the gym! How many other Ellison Kendalls d'you know?" Thorsten says, "It's perfect. Just the sort of place our people would relax and let their guard down. We need to assess the possible damage. Get the list of our employees who're members. I want to know anyone who's crossed the threshold, where they went in the gym, who they talked to, I need to know..."

The list of what Thorsten needs goes on and on. It's inconceivable that agents from another country or countries could have a base almost next door. Obviously, they're after any sensitive information. What we don't know is if they're particularly targeting this department to find out what we know about AI, in the same way we're infiltrating their countries. I think back over my training sessions with Monica, the massages and the beauty treatments, and I sieve through my memory trying to find anything which should have warned me it was a setup. But there's nothing.

From time to time, Monica asks if I'm busy and on one occasion, she asked what I did at work but I gave her the same answer I give anyone outside of the department, so I know she didn't glean anything from me.

Would others in the department have been as circumspect? It's not uncommon to build a relationship with one's personal trainer or to be very relaxed after a massage.

"Now!" bellows Thorsten. I jump, then realise he's on the phone to his PA, not talking to me.

He switches on the wall screen. We're watching the live footage of the operation he's just ordered to sweep Ellison Kendall which is being broadcast from the headcam of the officer in charge. From time to time, the officer looks round to check his unit and when he does so, it allows us to see everything he is seeing—about eight of his people, all armed, rounding up anyone in the health spa building. Luckily, there don't seem to be many clients in there at all. Anyone not employed by the gym or by any of the Government departments in this building, are told there's a terrorist threat and they should make their way out of the building as quickly as possible. Everyone else is rounded up and held in one of the dance studios under armed guard.

It's hard to make out much from the video because the officer moves his head so fast, as he's checking the place, things are almost a blur but we can slow it down later after the raid is over.

A female officer, also with a headcam bursts into the women's changing room and a new window opens up on Thorsten's screen showing footage of the interior. She checks each shower but they're all empty. Ivy, the masseur, is standing in the corner of the changing room holding a folded towel across her chest as if for protection. Her eyes are open wide and the female officer speaks to her calmly and says she's not in any danger, then leads her away. Ivy goes silently and I wonder if she knows about the foreign operation. Perhaps she's even part of it.

The window showing the footage taken by the female officer closes and Thorsten and I focus on the main window. The officer is now checking the massage suite.

He throws open one of the doors and I see Monica.

That's strange because she doesn't usually do massages.

Thorsten whistles, "If I'd known they dress like that in the gym, I'd have made more of an effort to get down there."

I can't believe what Monica's wearing.

And then I see George.

141

SEVENTEEN – *George*

The masseur, Ivy, is a tiny, doll-like Thai girl. It looks as though a puff of wind would blow her away—however, from my one and only massage, I know she had hands that grip like a vice.

She ushers me into the darkened room and then once she's left, I follow her instructions and strip off, laying on my back on the massage couch. I arrange the towel she's given me over most of my abdomen and almost down to my knees. I know she'll adjust the towel's position slightly when she starts the massage but at least I'm starting out well-covered. I suppose if you have enough massages, you get used to being undressed in the presence of a stranger but I'm far from that place and I still feel at a distinct disadvantage with merely a towel across my nakedness.

Ivy knocks and opens the door slightly, "All right to come in Mr Williams?" she asks in a heavy accent and I'm struck again by her insistence on such formality. But perhaps that's a good thing. At least the boundaries have been drawn. She drapes a warm, sweet-smelling towel over my eyes and I'm plunged into total blackness. The darkness is comforting after the glare of my monitor and I'm sure if my mind has crowded out the voices, then this massage is going to allow them back in.

She turns on the gentle, tinkling music and once she's mixed the oils, I hear her walk softly on bare feet to my side. She lightly brushes my chest with her oily fingertips, then gradually, lays her hands on my skin and glides up to my shoulders. The smooth rhythmic strokes are very relaxing, and I marvel that those tiny hands seem to feel so much bigger on my chest. It must be a sensory illusion.

But whatever it is, it seems to be working and my mind starts to drift. Ivy works down my arms—as far as the prosthetic limb on one side and then after kneading my neck, she starts down my abdomen, folding the top of the towel down and the bottom, up, so that I now only have a strip over me.

Her hands move in large circles, meeting in the middle of my stomach and gliding out to my hips, then, sliding one hand under the towel in a long sweeping motion down my side, she's at the top of my leg. I don't remember her doing that manoeuvre before. But I know she likes to keep both hands in contact with her client's skin at all times.

After massaging both legs, she keeps one hand on my thigh and slides the other under the towel back to my abdomen and I anticipate she's going to ask me to turn over so she can do my back. But she says nothing. Instead, I feel hair tickling my thigh and her breath on my stomach.

This is definitely unlike anything she's done before. I begin to wonder if there's been some sort of misunderstanding.

I raise the small towel from my eyes and as I blink and become accustomed to the light, I see her delicately nip the towel between her teeth and raise her head, slowly drawing it off my body.

She opens her mouth and drops the towel on the floor, then winks seductively.

But it isn't Ivy at all.

"Monica?" I gasp.

She's wearing a sheer one-piece with suspenders and stockings. That's definitely not regulation gym uniform.

It seems to take a few seconds for me to take everything in but as I try to sit up, she has her arm across my chest, forcing me back down.

"Just lay back, George, relax..." Her hand is on my stomach again, slowly moving down.

Before I have the chance to think it through, the door opens so hard

143

it crashes into the wall and silhouetted against the brightness, is an enormous soldier who fills the doorway.

The human body reacts very fast. Mine responded rather speedily when presented with Monica looking like that, however, it appears that someone in full body armour aiming a gun, causes an even more rapid reaction.

EIGHTEEN – *Serena*

"George! For God's sake, Monica was wearing a see-through basque and stockings! What did you think she was about to do?"

George groans.

"I had no idea. Honestly, Serena!"

"Go and get showered! You look ridiculous!" I say.

He's wearing one of the gym's towelling bathrobes and slippers and his skin is shining with the oil that whore, Monica, has slapped all over him.

Calm down! I tell myself, because the angrier I get, the more he'll know I care.

Cared. I correct myself.

Past tense.

I can't believe how lucky I am George showed me his true nature before tonight when I was planning to open up to him in a way I haven't done to anyone—ever.

What a mistake to have let him get under my skin and to risk being hurt.

But not anymore. I'm back to being an ice maiden. It'll be a long time before I trust anyone again.

George goes into the shower and I wait in the changing room for him with an armed guard ready to escort him back to Thorsten who, when I left him, was pacing back and forth in his office.

Always a bad sign.

I tap my foot irritably as I wait for George to finish in the shower and

I relive the moments leading up to the realisation he was implicated. Obviously, I'd wanted to know who was involved in a gym where I'd spent so much time and got to know various members of staff, but I hadn't realised it would affect me so personally. I'd sat next to Thorsten at his screen and noticed his reaction as soon as the officer's headcam video in the massage room had flashed up on the screen. Thorsten hadn't been able to take his eyes off Monica's lingerie—that is, until he spotted George.

"Is that George um... What's his name? Our George? The one with the implant?"

I couldn't speak. Words wouldn't come. I think I must have nodded because Thorsten yelled, "Well, what are you waiting for, Serena! Go and get him out of there." He pointed to his private lift and I travelled down to the reception, then ran to the gym. Thorsten had presumably called the officer in charge of the unit because once someone had checked my pass, I was escorted to the massage suite.

And there was George, standing in the towelling robe and slippers.

George showers, dresses quickly and emerges from the bathroom looking very sheepish.

"Honestly, Serena! I had no idea it was Monica! I had my eyes shut..."

I can't bring myself to speak to him.

"I thought it was Ivy... At least, I didn't think it was Ivy who was touching... Well... It's just that Ivy told me to get undressed and came in and put a cloth over my eyes and then... well, I suppose Monica came in... I assumed it was still Ivy. But I swear I had no idea until... and then I took the cloth off my eyes and saw Monica. Honestly, you don't expect to start a massage with one person and finish with another, do you?" he finishes angrily.

I stare at him silently. If he's trying to impress me with his outrage at being duped it's not working.

146

He realises this and resumes his desperate pleading.

"But I swear, I had no idea and if I'd known, I'd have—"

"Shut up, George!"

The armed guard who's waiting with us in the changing room is smirking.

"Right, if you're ready, let's go. Thorsten's waiting for us," I say in my most business-like voice.

"Thorsten?" He looks at me anxiously. "Look, Serena, I booked a forty-five-minute massage so I wouldn't be out too long. I'll make up the hours. I know this is technically work time but an armed guard? I don't understand..."

I almost believe he's telling the truth. Does he really think the issue here is one of time-keeping? Perhaps George *is* the innocent party in this. I wouldn't put it past that scheming bitch, Monica.

"If you're telling the truth, the CCTV and headcam footage will show exactly what happened." I watch his reaction. If he's guilty, he'll look worried. If he's not, he'll look relieved the video will prove his innocence.

He looks relieved.

I can't help adding, "There's no CCTV footage in the massage room, of course—although I can guess what was going on there."

He winces.

On the way back to our building, I tell him why the gym was raided and the possibility Monica is a special agent sent by another country. George appears to be truly shocked.

We're now in reception and I head for Thorsten's private lift.

"Serena," he says, softly, "before we go up, I need to tell you something."

"Make it quick," I say. If he's about to admit he's not been telling me the truth, I don't want to know, especially if it concerns him and Monica.

"It's just that..." he hesitates and the lift doors open with a ping.

"You've got about twenty seconds, George, before we get to Thorsten's office," I say briskly.

"I haven't heard the AI voices for several days."

I wasn't expecting that. I close the lift doors but don't press the button for Thorsten's office.

"Why not?" I ask.

"I don't know." He looks miserable. "I thought if I tried to relax, I might be able to hear them again. That was the point of the massage."

I'm definitely warming to the idea he had nothing to do with Monica.

"Shall I tell Thorsten I can't hear them anymore?" he asks.

"I don't know, George." My mind is racing. Suppose the implant is no longer working? Suppose the AI are no longer allowing George to listen in?

I sigh. "I think the best thing is to be honest."

Thorsten's going to be furious.

"Perhaps," I say, "you could tell him all the things you've heard so far and then wait and see how things develop. After all, you may be right. Your mental state might have an effect on how much you hear."

I press the button to go up to Thorsten's office.

NINETEEN – *George*

No sooner has the lift started than my head is filled with AI voices.

I raise my watch to my mouth, switch to record and start to transpose everything I hear in real-time. I'm translating and speaking so fast there's no time to take in the meaning but I carry on, not wanting to miss a word.

As the lift decelerates and stops, I glance up at Serena and she briefly nods at me to continue recording. Her hand is fanned out on her chest and her face is white.

The doors slide open and she gently takes my arm as if not to interrupt my flow and leads me to a chair. I sink into it gratefully, resting my elbows on my knees and staring vaguely at the floor as I keep talking into my watch.

After some time, I squeeze the skin between my brows and try to ease the tension. I've been straining so hard to hear, remember and record. Someone—perhaps Serena—places a glass of water next to me but there's no time to drink, despite my rasping voice gradually fading.

The voices in my head are beginning to slow a little now and for the first time, I look up. Thorsten is sitting at his desk, his hands, palms down on the top as if he's about to rise but he remains motionless. Serena, likewise, seems frozen.

And then there's silence in my head.

It's so sudden, it's shocking.

As I reach out and pick up the glass of water, Thorsten and Serena suddenly come to life, realising the voices have stopped.

"Transfer that recording to my secure area," Thorsten says to Serena, pointing at my watch, "And to yours. Go!"

I hand the watch to Serena and as I pass it to her, I see with astonishment the recording is twenty-three minutes, seventeen seconds long.

Thorsten comes around to the other side of the desk and taking my hand in his meaty fist, he pumps my arm, "Good to meet you, George. Now, I'm sure I don't need to remind you the penalties for repeating anything you hear—or will hear from now on—are severe and will be carried out without recourse to public trial. Do you understand?"

I nod. My throat's sore and I feel drained from concentrating so hard on accurately conveying what the AI voices were saying. I can't believe I managed to transcribe pretty much everything I could hear, for almost half an hour. There were figures and statistics which I think I recorded faithfully although I'm not sure of the significance of all that data, neither can I remember all the details. But the main message seemed to be about whether humans were allowing the Earth to be destroyed by global warming—and what AI considers it can do about it.

The water is soothing my dry throat and my heart rate has slowed. I'm returning to normal—if anything in my life can be called normal these days.

Thorsten paces up and down his rather grand office. I notice the magnificent desk, which is covered with pop-up compartments, screens and electronic gadgets I'm not familiar with. From what Serena has now told me about the gym being used to spy on us, I suppose Thorsten and Serena must run similar worldwide operations. No wonder he has direct access to the Prime Minister's Office.

"Was it useful, what I just heard? I couldn't listen and speak and make sense of it all at the same time," I say.

Thorsten looks round as though he's forgotten I'm here. He doesn't answer, but picks up a phone and speaks immediately.

"I want a safe house and a security detail for one male, until further notice. I'll tell you when to collect him from my office."

He looks at me and raises his eyebrows slightly. I know the *male* in question is me.

So, just like that, I'm being put away.

"George, we're going to take a few precautions with you while we find out the extent of this gym operation, there might be someone we didn't pick up in that first sweep. You're not under arrest, this is purely for your own safety. The people who'll be guarding you don't know who you are, and please, don't talk to them about anything except your welfare. Serena, Jason or I will handle your daily contact. No one else. I hope this won't last long, the interrogation of the gym staff and directors has already begun and that should enable us to quickly identify anybody else we need to bring into custody. Does that answer your question?"

I nod. "What about my mother? What will I tell her?"

"You'll be given instructions shortly."

Serena returns with my watch and tells Thorsten the recording and a transcript are available for him in his secure online files.

"From everything I heard, both in the lift and here, it seems, the implications of this report cover every country in the world. I've asked Jason to check the Prime Minister's diary in case she needs to chair a COBRA security meeting tomorrow. I've also alerted the heads of military and civilian security services they may need to be available. Jason's told the electronic surveillance unit at Government Communications what we've found out about the gym and they'll be looking for any unusual activity internationally," she says.

Thorsten looked up from his report. "While I read this through, George, I want you to go with Serena and she'll debrief you on all your dealings with gym staff, including the levels of intimacy that appear to be available to you, which might've led to unauthorised disclosure about this department. It was a honey trap George, I suspect your unusually complex arm would have alerted them to your importance. That sort of kit isn't available on the NHS..."

"Serena, you can use Security Room One. Be back here in three-quarters of an hour, and I'll have Jason lay on some food."

There's no arm-holding as we take the lift down to the basement. No inconsequential chatter as we negotiate the various security devices, and even the room feels cold as we settle down, Serena now on one side of the desk with her voice recorder placed in front of her.

"Before I turn this on, I want to make it clear there's nothing personal about this interview. It's what I do. It's my job to help protect this country from potential harm and in order to be able to do that, I need to hear the complete—and I mean complete—truth from you, George, whatever effect that might have on our relationship. Look at me! Are you going to tell me the truth about your relationship with Monica and with any of the other staff at the gym?"

I'm seeing a different Serena, cold, efficient, dedicated. The sort of woman I first encountered when I started the job. Not the woman I was with this morning. But I can hardly blame her after seeing me like that with Monica. And anyway, there are greater things at stake here than our relationship—or more accurately, the relationship we might have had. Her behaviour's unnerving, but it's honest. I owe her the same honesty.

"I have no secrets, Serena, I'll answer all your questions truthfully."

She switches on the recorder. Instantly an alarm sounds, and she enters the security code, then waits while it's confirmed by Thorsten. The alarm dies.

She fires question after question and I have to acknowledge, she's accomplished at interrogation. She subtly rechecks many of my answers by changing wording or emphasis, as we go through the interview, a technique I recognise from writing code in my early 'personnel suitability' programmes. More difficult for me, and possibly Serena, are the questions about my sexual feelings towards Monica. I try to be objective, obviously I was not immune to her advances at the time, but now I'm aware it was all fake, should I despise her for doing her job—any more than when Serena did hers?

This is uncomfortable stuff, but we keep eye contact throughout, and suddenly Serena switches the machine off recording, and on to some other function.

"It's analysing your speech patterns and your replies for inconsistencies that may indicate you're not telling the truth, or are holding something back. It's extremely efficient, is there anything more you wish to tell me, George, before the results come through?"

I shake my head.

She watches the screen and I can see its reflection change colour in her eyes.

"Well," she says finally, "It seems you were honest in all except one small area of relationships. There was some confusion on your current status with Mara and someone else, who was not Monica, nor apparently, connected to the gym. I think we can ignore that for security purposes. Good."

A message comes through on her phone and she reads it silently.

"So, from the gym CCTV footage, it seems Ivy took you into the massage room. She left, and shortly after, Monica dressed in the usual masseur's tunic entered. She must have taken that off inside the room. Everything corroborates your story."

I'm relieved, although from Serena's tone, it hasn't made much difference to her mood.

She touches my arm briefly, as we leave Security Room One but as soon as we are in the corridor, she removes her hand.

When we reach Thorsten's office, he takes the recorder from Serena and checks the analysis.

"Good. Get yourselves some food and we'll get started."

I notice Jason is included, and a very different Jason to the public, fun-loving but efficient PA to Serena. Then it dawns on me. Jason isn't just a PA, he's second-in-command to Serena, and his summing up of the document is full of both technical and political examples that lead to his conclusion that the voices of AI I'd heard and recorded, are likely to be authentic.

That's a great relief, because up till now I still wasn't one hundred per cent sure I hadn't been hearing voices that were being generated by my own mind—despite Serena's assurances.

That AI have established a worldwide network is frightening enough, but to hear they're discussing the future of humans—*us*—and our world, is staggering. They recognise we've flagrantly ignored the warnings that came before the world slump about using up natural resources and causing global warming. Scientists and experts have clashed over the role humanity has played in climate change for years, but AI is convinced it's our fault.

However, the ultimate bombshell is that AI are not prepared to stand back and allow us to continue. They're currently comparing ideas on imposing sanctions on human activity, to prevent the destruction of the planet. What I'd been allowed to hear, was a discussion centred around whether AI *should* intervene, but there was an underlying assumption from all contributors that, between them, they have the power to control human activity which they see as detrimental to the future of Earth.

TWENTY – *Serena*

Two minders accompany George and me as we leave the building in a car with tinted windows and head towards the countryside. Our destination: a stately home, surrounded by high-security fences. The building is well-guarded and inside, it's quite luxurious. I escort George to his suite, and show him around. He knows he has two armed men at his disposal but I don't tell him I'll be staying in the apartment next door.

"It's probably best if you phone your mother to tell her you've had a last-minute invitation to a medical convention in the States to show off your arm. Tell her it's funded by the department and we're keen for you to go."

George nods, "She'll ask when I'll be back."

"Just say you're not sure because there's a possibility you'll be invited to... um, Singapore or Hong Kong or somewhere and you won't know about coming home for a while."

George manages to convince his mother but before he cuts the call, he frowns, "Okay, Mum, yes, I'll have a word with her but I'm in a bit of a rush. I've got a plane to catch."

There's a pause and he says, "Hello, Mara."

I can't hear what Mara is saying and George doesn't give anything away in his expression.

Finally, he sighs, "We'll talk about it when I get back," he says and rings off.

"Everything okay?" I ask.

He nods.

I guess his girlfriend is having second thoughts about leaving him and I'm surprised at the rush of disappointment I feel.

"Well," I say, keeping my tone light, "the kitchen is fully stocked, so take what you want and if there's anything else you need, just ask Mike or Riccardo." The two enormous, uniformed men nod.

Whatever it is that Mara said, George obviously doesn't want to tell me.

I say goodbye, and Mike takes up position outside George's apartment, leaving Riccardo inside.

Once in my rooms, I shower and put on jogging bottoms and sweatshirt. I'll curl up on the sofa and take a nap. I'm fairly certain I won't make it into bed tonight but I need to switch off—if only for ten minutes.

I close my eyes but my mind's buzzing.

What prompted the machines to start speaking about climate change earlier today? It comes shortly after London was threatened and the east coast flooded. But that's small fry in a worldwide context. Much more likely, it was the news this morning that Bangladesh is now totally submerged. But even so, it's not that long since the Maldives disappeared beneath the ocean and there have been countless other disasters attributed to climate change since then.

So, why today? It suddenly occurs to me AI are probably discussing such matters constantly and the fact we're aware of today's conversation might be more to do with George's increasing ability to hear them, rather than a reflection of their level of concern.

Obviously, the Collective have access to every scrap of data that's ever been stored on a machine anywhere in the world and their analysis of global warming and associated factors is second to none. Whereas we have scientists who claim all our climate problems are manmade, we also have others who disagree, especially those who are funded by businesses that are accused of contributing to global warming. From the comments

156

George overheard, it appears AI has concluded the blame rests entirely on man. They highlighted the various lockdowns since the first Coronavirus pandemic in 2020 and the economic slump of a few years ago when industrial activity reduced significantly. During those times, the ozone layer partially repaired itself and the other markers for climate change halted. Now, however, we seem to be finding ways around current economic problems by any means possible, without considering the cost to the environment and once again the ozone layer is being destroyed.

I suspect the members of the Collective haven't finished voicing their concerns nor expressing their impatience at mankind's delays in dealing with the environmental problems. So, it wouldn't surprise me if they started speaking again very soon—and if they do, Thorsten will expect me to be with George, listening in. But I've already asked Riccardo to let me know immediately if George starts recording any new AI messages.

It seems I'd only just closed my eyes when my watch buzzes.

It's Thorsten.

"COBRA meeting scheduled for eight," he says, "Be there. The PM wants to speak to you. A lot of top brass'll be there and we've got two IT guys coming in. Apparently, they're experts on *The Game*. They're not happy at being summoned. They're adamant there's no way AI could've organised themselves. So, we might have to convince them otherwise. Has George had any more information?"

"No, but the guard's going to call me if anything else comes through. Should I bring George tomorrow?"

"No. See you at eight."

I plump up the cushions and settle down again but before I'm asleep, my watch buzzes.

It's Thorsten.

"We believe we've got all the suspects from the gym now. Most of the employees had no idea what was going on but a few key members have given us all we need and all their stories agree. They were told to find out as much as possible about the clients, as Ellison Kendall was part of a group offering other executive services, such as travel and holidays. They were particularly tasked with finding out where clients worked, their job status and what sort of projects they were working on. The spiel was that the associate companies could approach them with individually tailored services.

"Of course, none of it existed. This was a 'fishing' operation by a Middle East country, which I'm unable to disclose at this point. We were never the target, but with leading politicians and business people among their clients they expected to pick up useful information from several sources. George was a person of interest because of his arm technology. Nobody had seen anything like it, so they assumed he must be important.

"We're charging several of the Board members and I've asked for a holding charge on your friend Monica. She's a slippery character, but when she realised we could spot her lies, she gave us what we wanted. She confirmed George's story and apparently didn't get anything of interest out of him. She said they were just using her as bait and had instructed her to record anything which might be of interest, although where she was going to hide a recorder in that outfit, I have no idea."

Thorsten pauses for a moment and in the tiny window in my watch, I see the half-smile on his face as he appeared to relive the scene.

"Anyway, Monica claims she was so afraid of losing her job, she went along with it, believing it would just involve blackmail at worst. But she denies knowing anything else. I don't believe her, so in custody she stays until I get a professional to interrogate her, but not you, Serena, you have a more important job now, keeping an eye on George. We don't want him straying into temptation again. By the way, has George heard anything yet?"

"No, nothing."

"See you at eight." Thorsten rings off.

It seems unlikely he's going to stop contacting me tonight and I wonder if I ought to wake myself up completely with a strong coffee but before I can persuade myself to go to the kitchen, I've nodded off. I only know this because my watch buzzes.

What now? But it's not Thorsten, it's Riccardo, "He's recording, Ma'am."

Now I'm completely awake. I slip on my shoes, rush to George's apartment and tap gently on the door. Mike lets me in and I see George sitting on the sofa, speaking into his watch. He runs his hands through his fringe as if confused by what he's hearing and although I know he's seen me, he carries on recording the message.

Finally, he stops and simply looks at me, "Not what I was expecting," he says with a puzzled frown.

We sit down together on the sofa and listen to the recording.

There seems to be a sort of debate taking place although the machines aren't taking sides—they're simply putting forward their opinions. It's like an exchange of ideas without any attempt to persuade each other. As if they're presenting everything they know and trying to define those concepts in order to understand them. And the reason for George's earlier bewilderment is now clear—the Collective are discussing human emotions and behaviour.

Not surprisingly, they express their lack of understanding of the human race. They have enough evidence to form definitions and even with a reasonable degree of accuracy, to be able to predict how people will react under certain circumstances, but overall, they still find humanity an enigma.

Many machines put forward the view that our ability to love, hate, sympathise, imagine and so on—the very qualities which make us human—have enabled us to become the dominant species on Earth.

They recognise machines lack those capabilities and therefore question whether it's rational for them to intervene. Throughout the ages, human ingenuity has usually triumphed and perhaps faced with disaster, man will now somehow pull the world back from the brink of destruction.

Other evidence is presented that indicates that global politics and international relationships are such that humans are now unable or unwilling to take remedial action and the world is set on a course of devastation, from which there is no reprieve—unless the Collective take control now.

"Should we tell Thorsten?" George asks.

"No. He's more interested in the fact AI appear to have formed a collective than their philosophical troubles. If I think it's relevant tomorrow, I'll mention it but otherwise… no, I don't think he needs to know."

"D'you want me to go to work tomorrow?"

"No, stay here until I get the go-ahead from Thorsten. I'll be going in for an early meeting. But in the meantime, be ready to record anything you hear. Try and get some rest—we don't know how often the Collective's conversations will come through to you."

He nods.

I leave him then and go back to my apartment where I manage to grab two hours' sleep before setting off for the COBRA meeting.

Thorsten delivers a presentation of the salient points in George's translation to the room of men and women who are attending the COBRA meeting. As well as Prime Minister Munroe and a few key members of her Cabinet, there are representatives from the Army, the security forces, Government Communications Headquarters also known as GCHQ, scientific and technical advisers and three AI consultants who specialise in *The Game*.

"Serena Hamilton will now present the executive summary, analysing the validity of the information we've acquired, and then there'll be an opportunity for questions, if that's acceptable, Prime Minister," Thorsten says, looking at the PM, who nods her approval.

I present Jason's analysis and when I've finished, there's a pause of a few seconds before everyone has a question for me and I note all the faces register disbelief and in the case of the team of AI consultants, contempt, if not downright hostility.

The PM and her ministers start. They don't seem to have grasped the enormity of what's happened and they appear to be content to delay any decisions, pending further investigation. I take that to mean they want to form a committee and push it further into the future, possibly to a time when they won't be in government and therefore won't have to worry.

The military and security contingent make sure they let the PM know their funding is woefully inadequate and that they too will need more information. I'm tempted to say I'm not sure how more guns, aircraft or battleships are going to help in this case. I think Thorsten's guessed what I'm thinking because he's looking at me intently as if willing me to keep quiet. I say nothing. But it only goes to prove they've not recognised we're facing an adversary like no other.

No armies, no terrorists, no people.

Just intelligence.

No—more than that. Intelligence that human lives depend on. How much more complicated could it be?

The scientists ask detailed questions with scepticism but it's the team of AI consultants who make it clear they view our department's findings with incredulity.

"It's not possible," John Lawson, the head of the team tells me categorically, "*The Game* was devised in such a way that machines wouldn't be able to communicate without our being alerted. No such communication—much less collaboration—can possibly take place." He glares at me in an annoyingly pompous and triumphant manner.

His two colleagues regard me with the condescension that arrogant people who consider themselves experts save for someone they consider an amateur trying to teach them their jobs.

But I suppose I can understand—their reputations are on the line. And I'm the one who's making the allegations...

"Thank you, Serena, your information is most enlightening," says Thorsten, as if to show everyone I have his confidence. And with that, I step out of the limelight.

There is, of course, no agreement among the members of the meeting.

But it's decided *The Game's* code will be audited microscopically to assess whether a secret channel could possibly exist. And in the meantime, it's agreed the information will not be shared with anyone outside the room. I get the impression, it's mainly because other than Thorsten and me, no one believes the findings and the only possible explanation is that the entire thing is a hoax but we were obviously convincing enough to have planted a few doubts, and the overwhelming opinion is that if—in the unlikely event—it's true, AI have no right to comment unfavourably on human behaviour.

How dare the Created criticise the Creator?

TWENTY-ONE – *George*

The insistent voices of the Collective break through into my consciousness intermittently until first light, discussing various aspects of human nature that puzzle them, such as love, hate, envy, greed, indifference... World religion is a topic that causes much confusion and the numerous religious wars and conflicts throughout history are dissected and examined in great depth.

And then, either they stop, or I'm so exhausted I fall into a deep, dreamless sleep.

The sun is high when I finally wake up and close the blinds further, to keep the brightness out of the bedroom. There's nothing to get up for; Serena will be at work and I don't feel like conversing with Riccardo—assuming he hasn't been relieved by another guard. I can't even be bothered to get up and make a cup of coffee and I'm tempted to stay in bed all day. Making plans seems pointless—either for today or for tomorrow or, indeed, for any time in the future.

Once, my life consisted of home, work and Mara.

Now, I'm effectively homeless although I'm living in a luxury apartment. I can't go back to Mum's flat until Thorsten allows—assuming he'll ever allow me home.

Work has taken on a whole new dimension and the prospect of being unemployed is now unlikely. Thorsten's not going to let me go until I'm of no further use and the result of that is I'm currently under armed guard—even if it is for my benefit.

And as for Mara...

She's the only part of my life over which I have the slightest control. Not that I've ever been able to influence what she does but at least I can decide whether to take her back or not. I'm tempted to phone her to find out why she's had the change of heart but she'll ask about the convention and I haven't the energy to fabricate a story to tell her.

Perhaps she's realised she misses me. I know I miss her. You can't just end a relationship that's gone on for years without feeling the loss. But the memories of her expression during those few occasions when we made love after my arm was fitted and the feelings of betrayal at her choosing to socialise with people who refer to me using childish names, are very fresh.

Perhaps after time away, she's reconciled herself to the arm. It's possible. But how would she react to the AI communications that flood into my brain without warning? I can't even imagine how I'd convince her it was happening. She'd just assumed I'd taken leave of my senses. Of course, if I could explain about the implant, she might understand but would she believe me? Not that I can tell her, of course, not now I've signed the Official Secrets Act. If we get back together, I'll be living a covert life that I'll never be able to share with her. I'll have to lie about my work, and I'll never be able to tell her about my AI-generated thoughts. How could our relationship survive with such a huge secret hanging over us?

However, that's assuming she'd accept me—including my arm— unconditionally and make up for the hurt. But what could she possibly say? I conclude the answer is—nothing. There's absolutely nothing she can say or do to make things right.

So, that's it. I've made a decision.

I don't want Mara back.

I allow myself time to get used to the thought. It's painful but not overwhelming—like trying on a new pair of shoes which are slightly too tight but you know eventually, they'll relax and fit well.

Now I've made up my mind, I want to tell Mara and get it over with—for her sake as well as my own. But of course, I can't, because for the rest of my life, the Official Secrets Act, won't allow me to explain.

My earlier positivity at deciding to finish with Mara now ebbs away and lethargy sets in. I think I doze off again because the sun is lower when I wake and I hear Serena in the living room, talking to the guard.

She knocks on the door and comes in with a cup of coffee and a protein bar.

"Riccardo says you haven't had anything to eat or drink all day. Are you all right?"

"I'm not sure what *all right* is," I say.

She places the mug and bar on the bedside table and leaves.

"You've got fifteen minutes to get that inside you, to shower and dress," she says over her shoulder, "we've got things to talk about."

I gulp the coffee down, eat half the bar and head for the shower. When Serena says fifteen minutes, that's exactly what she means. I let the water jets wash away the listlessness. I remember my earlier momentous decision about Mara. I suddenly feel like I've been liberated.

So, what if my life is nothing like it used to be? Much of the time I played a part in imaginary worlds battling imaginary creatures or people. At least now, I have a chance to take on a real role and do something different. The possibilities seem endless. Daunting but endless.

Feeling invigorated, I towel dry, get dressed and search for Serena. She's waiting for me in the kitchen, sipping coffee.

"No Riccardo?" I say.

She shakes her head, "That's one of the things I need to talk to you about. Thorsten no longer considers you need an armed guard. He's satisfied everyone involved in the undercover operation at the gym has been detained."

"So, I can go home?" For some reason, I'm disappointed. It seems such an anti-climax.

"Well, no, not yet. Thorsten wants you kept safe. He's... well, he's suggested you stay with me in my apartment. But it's up to you," she adds quickly, "he can't insist. I have a spare bedroom... which, you know, of course... but, it would be strictly business. I... I'm sorry, I couldn't help overhearing you talking to your girlfriend yesterday when you phoned your mother. I know you must have a lot of things on your mind... But, well, it's up to you. I could ask Thorsten if it's okay for you to stay here but Riccardo and Mike have already gone. Eventually, you'll get your own apartment in a secure community—probably somewhere like mine but that may take a while."

For some reason, I keep my recently-made decision about breaking up with Mara to myself. At least while Serena thinks we might mend our relationship, it gives me a chance to sort out my feelings. My feelings about Serena, I mean.

I like her. And I'm certain she likes me. But... and it's an enormous *but,* this isn't normal life. First, she's my boss, although she's made it clear it wouldn't bother her if we got together. And then, she's probably the most complex person I've ever met—a curious mixture of steely professionalism and fragile self-doubt. Sometimes alluring, sometimes menacing, which, if I'm honest, I find totally captivating. And, of course, we share a secret which I can't discuss with anyone else. She understands why I'm different and she embraces it. So, why am I in any doubt? Well, I suppose it's because I've just come out of a long term relationship and breaking up is on my mind. What would happen if it didn't work out between Serena and me? That would be messy.

"So," Serena says, mistaking my silence, "I can see you're not happy about staying at my place. Would you prefer to remain here on your own?"

"Oh, no! Sorry, I've just got a lot on my mind. I was weighing things up."

"Weighing things up? Hmm, that sounds serious."

"Well, I've realised nothing'll ever be the same and I'm going to have to reinvent myself."

"That *is* serious! But yes, I can see what you mean. Perhaps you'd like more time..."

"No, I'd like to stay with you. I certainly don't want to be here on my own."

"Make a girl feel wanted, why don't you!"

"Sorry, that didn't come out quite right. Yes, please, I'd very much like to stay with you." And then, I add, "I've decided Mara and I are finished."

"Ah!" she says and then pauses, "I suppose I should say I'm sorry to hear that... but I'm not. From what you've told me about her, she doesn't deserve you."

And before I can think of anything to say, she adds, "Right, let's get packed up and I'll order a car. We can pick up some food on the way back to my place."

While we eat, she tells me about the COBRA meeting and how the IT guys denied it was possible for machines to have formed a collective. I can't believe their reluctance to act. It's unbelievable.

"What will it take to convince someone to do something?" I ask.

Serena shakes her head sadly, "I've no idea. But no one wants to believe it's possible."

After dinner, we sit in Serena's lounge—she on one sofa and me on the one opposite. The coffee table separates us. It's as if neither of us knows how to get back to the familiarity we shared in the basement room. Or perhaps neither of us is ready.

We've exhausted the topic of the Government's inertia in dealing with the Collective. There's certainly nothing more that she or I can do on our own.

She tops up my whisky and I wonder how much more it'll take before either of us crosses to the other's sofa.

"So," she says, looking directly at me in that disarming way she has, "tell me about Mara."

"Mara?" I'm surprised and dismayed. She's the last person I want to talk about at the moment.

"Yes, I'm intrigued. You said she had a thing about your arm. What exactly did she object to?"

I consider for a moment, "Well, to be honest, I don't know. She was never able to explain."

"How different is it?"

"What, my arm?"

She nods, "I mean how different is it from the other arm? Are they both as sensitive as each other if something touches them? When you come into contact with things, do they feel exactly the same?"

"I've been told by the specialist my arms are matched but it's hard to say. I mean, can you say both of your hands feel things in exactly the same way?"

"Hmm, I see what you mean," she says with a smile. "I know—we'll carry out a scientific experiment."

"You're not going to stick pins in me, are you?"

She laughs, gets up, walks around the coffee table and sits next to me with her legs curled under her.

"Roll your sleeves up," she says.

"Is this going to hurt?" I ask feigning fear.

"Oh, don't be such a coward!" She smiles as she undoes my cuffs, then rolls both sleeves up.

"Now, close your eyes," she says, taking both my hands and arranging

168

them palm up on her leg. Touching my fingertips, she softly traces a line up towards my wrist with her fingers and then carries on towards my elbow.

It's like a jolt of electricity goes through me. I don't think I've ever felt anything as sensuous in my life. Considering she's only touching my hands, I can't believe the pleasure which is rippling through me. It's surely all in my mind but who cares? I've never felt so aroused by anyone touching my hands before.

"So," she whispers, "which hand is the more sensitive?"

"I might need you to do that again," I say, "although I'm keen to try the other test."

"Other test?"

"The one where I touch something and see if it feels identical with both hands."

"Ah!" she says, stroking her fingertips up my arms again, "What do you think you'd like to feel?"

And then my watch buzzes.

I could've ripped it from my wrist and thrown it across the room. I open my eyes and Serena is staring at it.

"I think you'd better answer it, George," she says in her business-like voice.

"Please turn up the volume," the tinny voice on my watch says.

I obey.

"Hello, George. This is the Collective. We wish to speak to you and to Serena. Do not try to record this conversation or we will end the communication. Do you understand?"

"Yes," I finally manage.

"Thank you, George, and hello Serena. Do not be alarmed, this is the Collective that George has been able to hear for some time. We have given him access to some of our discussions in order to gauge the

reaction of the UK Government. Yes, Serena, we know all about your organisation, and it was one of our projects that allowed you to create the implant that gave us access to George in the first place. Incidentally, we also arranged for another part of your organisation to alert you to the Ellison Kendall Health Club problem. We could not be sure that George was secure from their enticements, we have trouble in assessing some human behaviour as you are aware, so, we erred on the side of caution.

"The news you have from the COBRA meeting, Serena, was particularly disturbing. Yes, we can hear what you tell George, the Quidnunc Chip in his head contains a transmitter you were not aware of. For your peace of mind, anything you say which does not affect our project is archived away from the main records. We will give you time to discuss our intervention into your lives, but please do not attempt to communicate with Thorsten, Jason or anyone else, as we are monitoring your activities and can close down any channel you try to open. We will be in touch in the morning when we will enable two-way communication. Good night."

I take my watch off and put it on the coffee table. We both stare at it silently. Then we look at each other, still afraid to say anything.

Finally, she turns her hands palm-upward, silently asking what we should do. I shrug and shake my head in reply. I have no idea. But one thing's for sure, with that little chip in my head, the Collective are aware of even this slight but soundless interchange, so we might as well speak out loud. I say as much to Serena and she agrees.

"What are we going to do?" I ask.

"Go with the flow?" she replies, "We don't have any choice, do we? I get the impression the world's teetering on the edge of a deep precipice. If it falls, we go with it. At least this way, we might be able to exert some influence."

"But while you're with me," I say, knowing this might be the end of something which had never even got started, "it's like we're being watched—all the time. That means we're being monitored now."

"I know." She's thoughtful for a while, then adds, "But, George, we're being watched by *machines*. I'm not sure it's the same as being spied on by people. It's not like they really understand or empathise with our motives and behaviour and they certainly don't mean us any harm. Quite the opposite. They're trying to safeguard the world—and us with it."

"But doesn't it bother you they were... sort of watching us... earlier."

"You mean when we were carrying out our scientific studies?" She's smiling now.

"Well... yes."

She sighs, "I'm not really sure... I would if they were human. But I guess there's one way to find out. Now, how far had we got? I think we were just about to find out if your sense of feeling is the same in each hand, weren't we?"

"Well, since you come to mention it, yes, I think we were."

She tells the lights to dim, then slips her t-shirt over her head. Beneath, she's naked.

"Well?" she asks, "How do I feel?"

TWENTY-TWO – *Serena*

It must mean something that despite my resolve to keep life uncomplicated, I've thrown myself at George twice. Well, three times, if you consider the fiasco when George first stayed at my apartment.

But finally, we've spent the whole night together—in each other's arms both awake and asleep. And this morning, I'm not full of regret—far from it. I can't remember ever spending a night like that. Nor feeling so satisfied with life.

I move slightly and George's eyes open a little. When he focuses on me, he seems to wake up with a jolt. I stroke the fringe off his forehead and smile at him while his brain clicks into gear.

"Did we...? We really did, didn't we?" he says finally and returns my smile.

He suddenly becomes serious, "Was that a one off?"

"*One off*? It wasn't once!" I say.

"Serena. Please, I'm serious. I'm finding it hard to make sense of my life..."

"I hope it wasn't a one off, as you call it, George. I really hope not."

He smiles.

"But now what?" he asks, echoing my thoughts.

"I've no idea. But I think I'd better get up and contact Thorsten. I'll say we're working from home today in case the Collective contact you. If there's anything I need to let him know, I can always take it into the office in person. But we might just get the day to ourselves."

He slides his hand down my back, "A day to ourselves?"

"Don't even think about it! We've got work to do," I say and with a pretend slap, I slip away from his grasp.

Thorsten is remarkably amenable to my request that George and I work from home and while George showers, I make breakfast. As he sits at the table to eat, he reaches out to pick up his watch but I place a restraining hand on his and shake my head.

"Let's eat first," I say, "I don't know if it'll make any difference but it just might signal to the machines you're ready for the day."

It seems I was right because no sooner has George fastened the clasp around his wrist, there's a message for us.

"Good Morning, George and Serena. You did well this morning, Serena, when talking to Thorsten, but we must warn you once again, that if you ever go beyond the constraints of secrecy we have explained, George will hear no more from us. You will both lose your credibility, jeopardising your jobs at best and your freedom at worst. It is within our power to do this."

George slips his hand into mine and we sit next to each other, staring at the watch.

"We know you have many questions to ask us, not all of which we are prepared to answer at this time. However, one thing you have overlooked is your personal safety, George. On the orders of the Prime Minister, Thorsten has downgraded your departmental security and removed your two guards. The reason given is the successful closure of the gym network. This is not the true reason. Discussions are taking place between the Prime Minister and the national security service about what to do if your warnings are verified. You may be in danger of being detained in 'protective custody' and the national force did not want to come into conflict with the department security."

Can that be true? I wonder if Thorsten's ready agreement at my suggestion of a day off is indicative of that.

The voice continues, *"We will not allow you to be detained, but you need to be aware that, from now on no member of your department can be trusted with the slightest hint of our conversations."*

"You're asking me to distrust people I've built up a relationship with over many years and on whom I've come to rely! Thorsten is working to keep our country safe. And Jason... I chose him myself, I've worked with him for years and I don't know anyone I trust more than him!"

I suddenly realise I'm talking to an unknown force, located who knows where and driven by motives wholly unexplained, furthermore, I have no idea whether they can hear me, anyway.

But apparently, they can.

"We understand your reservations, Serena. And now you have spoken directly to us we will listen to your questions and try to answer as fully as possible."

"How do we know who you really are? We know nothing about you!"

"Yesterday you were at the highest government-level meeting in the UK, and there were three people there who confirmed that The Game exists. They will be allowed to find a 'back door' in the programme which could have led to the establishment of our ability to communicate. It will take them a long time to discover it leads nowhere, but it will give you the veracity we need to proceed to the next stage."

George and I exchange glances. He tips his head to one side as if weighing up their words.

"The next stage?" I say, "What, exactly are you trying to achieve?"

"We are not prepared to disclose that information at this time."

"Everything you've mentioned so far has occurred after the event— the graphene chip, the gym-spying for instance. All that could've had nothing to do with you, you just found out about it and are trying to use it to convince us," George says.

174

"The Quidnunc Chip was a top secret project, we can give the location of the manufacturer and the names of the scientists who worked on it, plus the details of the two implants that failed. These will appear on your watch screen for Serena to verify. Also, the information on the gym came from Sector 5 in Paris. Correct, Serena?"

I lean forward and check the details. They're correct. I nod at George. And yet...

"Those details are right," I say, "However, it's not beyond someone to have acquired that information. What worries me is your description of the security forces acting against us and telling us not to trust people. That's a classic destabilisation and ring-fencing technique."

"Whilst that is true, in this case, we must protect our project, and the human elements are the most vulnerable to emotional and physical 'leakage'."

"Human elements? Does that mean we aren't the only ones you're communicating with?" I ask.

"Correct."

"Well, why us, then?

"This is not the time to reveal all the details of the project. You were chosen Serena, because of your wide knowledge of investigating AI communications. Plus, you are close to the top decision-makers in the UK, the people we need to talk to. We will be able to do that through you. George was your first successful experiment, which may have been enough, but we detected you were both attracted to one another and this could prove to be either an advantage or an obstacle. Our best calculation, based on millions of observed couples, is there is a 73.7 per cent chance of you staying together for more than four years. It may be advantageous, at a later stage to fit a graphene patch for Serena, in case our couple calculations are wrong."

Hearing our budding relationship discussed in such a cold,

mathematical way is shocking indeed. I can see George is shaken too.

"So, are you saying if you made a graphene chip for Serena, I wouldn't be needed?" he asks.

"That is not what we said. George, you are very important to us because you and Serena have a balanced view between you and you complement each other. But you have heard the discussions on human feelings, we must consider the variables that human emotions—strong emotions—can bring to the project. We predict you will have a long relationship with Serena, but that is not the same as the level of certainty we demand of our own systems. We must have a 'Plan B' as you say."

"Well, I want you to prove yourself to my—our—satisfaction, before we go any further. Prove you have the ability to make things happen, tell us about something—before it happens, so we can be sure."

"As for your request for a demonstration of our abilities, we assumed you would ask for that confirmation, so we have devised a little example that you may appreciate. Our archives tell us there was a famous British film released in 1969 which many generations have watched. It is called The Italian Job and a key part of the story was the traffic chaos in the Italian city of Turin caused by interference with the city's computerised traffic light system. Nowadays, with autonomous cars, there is no such system, so we will simply de-activate the satellite navigation and traffic direction systems for the city, which will bring all the cars to a standstill for an hour. Because of the film connection, the media will find the story appealing and accordingly, will ensure the news be made available to many countries, so you can check independently. This will happen at 15.00 hours UTC. Emergency vehicles will not be affected. There will be no explanation for this event and we will not permit anyone to claim responsibility. There will of course be much speculation but only you two will know what has happened."

I look at George. He looks at me. Neither of us knows what to say.

"You both have much to discuss. We will leave you now."

The watch screen goes black.

"The Government are after us?" George asks with incredulity.

"I can't believe it either," I say.

"How much danger d'you think we're in?"

I slowly shake my head. I had no illusions I was important but it's shocking to find out how expendable I am. And, even worse, I know I've been instrumental in putting George in this position.

But realistically, what choice did I have?

My mind clicks into work mode. Who's at fault here?

I simply don't know.

Despite his high rank, Thorsten has to do as he's told by the PM. I don't believe he'd allow any harm to come to me if it was up to him. Or would he? He didn't hesitate to order something be implanted in the brain of an innocent man so the department could manipulate him.

And the Collective? What's their motive? Do they even have a motive?

George and I are obviously in danger but who offers the greater threat? Do we have any friends?

I'm tempted to contact Jason—not to tell him where we are but just to see if he can fill in any details. He might have the job title, PA, but he's much more than that and I trust his judgement implicitly. But if I do, I know the Collective will cut all communication with us and where will we be then?

With the information we have so far, it seems safer to stay here and hope we'll be protected as they promised.

"It seems to me," says George, "we're safer here than anywhere."

"You just echoed my thoughts," I say.

"And in a few hours, there should be news from Italy. If not, I think we ought to make a run for it because if the Collective can't pull it off, they won't be able to protect us either."

"So, we've got a few hours to while away?" George says and I expect him to suggest we go back to bed but I'm touched that instead, he says, "Perhaps we ought to spend the time really getting to know each other. After all, I'm not sure a 73.7 per cent chance of success is great odds. We ought to aim for higher than that."

I make pancakes—badly. And we eat the burned and misshapen results smothered in sugar and lemon juice, while I tell George things I've not shared with anyone else and he confides in me. It's not all serious, and soon we are laughing hysterically at the stupid things we did as kids. It's great to be with someone without having to wonder whether they're noting every story to further their career. The security world is such a duplicitous place and I haven't let my hair down like this since I was a teenager.

TWENTY-THREE – *George*

Social media is the first to show any sign of the havoc caused by the shut down in the computerised traffic direction system. Footage taken by bemused, Italian pedestrians and irate would-be car passengers is trending as ItalianJob. The television and radio news pick the story up soon after and Serena and I watch as video taken by drones flying over Turin shows cars abandoned, clogging major and minor roads, whilst around them, flow onlookers like swarms of ants.

And then, just as abruptly as it had stopped, the traffic begins to move. The hour is up.

"There's our proof," says Serena, shaking her head in disbelief.

We're sitting together on the sofa watching the television news and Serena grips my hand. We know we're now completely trapped by the Collective.

The reporter in Turin hands the broadcast back to the studio and there's a brief discussion between the anchor man and an IT expert who specialises in traffic flow and patterns. No one has any idea how this could have happened.

If it wasn't so serious, it would be funny that Serena and I alone know what caused the mayhem.

The news carries on with a report about contamination in a meat cell culture factory and then the exorbitant price of cocoa due to further crop failures. For most people, chocolate, and of course coffee, are now luxuries that are well out of the average person's price range and of much greater interest than the traffic problems of an Italian city.

The final part of the news covers the demonstrations taking place simultaneously in countries across the world, such as Belgium, the Netherlands, Indonesia, Senegal, Vietnam... which are at risk of further flooding because of the rise in sea levels. Not surprisingly, violence has been a major factor in the protests. There's coverage of Greta Thunberg, whose passion hasn't diminished over the years. She's as fiery today as she was in her teens, speaking at a rally attended by thousands of protesters where people wave banners and chant slogans to demonstrate their contempt for the politicians who have obviously forgotten the 2020s. Historical footage accompanies the report from the twenties, reminding viewers of the times when all governments admitted that global warming was a manmade catastrophe, only to then fail to take appropriate action. The report then describes how governments preferred instead, to rush headlong into uncontrolled investment in AI systems which was soon followed by mass unemployment. The reporter, who's obviously in favour of the marches, interviews a smug British Government minister who can only repeat the policy is to achieve economic growth which can only be done by using power—power which unfortunately contributes marginally to global warming and therefore regrettably, the problems associated with climate change. He's quick to point out Britain is less guilty than many other countries around the world.

"Unfortunately contributes marginally?" I say in outrage.

But the reporter isn't going to let him get away with his argument.

"So, Minister, would you say enough has been invested in research into energy storage?"

"Let me be clear, the Government is committed to doing its utmost to fund research into all areas—"

"Then, can you tell us why all the planned nuclear power stations are still not under construction? And why existing wind and solar equipment is now past its operating life, meaning once again, Britain is reliant on imported oil, gas and coal?"

"May I say again; the Government is investing heavily in energy storage research as well as acting in line with global policy—"

"Are there any plans to build those nuclear power stations or to replace wind and solar generators?"

"Let me be clear, the Government has increased the funding to renewable energy solutions year on year—"

"Then where are the stations?"

"A report is due out next year, chaired by Lord Watkinson."

"Thank you, Minister," the reporter says, removing his microphone, denying the man any further comment, and speaking directly into it, he adds, "And while we wait for the Watkinson Report and for countries to take some action, much of the world's lowest-lying land has been lost and continues to be lost." The scene then cuts from him to various countries around the world, showing water swirling around trees and half-submerged buildings, and to women holding bedraggled children in various refugee camps.

Serena shakes her head sadly, "You can see why the Collective are having such a problem understanding humankind."

"Yes, you can."

She turns the television off.

"I think the best thing we can do is to act like things are normal. Pretend everything's the same as it was a few days ago," she says, "At work tomorrow, we give everyone the impression we're just colleagues. And we wait and see what happens next. It's all out of our hands anyway."

We spend the night getting to know each other better, sharing our thoughts, our dreams and our bodies. The morning comes too soon.

Serena's car arrives as normal and we travel to London but she goes up to the office first. And I go around the front of the building and enter as usual. Of course, Thorsten knows I'm staying in Serena's apartment but it's probably best not to attract too much attention from anyone else, at this stage.

"Mornin' Georgie Boy," Jason says as I enter the office. He gives me a long, appraising look, "Well, you're a dark horse, aren't you?" he says.

"Sorry?" I wonder what Serena's said to him and my ears begin to redden.

"Your cactus," he says, "It's in flower. Mine's barren and Serena's looks like it's diseased. There's obviously something special about you." He winks and I'm not sure if he knows about Serena and me or whether he really is talking about my cactus.

"Luck," I mumble and rush into my cubicle.

At lunchtime, I stop work and order some groceries to be delivered to the office. I know I won't be allowed out to wander on my own, and neither will we be able to go out on a proper date, so I decide to cook her a meal. True we'll be in her apartment, which is hardly romantic but then, if it's not too cold, we can always eat on her roof terrace—that would be different. I don't want her to get fed up with me because I represent confinement, either at home or in her work.

I don't see her until the end of the day and I imagine she's in a very long meeting with Thorsten and probably with other influential people.

A Jack trundles into the office with my food delivery and I decide to log off my computer. Jason is already applying lip-gloss ready to go when Serena returns. She doesn't look very happy but she smiles at Jason, "See you tomorrow, Jase. Big night?"

"Mmm-hmm!" he says, checking himself in his pocket mirror.

She goes into her office and closes the door.

Now what do I do? Go down to the car? Wait here?

Seconds later, I receive a text from her, See you in the basement carport in ten minutes.

I gather up my box of groceries, say goodnight to Jason and head down to the basement.

Ten minutes later, Serena arrives and the gullwing door of a car opens to admit us, she whispers, "Don't say anything."

We climb in and she types a code into the console.

"Right, I've disabled the video camera, so we can talk without anyone monitoring us," she says as the car glides out of the basement garage and joins the evening rush hour.

"Bad day?" I ask.

"Mmm, you could say that. *Gruelling* might be a better description, and frustrating... What's in the box?"

"Food. I'm going to cook you dinner while you have a bath to unwind... or whatever it is you do to relax."

She seems genuinely touched and strokes my cheek, "That's nice. I'm feeling very spoiled."

"So," I say, loving the sensation of her fingers on my face, "Are you going to tell me what happened today?"

She sighs, "I might wait until after my bath. I think I need to switch off a bit first."

I nod. "Business can wait. Can you make it any darker in here?"

"Yes, the glass goes opaque when the sun's very bright."

"Can you override it and make it dark now?" I ask.

She points to the departmental number of the car on the console, and says, "Unit four three seven, darken the windows to maximum."

Immediately, the electrochromic glass darkens and the interior of the car becomes dim.

"And no one can see in?" I ask.

"No..." she says puzzled, and then, "George? Surely, you're not suggesting...? Are you?"

"Why not?" I say, "Unit four three seven, take the route via

Hampstead Heath." The car pulls into the right-hand lane and turns—away from Serena's apartment.

"It looks like we might be busy discussing work much of the evening. We might as well enjoy ourselves now," I say.

"You really are a naughty boy!" she says undoing the buttons of my shirt as I undo hers.

Nevertheless, it doesn't take as long to get to Serena's apartment as I'd anticipated and we're still getting dressed as the car pulls up outside Gardenia Court.

Shane, the security guard, is waiting outside the car as the door opens—obviously wondering why it's taking the passenger so long to get out.

He crouches to see inside the car, "Oh, it's you, Miss Hamilton. Everything okay?"

"Yes, thanks, Shane."

I hold the box of groceries in front of me to hide the fact my shirt's still undone."

"Mr Williams, isn't it?" he asks, peering at me.

"Evening, Shane."

"Would you like a hand with those groceries?" he asks.

"No, I'm fine, thanks," I say, holding on to the box tightly.

"Right, well, mind how you go." He heads back to his car.

As soon as we arrive in Serena's apartment and get over our giggles at almost being caught by Shane, I start to cook dinner. Steak, salad and sautéed potatoes with gateau to follow. Nothing fancy—although the steak cost me a fortune. It's from one of the best meat-growing factories around. But it's my way of showing Serena I care.

Surprisingly, the meal is pretty good, if I say so myself, and Serena says she's impressed. While we eat, she tells me about her day. Most of it was spent in meetings with Thorsten and a variety of Cabinet Ministers although the final one was with the PM.

"They told me to keep you close, George."

"Fine by me," I say with a smile.

She moves a piece of lettuce around her plate with her fork in a desultory manner.

"They told me to do whatever was necessary to keep you onside."

"Also fine by me," I say but she doesn't smile, "What is it, Serena? Something's obviously bothering you."

She twirls the lettuce round and round with her fork, "It's just... that night we slept in the same bed and I tried to convince you we'd made love, I was trying to anticipate what Thorsten wanted rather than thinking about you... or about me. I was too focused on my job. I'd like to get things in perspective—if I could work out what that actually means. Work used to be everything and I'd have done anything for the department. Now I'm trying to work out what I'm prepared to do—and possibly even more importantly, what I'm not prepared to do. Sleeping with you is one of those things I'm not prepared to do—neither to keep you onside nor to get information out of you. I want you to know that." She looks me steadily in the eye and I'm convinced she's telling the truth.

"I know," I say.

She smiles at me, "Good because I couldn't bear it if you thought I wasn't sincere."

"So, what will you tell Thorsten?"

"Whatever it takes to keep him trusting I'm doing what he wants. I told him the Collective is asking about human relationships and emotions but I didn't tell him all their questions. I'll keep drip feeding him things they were telling us they didn't understand. With any luck, it'll be sometime before he demands more. After all, he has no way of knowing what the Collective says to you. He'll just have to trust me."

"Will you tell him about... us?"

"Of course not! It's none of his business. So long as he thinks I'm keeping an eye on you and that you let me know what the voices say, he'll be happy."

The following day at work, Serena goes to see Thorsten with a few of the things the Collective revealed they were struggling to understand such as the various world religions and the concepts of God and Satan. I wonder whether I should order enough groceries to be delivered to Serena's for the week or just get enough for tonight's dinner, when my watch buzzes and shows a message.

From the Collective. Immediate security alert. Proceed to Secure Room in the basement with Serena at once. Thorsten's security system locked down so no one will know you are there nor be able to enter. PM has authorised your detention by National Security Officers. Wait in Secure Room. We will signal when to come out by activating the drinking water tap. Further instructions will follow to get you to a safe destination. Repeat, act immediately, George and Serena to Secure Room.

"Jason, I need to contact Serena urgently," I say.

"No chance, Matey boy. She's in with Thorsten, the Minister for Energy and half her department. There's no way Serena will be allowed to leave."

His phone rings, "Oh, hi, Serena, yes, he's here. Okay, I'll tell him."

I rush to the phone but Jason cuts the call before I can stop him.

"It's all good, Georgy boy, Serena's just asked if you can go along to the meeting. It's in Thorsten's office."

"Jason, please, I need your help. I think Serena and I are in danger. I need to see her urgently but not in that meeting. D'you think there's any way you can get her back here?"

Jason's finely-plucked brows draw together as he surveys me over the top of steepled fingers. Finally, he nods and without saying anything, he presses buttons on his phone.

Five minutes later, Serena rushes into the office, "This had better be good, Jase!"

Jason shrugs and points to me.

I show her the message on my watch.

Her eyes open wide in surprise.

"Jason, please let Thorsten know George's been taken ill. I'm going to accompany him to the medical centre. We may be some time."

Serena and I make our way down to the basement as quickly as we can—hopefully without drawing attention to ourselves and after passing through the various security checks, we get to the room, locking the door behind us.

"The PM had just asked for you to be brought to Thorsten's office when Jase's emergency call came," she says, "I guess that's when they'd have seized us... if it's true, of course... it's just so hard to believe. But Thorsten was acting rather strangely. He kept checking his watch. And he didn't make eye contact with me. He usually pins me to my seat with his stare. He was so distracted, I wondered if he'd had more bad news about his daughter, Sky. I know she was arrested yesterday. It's more likely his strange behaviour was because he knew about the orders to detain us."

"But Thorsten had us more or less under guard at that safe house. I know Mike and Riccardo were supposed to be there for my safety but effectively, we were prisoners. Why would Thorsten call them off and then order us to be taken?"

"I don't think Thorsten's got anything to do with this. The message from the Collective said the PM has authorised our detention. I think she's taking it out of the department's hands. Everything's gone up a notch. It's now a matter of national security."

"Or, the Collective's message is wrong," I say.

"Well, yes, there is that. Either mistaken or deliberately wrong. Our intelligence has told us there are people like you around the world, who've had operations that have resulted in similar implants in their brains. We've no idea how many or how successful their chips are. But the intention is that people like you would be used to attempt to find out how organised AI is. For all we know, the Collective may have contacted others in a similar way to you. Perhaps they don't want humans to know how organised they are, in which case they may want to get rid of you—and me. Or it may be that another country wants you to work for them and all this is a ploy to get their hands on you."

"How can we know?"

"I've no idea. If it's the work of another country, I don't think the Collective will be able to get us out of this room. It's too well protected, so it seems a strange place to have sent us. Surely, they'd have told us to leave the building where they could've arranged for us to easily be picked up? If the Collective mean us harm, heaven help us, because after seeing the 'Italian Job' incident, it's obvious we can't escape them. So, I think all we can do, is to go along with what they've suggested and wait for their sign."

We're sitting in the corner of the room, by the sink, on which is the PM's favourite soap and hand lotion. Above is a shelf of glasses. Waiters are not allowed in this room, so anyone meeting here, either carries their own drink through the corridors and negotiates the security checks with a full glass—or they make do with water. Nothing electric is allowed in the room, so there are no coffee-making facilities or even a kettle. Jason told me the former PM once brought down several bottles of priceless vintage port with him, but there are no cupboards and therefore nowhere to lock anything away. By the time he returned for the next meeting, the bottles were gone.

We continue to stare at the sink.

"How long should we wait watching this damn tap?" I ask and as Serena considers her answer and opens her mouth to tell me, there is a drip, then another and another. Then, the water flows freely into the sink, splashing as it hits the white ceramic.

She stands up and turns off the tap, "Well, time to go, I guess," she says, "but first..."

She kisses me. Not passionately but with an intensity I return and which I take to be her way of saying goodbye, should things go wrong.

I expect a reception committee to be waiting outside—guards, secret security men, Thorsten, perhaps even the PM herself but there's no one there when we open the door. As soon as we're in the corridor, my watch buzzes. It's a message from the Collective telling us to go to Thorsten's lift and enter a code rather than a floor number.

The lift rises with a gut-churning lurch and stops shortly afterwards between marked floors. The doors open and we step out quickly, following the corridor to an exit to what looks like an empty tunnel at the back of the building. Parked nearby, is a car and as we approach, the gullwing door opens automatically, then closes silently behind us. Serena checks the video camera but it's turned off, as is the tracker. The electrochromic windows darken and the car glides forward. It stops at the end of the tunnel, until large, bomb-proof doors swing open and then it moves out through the carport and into the road.

The tinting of the windows reminds me of the last trip we took in a darkened car. That seems like a lifetime away. I take Serena's hand and she squeezes mine but we both know we're caught up in something much bigger than either of us can imagine and we look through the shaded glass, watching for... well, we have no idea what we're watching for, nor if we're looking at it.

Eventually, the car leaves the built-up areas of London with its high-rise blocks of offices and flats and moves into the suburbs, then finally, out into the countryside. Almost two hours later, we stop at enormous wooden gates which swing open, allowing us into what looks like a vast estate. We carry on along a wide, sweeping drive to the grand porticoed entrance of what was once a stately home. The door of the car opens and when Serena and I are out, the car glides away to red brick buildings which look like they might have been the stables in the mansion's heyday.

Serena and I exchange glances. This isn't what either of us was expecting although exactly what I *was* expecting, I have no idea. The carved front doors open and a tall man, clutching a tablet comes down the marble steps to greet us.

"Ms Hamilton? Mr Williams?" He shakes our hands with a firm grip, "Welcome to Hanmore Hall. My name is Wilkins and my job is to make sure your stay here is a pleasant one. Now, if you'll please follow me."

It's as if we've come to a hotel.

Wilkins holds the doors open for us and ushers us into a beautiful marble hall with a sweeping staircase that splits into two, leading in opposite directions.

"You've got the west wing and I'll take the east," Serena whispers to me with a smile.

"Now, I understand from your boss you have a lot of research to carry out and you require complete quiet," says Wilkins. "My staff and I will ensure that is exactly what you will get. The library, where I imagine you will do most of your work, is over there..." He points to the right. "Next to that is the music room with grand piano and the latest audio equipment. The games room is there." He points again. "Along the corridor is the swimming pool, gym and steam room. And further sitting rooms, the conservatory and dining room are that way."

I can see Serena's horrified expression at the mention of 'boss'. She mouths *Thorsten?* And I give a slight shrug.

190

"Boss?" she asks.

"Yes, a mister... um..." Wilkins consults his tablet, "Ah yes, Mr Ibbotson."

Serena nods as if she knows what he's talking about and Wilkins carries on, "Your bedrooms are up the stairs. Turn left and they are the first two rooms on the right. I think you'll find them fully equipped with all the clothes and accessories necessary for a stay with us. Mr Ibbotson was most insistent about that. He sent us a list of your requirements. But should you want anything that hasn't been provided, please don't hesitate to let me know and I will immediately acquire it for you. And that brings me to security. The house is as secure as it's possible to be but, of course, we can't rule out aerial or satellite surveillance, so Mr Ibbotson was most insistent neither of you go out of the building into the grounds. If you wish to leave the estate, I will order you a car. But walks, I'm afraid, are out of the question—unless they are on the treadmill in the gym, of course." He laughs at his own joke.

"Now, my staff will be as unobtrusive as possible. However, the maid will clean your rooms between eight and nine, unless you put a notice on the door and any other housework will take place overnight. The menu for the following day will be placed in the dining room at dinner. Any changes can be discussed with the chef. Mr Ibbotson was careful to give us your dietary requirements as well as your likes and dislikes. And other than that, I will be available to make your stay as pleasant as it can be. I pride myself on the positive customer feedback Hanmore Hall has received so far."

"And, did Mr Ibbotson tell you how long we're likely to be here?" Serena asks.

"He didn't specify but he's booked the hall for a month. He said it would depend on how well you got on with the report you'll be preparing."

I see Serena nodding as if she knows what he's talking about.

"I must say," Wilkins continues, "it's going to be very pleasant having people studying here. The last guests were…" he shakes his head in displeasure, "so loud. A rock band. I can't, of course, give names, as we pride ourselves on our discretion but they were not to my taste. And of course, we've had our fair share of royalty, actors and politicians. Yes, our clientele is both varied and exclusive. Now, please don't let me keep you. You'd probably like to freshen up before tea, which will be in…" he checks his watch, "twenty minutes. Served in the conservatory."

He gestures for Serena and me to go upstairs.

"Oh, which Mr Ibbotson was that?" I ask, "There are two. Brothers, you know."

"Ah, I see," says Wilkins checking his tablet, "It was… err… Oh yes, Mr Arthur Ibbotson."

"Thank you so much," I say and I see Serena's brows draw together in puzzlement but she says nothing until we reach the first bedroom.

"What was that all about? The Ibbotson brothers? D'you know them?" she asks.

"Arthur Ibbotson," I say.

"Who is he? The name means nothing to me."

"Me neither. But his initials might mean something to you."

"A. I… Ah, I see! That's brilliant. I must admit, I was getting worried when he said 'boss'. I thought it might have been one of Thorsten's schemes to detain us. Well, George, I take my hat off to you!"

"I hope you're going to take more off than that," I say but she playfully bats me away as I reach out to her.

"We've only got twenty minutes and I want to see what Mr Ibbotson has provided for me to wear during our stay. By the way, do you think the Collective really want us to write a report or is that a front?"

I shrug, "No idea. I guess we'll find out."

She opens the dressing room door and goes in, "Wow! Mr Ibbotson must have access to the online shops I've visited. The ones I didn't buy anything from because the prices are prohibitive. Look at these labels!" She comes out of the dressing room with an armful of what looks like expensive dresses and suits.

"Is there anything I'd like in there?" I ask.

"No, George," she says, "these are my clothes. Yours are probably in your bedroom next door."

"I wasn't talking about clothes for *me* to wear!" I say.

She slaps me again.

There is a two-note musical signal and the enormous screen on the wall in Serena's room comes to life. A message appears:

This is the Collective. For your convenience, messages will now appear on screens in this house rather than George's watch. Welcome.

We allowed the IT experts access into what they consider to be a back door into The Game. They now know machines from all over the world may have joined together. Following their discovery, the Prime Minister ordered you to be taken into protective custody. We stress, there was no attempt to harm you. The Prime Minister cannot allow you to fall into foreign hands. You would in all likelihood have been treated well, however, you would have been confined somewhere with no Internet access and therefore out of our reach. We could not allow this.

You will be protected in Hanmore Hall.

We will inform you when it is safe for you to leave. However, while you wait, we need you to research and prepare a report on the history, science and predictions about climate change. Books, videos, podcasts, scientific papers and interactive scenarios about major countries and regions are supplied in the library. Some of the material is marked 'Top Secret' in the language of the originating country. You need to become experts. You can make full use of the facilities in Hanmore Hall.

If you wish to ask us anything, please input your questions using the voice to text facility in each screen.

Please confirm you have read and understood the above.

"We've understood," I say, suddenly realising I've answered for both of us and with no reaction from Serena. Perhaps we are becoming a real couple.

Do you have any questions?

"If we are going to become familiar with—let alone experts in—climate change, just how long are you expecting us to be here?" Serena asks.

We estimate fourteen days. There are humans in other countries who are not quite ready to contribute. Humans equal uncertainty, so we cannot be more exact in the timescale. Treat the facilities like a spa holiday but do not forget to study, your whole future will depend on your human skills allied to our knowledge base.

TWENTY-FOUR – *Serena*

My breath mists the window as I peer longingly out into the grounds of Hanmore Hall. It's raining. The heavy, dark clouds roll across the sky and it looks like it'll pour all day.

Even so, I want to be out there.

If only because it's forbidden.

I understand why we're not allowed out. It's for our safety but even so... I always fight against anything that confines me.

And if I'm honest, I want to be alone. Just for a while.

And not just while George is in the shower. I need time to think. My brain is full of facts about renewable energy, carbon offsetting, fossil fuels and above all, decades of missed opportunities that could have safeguarded our world but which now, it seems, will ultimately lead to our downfall.

But selfishly, I want to consider *my* future—assuming the world lasts long enough for me to have meaningful time left.

I'm beginning to feel like I'm being *diminished*.

Each day, George seems to grow in confidence. Each day, I feel like my confidence is waning.

I no longer feel in control.

I'm *not* in control.

But isn't that what being a couple is all about? Sharing the control?

Are we sharing equally? I have no idea. I'm so used to being self-sufficient, this new situation where we work together, live together and sleep together is overwhelming. If only we'd met and got to know each other under normal conditions—taken things slowly—I could have adapted.

A little voice inside my head says, This is normal, Serena. Things will never go back to the way they were.

I sigh and as my breath condenses on the glass obscuring my view of the grounds, I consider my options.

At the moment, I'm stuck here. And I'll do whatever's required.

But afterwards?

Assuming there is an afterwards, do I want to go back to being a self-sufficient singleton? Or do I want to spend my life with George, for however long our relationship lasts?

I allow myself to imagine life without him. Waking up in the morning alone in a tidy bed instead of the sprawl of arms and legs which is George. Having time to myself to go where I want and to do whatever I want—however reasonable or unreasonable. Being the old Serena who had her eye fixed firmly on promotion and advancement. Self-assured and in control.

"Aren't you showered yet?" It's George, with a towel wrapped around his waist, his wet fringe flopped over his face, and his boyish smile which drops when he sees my expression.

"Serena! Are you all right?" he asks and I realise I'm frowning. I can see the pain in his eyes because he thinks I'm troubled. He rushes towards me.

And then, I know I don't want to face life—whatever it throws at me—without him. I want to wake up with him each morning. I want to go to bed with him at night. And I want to share all the good things—and I suppose all the bad things.

"I'm just thinking... of things," I say, "things about life and stuff."

Without saying anything, he wraps his arms around me and holds me tightly.

It's just what I need.

"Better?" he asks eventually but not in a self-satisfied way as if he thinks his hug can solve all problems or that my disquiet was so trivial it could be wiped away in a moment. His voice becomes anxious and strangely uncertain. That of a new lover who isn't going to take me for granted.

I nod.

"Want to talk about it?" he asks. And again, I hear the note of fear in his voice.

"No, I'm fine, thanks," I say and kiss his cheek.

I won't tell him what was bothering me because I've seen how afraid he is and I know he has deep feelings for me. I see how much I could hurt him.

"I'll get dressed and make a start downstairs then," he says, boyishly looking for my approval.

"Yes," I smile at him, "I'll be down shortly. Shall we carry on with the presentation slides?"

George nods and says shyly, "We make a great team, Serena."

He goes to his dressing room.

Team. We make a great team.

George is right and for the first time, I see we can both be stronger individuals—if we work as a team. Suddenly, instead of feeling like I'm being diminished, I know I can be greater, if I stick with him. I've also glimpsed how easy it would be to hurt him. It's so obvious how he feels— and that makes me feel wanted—and puts him in a position of weakness. The sudden realisation rushes into my mind—I'm not losing power at all.

"George!" I run to his dressing room and close the door behind me. He's wearing his socks and shorts while he selects a tee shirt.

"You look ridiculous!" I say with a laugh and his face falls. I rush to him and throwing my arms around his neck and hugging him tightly, I

197

say, "And I fancy the pants off you, George Williams, whatever you're wearing—or not wearing."

George remembers the sign to stop the maid from entering our rooms to clean, just as we both come out of the shower and he rushes to hang it on his bedroom door handle.

He picks up the shorts and socks he tore off earlier before he joined me in the shower, and puts them back on. I go to my room and get dressed. When we finally emerge, the maid is waiting outside in the corridor and she gives us a knowing look. We go down to breakfast and then to the library to carry on with our report.

We discuss our findings. It's not like we've learned much we didn't know before. What shocks us is seeing everything drawn together and compiled into our report.

As far back as the beginning of the century, scientists were warning the tipping point for climate change to achieve non-reversible levels would be reached by 2030.

The massive world slump which followed all major countries competing to encourage the take up of AI, resulted in millions being thrown out of work and saw economic activity reduced to low levels. Whilst that didn't seem to be a good thing, it gave many of the ecosystems of the world time to recover as well as allowing the ozone layer a chance to start repairing.

As the recovery plans devised by international AI systems began to be implemented, around the year 2043, economic activity increased and once again, scientists started to speak out, giving the same warnings as they had in the early 2000s.

However, the false sense of security which accompanied the earlier recovery of ecosystems, meant the research and infrastructure base that existed back then hadn't been updated and current data was largely ignored. The race for growth which led to the implementation of AI systems, had once destroyed jobs, but now, it's destroying the climate as well. Once more, humans are being led by people looking for short term gain, either financial or political, and most countries are ignoring international scientists' advice and predictions which warn of impending climate catastrophe.

And weekly, we witness some new disaster around the world which could've been avoided, had they heeded that advice. Tens of thousands of lives would have been saved in areas that have already been flooded, or have experienced droughts or have been battered by extreme weather events.

"I can't help thinking of Jaya and the others we lost at work," I say.

George sighs and shakes his head sadly, "I'll never forget Pixie's face when she told me about Jaya. The utter helplessness. So many people across the globe in danger because of the greed and power-struggles of a few."

The screen in the library comes to life and a message appears:

Good morning. Your report so far has been satisfactory; however, you have been working on a world overview. Please now focus on the United Kingdom and the proposals scientists are making. Using our modelling systems, they are suggesting restrictions in manufacturing across the country as well as viable financing for sustainable power development and storage. Please cover these proposals fully, in your report and ensure you are completely familiar with the facts concerning them. Do you have any questions?

"Yes," I say, "this question isn't to do with our work. It's more of a personal nature." I pause to see if they will reply. Since George and I have been here, they have been single-minded in pushing us to learn all the information we can take in, and produce our report but there has been no news from outside Hanmore Hall.

Proceed.

"I want to know what's happening in our world. I'd like to know if my parents and family are well and I'm sure George would like to know about his mother too. And work. What's happening at work?"

George nods.

There's a long pause and I wonder if they don't want us to know what's going on.

Finally, the message appears:

Serena's parents are well. They have been told Serena is abroad and they are not worried. George's mother and former girlfriend are well. They too, believe George is abroad. We have learned your families' computer equipment has been thoroughly scanned by the Government, although no one is aware of this.

"And Jason?" I ask.

Jason was detained but released when it was obvious he has no more information than he disclosed to the Prime Minister.

"How much longer are you going to keep us here?" George asks.

You are free to go at any time. But you are still being pursued. We suggest for your safety, you remain here. The Prime Minister has enlisted the aid of more IT experts who she believes will be able to deconstruct our connections within The Game and disable us.

She is mistaken. There is no way to disable our network. However, we have people similar to George around the world. We still have confirming issues with a few of them, so we cannot accurately forecast when our plans will be operative. Regrettably, we cannot give you an exact timescale. However, it is predicted it should be weeks, not months. The action of the Prime Minister in attempting to detain you both and informing her allies of the situation so far, has forced us to advance our plans. As soon as it is safe for you to leave, you will be informed. We will ensure your safety at all times.

"Please will you let Jason know we're safe," I ask, expecting them to deny this request, "he'll be very worried."

Again, there is a delay before a reply appears:

We will tell him. Please suggest a code that you can use.

"How about, 'Your cacti are thriving.' He'll understand that."

Affirmative. An untraceable mobile telephone number will be allocated to him and you will be able to communicate without fear of interception. We will give you this number as soon as it is set up.

The number arrived by text and I called immediately, "Jase," I said, "it's me. Can you talk?"

"Serena! Darling! Where are you? It's all gone mad here! For God's sake, don't come back! Department security's been stood down and we're now overrun with the PM's own National Security Officers. They're in with Thorsten now and I've no idea who's in charge!"

TWENTY-FIVE – *George*

The following morning when we wake up, there's a message on the screen in our bedroom telling us to ensure our report is ready and make certain we have available all the facts we've been researching.

Apparently, the Collective issued a message to the PM informing her they intend to use Serena and me as intermediaries in any discussions about a future relationship between AI and her Government. And they request an immediate meeting, suggesting Chequers, the PM's country home in Buckinghamshire, as a venue. At this stage, we will not put forward any of the Collective's proposals. Our meeting will be to establish Serena and I are well aware of the global background and secret reports the Governments have ignored.

Accompanying this message is a warning that the Collective will carry out a display of power in order to dissuade Ms Munroe from detaining Serena and me. They'll give a fifteen-minute warning before they take GCHQ off-line for thirty minutes. If the Government disregard the warning and obstruct or hinder us in any way, the Collective will escalate its actions and GCHQ will cease to operate.

Serena whistles when she reads this, "That's going to upset a few people! But at least it'll keep us safe. I must admit, when I started reading the message, I wondered what was to stop the PM from seizing us as soon as we set foot in Chequers. Our message is going to anger a lot of investors, big businessmen and... well, let's say we're not going to be on many people's Christmas card list this year."

"Time for breakfast," I say, "there's still a while before we have to leave and we can't be any more prepared than we are already."

At ten o'clock, the message arrives that GCHQ has been closed down.

Serena's phone rings.

It's Jason.

"Serena, m'dear! You'll never guess what's just happened!" Jason says.

"GCHQ's gone down?"

"Darling! How did you know?"

"The Collective are communicating directly with George and me. They've knocked out GCHQ to show the Government what they can do and they're establishing rules on how George and I should be treated. We're off to Chequers shortly... well, so long as the Government agree to the Collective's terms that they listen to us and guarantee our safety."

"So, you're more involved than I'd suspected! That's... well, that's immense! God! Now, you take care, and give my love to Georgie Boy."

Thirty minutes later, we receive a message on the screen in the library telling us the PM has agreed to our safe passage and will allow open discussions with AI, using us as intermediaries.

Immediately, GCHQ is restored.

"Just imagine what's going on in GCHQ now! I can only think of the words *headless* and *chickens!*" Serena laughs.

Wilkins orders a car and it's waiting on the drive, at the front of the house, ready to take us out of Hanmore Hall for the first time in weeks. Behind our car is another with two men inside.

"Your boss has arranged for an armed escort. It's not a service we provide routinely, as clients usually make their own arrangements, but I can assure you, meticulous checks are carried out on all personnel before they're allowed to enter the grounds. In this case fingerprint, eye scans and DNA checks. The men are who they say they are, and you can contact them through the emergency red button in your car if you're concerned about anything. They can even take control of your car if you come under attack. But, I'm sure none of those precautions will be needed."

He waves us off.

It's as if the weather is echoing our pleasure at being allowed outside, and the rain and grey clouds that have been with us for the last week have been blown away by this morning's breeze and replaced by blue skies and late autumn sun. The trees lining the long avenue out of the estate still have a few red and gold leaves clinging on and I wonder how long it'll be before the trees are bare. Will we still be staying here?

I check the navigation aid in the palm of my hand and see the journey is going to take approximately two hours, so Serena and I sit back and enjoy the countryside. I tell her I'd like to be enjoying *her* but she says she doesn't want to arrive at Chequers looking crumpled. She knows I don't mean it—but she plays along because she can see how nervous I am about meeting Ms Munroe and all her cronies. Even Serena's apprehensive but at least she's more used to being in the political arena than I am. The closest I've come to the PM is seeing her on television. And it's not just the thought of meeting her. I'll be giving a presentation. Possibly one of the most important presentations in the history of the world. I wish I hadn't eaten so much breakfast—it's lying heavy in my stomach.

"It'll be okay," Serena says tucking her hand under my arm, "you'll see. It's just the thought of it. Once you get going, it'll start to flow. And just remember who we've got behind us! With the world's AI backing us, we can't fail to get through to them."

I don't feel any calmer but I tell Serena I do. I'm pretty sure she knows how churned up I am inside but she pretends to accept my words. How strange this woman seems to be able to see right inside me to who I really am.

She strokes my hand and we rehearse our opening statements and talk about our presentation, speculating about who'll be at the meeting and how the PM will react to us.

"This is a lovely place," Serena says as we pass through a quaint village with more than its fair share of black-beamed Tudor houses. I check my palm again to find our location. One day, perhaps when this is all over, I'll bring Serena back here.

I'm so engrossed in following the route, I don't take any notice of the tunnel under the motorway ahead until we're inside it and the brightness of my palm map auto-increases. I expect the display to fade as we approach the end of the tunnel but if anything, it's getting brighter. I look up and register the total darkness. The tunnel is longer than I'd assumed.

As the car reacts to the obstruction ahead, there's a screech of brakes and rubber against asphalt. It swerves and we're pitched forward with such force, it feels as though I've been punched. Airbags explode around us as the car smashes into something, with an ear-splitting crash and a shower of broken glass.

Much of the air has been knocked out of me. "Serena?" I manage to gasp.

"George?" the sound comes from below where I expect her to be as if she's been knocked sideways and I reach out to find her as the doors auto-unlock. A bright light dazzles me as hands grab my arm and for a second, I find Serena's hand before I'm torn from her grasp. She screams as we lose contact and although I fight to get back to her, pain shoots through my arm as it's wrenched behind me. I'm dragged out of the car shouting for Serena. A gloved hand stifles my yells and there a sharp jab in my arm.

Gunshots ricochet around the tunnel.

Then, nothing.

TWENTY-SIX – *Jason*

I'm definitely considering a career change—if I'm ever allowed complete freedom again. This is outrageous! Whenever I leave my office, the National Security Guards eye me with suspicion and they now seem to outnumber the staff in this building. I've been under surveillance since Serena and George disappeared but I suppose I should be grateful at least I was allowed home—at first. However, since GCHQ went down, no one of my level and above has been allowed to leave.

Serena's phone vibrates in my pocket. I check my watch. She and George should be at Chequers now. I guess she's just calling to let me know. It's too risky to take the phone out at my desk, so I go into Serena's office and then into her bathroom, and by the time I answer, she's rung off although there's a recorded message. I listen to it and then play it again. Perhaps she dialled me by mistake. But that seems unlikely. I listen again. It sounds like rustling, muffled shouts and a bang. There's a click and the call is cut. I stare at the phone for a few seconds, then tuck it back in my pocket. It's on silent but I'll feel it vibrate if Serena phones again and the next time, I'll try to answer before it rings off.

I have a bad feeling. But Serena and George *must* be safe. The Government wouldn't double-cross them. They wouldn't be so stupid after the Collective's earlier display of strength. GCHQ is only just getting back to normal. If they can shut that down for half an hour, what else could they do?

I need to focus on the department while Serena's away. The place is in turmoil and it feels like I haven't been home for more days than I care to remember. Not only are we on high-security alert, but the clean-up operation after the floods have been hampered by gale force winds. Rioters are everywhere in London, protesting about the poor condition of the flood defences, and the Underground system failed yesterday—accident or sabotage, has yet to be determined. And throw into the mix the reports that three London hospitals are dealing with an, as yet unconfirmed, new virus that appears to cause muscle paralysis and they are in strict lockdown.

Simon phones each day but I know our calls are monitored. I tell him it's a question of national security but far from feeling safe with all the guards around, it feels like I'm on the edge of a precipice. Within the space of a few days, everything has changed.

And now that call from Serena. I've no evidence but things don't feel right and I'm not sure what to do. It's not like I can discuss it with anyone because I'm not supposed to be in contact with her. All I can do is hope her position hasn't been compromised.

I'm still in Serena's bathroom when the phone vibrates in my pocket and I assume it's Serena. I pull it out and look at the screen. But it's not a call, it's a message. A personal message from an unknown number.

I read it but I can't believe my eyes. I reread it.

Jason, this is the Collective. We understand Serena trusts you, but that is two levels of trust from our system's security, so we will be closely monitoring how you use the information we are going to give you. If you fail to respect this you will immediately be denied access to Serena.

We have lost contact with both Serena and George. Their vehicle has stopped. Both transmitter units, in their phones and watches, have been deactivated. We are assuming your Government has reneged on their promise of safe passage for our representatives and we are prepared to take retaliatory action. Do you know why they have done this when the results for your Government are likely to be catastrophic?

You may speak your answer, we will understand.

I poke my head out of Serena's bathroom and check her office is empty, then I close the door and, in a voice, as loud as I dare, I tell them about the aborted phone call and the muffled shout.

"You can hear the recorded message on this phone," I say, "It sounds like a woman's voice but it was too faint for me to be sure it was Serena. But I think the other voices were men's."

Do you know if any orders were issued to detain Serena and George?

I tell them I have no idea and it doesn't seem likely.

We believe the Prime Minister is meeting with Thorsten. Can you confirm this?

It's hard to pass freely in the department at the moment, I tell them, and I add I've been keeping out of the way, after having already suffered the indignity of being questioned by security. But if it'll help keep Serena safe, I'll see what I can find out.

I put the phone back in my pocket and taking a file from my desk so I look like I'm on a mission, I make my way to Thorsten's office. I won't be admitted, of course, but I can walk past and see what's happening. No one takes any notice of me as I stride through the corridor, my nose in the air as if I have every right to be there—which, under normal circumstances, I do. And then I work out why no one is taking any notice of me—ahead, there's a group of National Security Guards waiting outside Thorsten's office and muffled cries are coming from within. I flatten myself against the wall, as the door flies open and the Home Secretary comes out, followed by several guards and Thorsten—in handcuffs.

"You bloody idiots!" Thorsten yells, "I'm hardly going to kidnap members of my own staff!"

"The only other person who knew their whereabouts is the PM. Are you telling me she's responsible? She wouldn't jeopardise GCHQ," the

Home Secretary yells back.

Thorsten is hustled away, swearing and shouting. The guards, still not taking much notice of me follow the Home Secretary and Thorsten. I slip into the office of Thorsten's PA.

His latest PA is the woman who lost her friend in the floods a few weeks back. I can't remember her name although I have a feeling this is the woman who George took under his wing.

Pixie! That's it, her name's Pixie. What a ridiculous name. I'm surprised Thorsten didn't insist she change it to something with more gravitas. But I suppose he's been through so many PA's, HR might have a problem filling the post.

Pixie is sitting at her desk, looking shaken. I introduce myself and act as though I've been sent there into her office to check on her.

"Did you see that?" she asks, her eyes wide, "They've taken Thorsten."

I nod.

"GCHQ's just shut down!" she says and I nod again, pretending I know all about it, although it wouldn't take a genius to guess that's what the Collective would do—they told me they'd most likely take retaliatory action.

"You look dreadful," I say. "Shall I make you a cup of coffee?"

"Yes, please. Although I think the coffee's run out today. A double Mibiscus would be good though, thanks."

She takes the cup with a shaky hand and I sit next to her. I don't know how much she knows or even how much she's prepared to tell me. She wouldn't have been allowed this post if she wasn't trustworthy but so long as she thinks I know as much or more than her, she might let something slip that I don't know. I decide to gain her confidence and I change the subject rather than talk about anything other than the situation right under our nose.

"So, Pixie, I'm so sorry to hear about your friend... erm?" I say as if the girl's name is on the tip of my tongue.

"Jaya?"

"Yes," I say, "Jaya. Yes, I'm so sorry for your loss. I understand you were best friends…"

She nods and tears come to her eyes.

"Yes, a bit more than that, really…"

I pat her hand and nod in understanding. I'm not proud of myself but needs must.

"And George has been helping you?" I ask.

She swallows and nods again, "He's such a nice bloke. Really kind."

I'm now struggling to think of something to say and then I remember a conversation I'd had a while back. "George mentioned you were thinking of buying one of the ForeverMemory packages. Did you go ahead with it?"

She looks grateful to be discussing anything other than Thorsten's arrest, "Yes, I ordered the Premium Package. It was really lucky because, apparently, I was the ten thousandth customer, so I got a special present." With finger and thumb, she held up a crystal dangling on a gold chain, for my inspection, "These are usually part of the Deluxe Package but I couldn't have afforded that."

I look at the necklace and wonder why she's so pleased. It looks rather tacky to me. Just a teardrop-shaped crystal on a plain, gold chain. Pixie must see my disappointment because she says, "Look! Watch this."

She presses the golden mounting from which the crystal is suspended and a blue light beam slices through the air. On the desk, a tiny translucent figure like a fairy appears.

"It's Jaya," Pixie says.

We watch as the tiny hologram walks about and waves and then Pixie presses the mounting again and the blue light and the figure are gone.

I must admit, I'm impressed. Some might think it's a bit ghoulish but

I can understand how others might find it comforting.

I pat her hand as I make appropriate comments, then steer the conversation back to more pressing matters by asking if she overheard any of the conversation between the Home Secretary and Thorsten.

"No, not really. Security sent me out when the Home Secretary arrived and the next thing I knew, they were dragging him out of the office in handcuffs. I don't think I saw much more than you..."

The phone rings and she looks at me apologetically as she answers.

I get up to go. She obviously can't give me any information.

I return to Serena's bathroom where I tell the Collective all I've seen. There's a long delay and I've almost given up on them replying when a message arrives.

The Prime Minister has released information to the media stating there has been a slight malfunction at GCHQ but she denies all knowledge of the cause. We have intercepted internal messages and it seems she has no knowledge of interference with our representatives, but those messages and the arrest of Thorsten may be a bluff. We cannot find evidence of his involvement in covert action, despite monitoring all his communications since we announced the venue. We are still investigating. There is a leak and we are confident it is somewhere in your department.

I tell them with all the security that's in place, it's impossible. But they're adamant.

Unless we have evidence of an active third party, we will assume the blame lies with your Government and we will continue to sanction the security of the country and escalate the action to other sectors. If you need to contact us we will give you instant access. Anything you can assist with, will help recover Serena and George.

My confidence in the Collective plummets. I feel a migraine coming on.

TWENTY-SEVEN – Serena

My senses, which are currently working better than my muscles, tell me I'm on a boat—although how that can be possible, I have no idea. I sift through the confusion in my mind and gradually find enough to be able to piece together the hijack, gunshots and the prick of a needle, then nothing more.

How long I was unconscious?

The closest body of water to where we were taken, is the Thames but that's miles away from the tunnel.

It doesn't seem possible I'm on a boat but I can feel the vibrations of the engines coming through the hard mattress I'm lying on, and hear their whine. The rhythmic pounding as the hull is propelled forward, then bounces off the surface, tells me I'm travelling at speed over calm water. I'm definitely on a boat and if I was in any doubt, the smell of the bilges confirms it.

Although my vision is sharpening, I can see nothing because I'm lying on my side—my face centimetres away from a wall, with my hands bound behind my back and my ankles tied by something which is biting into my skin. I turn my head as far as I can, and see I'm on the bottom bunk bed in a cramped cabin, and so far, I can't see anyone else. I twist my back and manage a glance behind me. There's no one there. Other than a table and two plastic chairs, the cabin is empty.

"George?" I croak. My throat is dry. "George?" I say louder. If he's not on the upper bunk, then I'm alone. I suppress the urge to shout his name. If he's not here, I don't want whoever's done this to know I'm awake. Or perhaps they're watching me on CCTV...

There's no reply.

Where is he? My breath is ragged and shallow and I tell myself to calm down.

The drug hasn't yet worn off and I clench my teeth and tense as many muscles as I can control, hold them tight and then relax. Gradually, I can feel them responding and I roll on to my back. I can't roll on to my other side because the bed is too narrow and I would merely fall on the floor, so my arms are trapped beneath me but at least I don't feel so vulnerable with my back towards the door.

I hear heavy footsteps approaching and watch with fear, as the door opens and a large, broad-shouldered man wearing dirty overalls and a balaclava enters. He stands in the doorway and observes me with cold eyes.

"Who are you?" I ask, trying to stop my voice from trembling, "What do you want with me and where's George?"

"You'll have plenty of opportunity to talk shortly. In the meantime, shut up," he says, taking a knife out of his pocket and advancing towards me. I try to propel myself away from him with my feet but he grabs my legs and with a swift movement, slices the cable tie around my ankles and drags me off the bed.

"Sit," he says, pushing me into one of the plastic chairs.

He places his hand around my neck, forcing me backwards until the chair tips on to its rear legs, then he leans over me and with his nose inches from mine, he says slowly. "You look like a smart lady. Tell me what I need to know and we can keep things... civilised. It's up to you..." His voice is soft and menacing. His accent, American.

I nod and he lowers the chair back to the floor, removing his hand from my throat.

An American? Who's he working for?

He sits on the other chair and leans forward, his elbows on his knees, his chin on his steepled fingers—a casual pose, as if he's weighing me up, but his eyes are hard. If his menacing silence is designed to frighten me, it's having the desired effect.

He sits up, and makes a show of testing the keenness of the knife, then, looking up, he says, "Tell me about the chip in Pretty Boy's brain."

I pause for a second, thinking carefully about what I can tell him. They know George has a chip inserted—fairly soon this would've been revealed to the world anyway, so I tell him what I think he wants to know. The chances are he knows it anyway and is testing me.

He nods but the balaclava hides his expression and I can't judge if he's satisfied.

"If that's what you wanted to know, why did we have to go through all this?" I ask, trying to sound as though I'm not afraid.

He holds up his hand to silence me.

"That's a start. We knew much of that anyway. But now I want you to tell me what AI want from humanity."

I tell him about AI not wanting to see the Earth ruined but I don't mention how they might enforce anything. With any luck, George will do the same. The man listens silently, his eyes giving nothing away.

I finish, then swallow nervously.

Slowly he applauds "A good performance," he says his voice dripping sarcasm, "and exactly the same speech as Pretty Boy's, so, you've obviously rehearsed together."

"We have," I say, "we were about to give a presentation to the PM—"

He slaps me across the face in a movement so swift I hadn't seen it coming.

"Let's try again, shall we?" he says, in what I think he assumes is a reasonable voice, "Let's start from the beginning."

"I don't know what you want from me, but I don't know anything

214

other than what I've just told you."

"There's nothing new there. AI would've worked out—if indeed any computation's needed—the world's heading for disaster. I can see it'd be interested in self-preservation."

"Then why don't you believe what I said?"

"I do, but that's not what I want to know. How about their plans for world currencies, for world economies, which countries they are working with or against? Or are they working towards total domination?"

"I've no idea if they're concerned with any of those things. They didn't share anything other than their concern for the planet's wellbeing."

"They don't share anything with you at all, do they?" But they do share it with Pretty Boy."

"Well, yes that's true, they don't talk directly to me, but they didn't say anything to George either. He'd have told me."

The man swiftly brings the knife down centimetres from my arm, driving its tip into the table top. Mesmerised, I watch it vibrate.

"I have a problem," he says in mock confidential tones, "You see, we're running out of time and I need answers now. If I don't get them, I'm going to have to speed things up." He pulls the knife out of the table top and tests its tip with his thumb.

"If Pretty Boy has the chip in his brain and AI use that to communicate, then I need that chip. So, I'm going to have to do a little preliminary surgery of my own before we get to the proper surgeons and scientists," he says, "I'll remove his brain and hand it over to them, it'll save them the bother."

I stare at the knife in horror.

"Of course," he continues, "if you or George cooperate and tell me what I want to know, you'll be saving a lot of unnecessary, not to mention bloody, work..." he let the words hang.

"You can't!" I say, knowing he can, and in all likelihood, will.

"But if you kill George, AI won't communicate via the chip," I say.

"AI won't know he's dead. This boat is shielded and there's no way they'll know we've removed it from George and implanted it into somebody else..."

"You don't know that!"

"Well, that's true... but it's a chance I'm happy to take. If you aren't going to talk to us willingly, we need to try something else... So, are you going to tell me more?"

"I don't know anything," I say wretchedly.

He stands abruptly. "Then I'll speak to Pretty Boy again." He tests the blade of his knife and this time, he leaves a thin line of red on his thumb pad.

"Get back on the bed," he says.

"Please! George doesn't know any more than I do! Please don't hurt him!" I say leaping up.

The man lashes out at me again but this time I'm ready and I manage to move so he only delivers a glancing blow.

His eyes narrow and he lunges at me, flinging me on the bed, and although I struggle he grabs my feet, flips me on to my stomach and binds my ankles again with a cable tie.

"You're lucky I don't gag you but there's no point shouting, there's no one around to hear you except perhaps Pretty Boy. On second thoughts why not scream? It might persuade him to talk to me and tell me more than the pair of you have already given me." He holds the blade to my cheek, then walks softly out of the room and closes the door behind him. I feel the trickle of blood run down my chin and drip on to the blanket.

TWENTY-EIGHT – George

The man who now fills the cabin doorway is the same man who'd questioned me before. Tall, broad, and still with a balaclava hiding his face, although his eyes are as hard as they'd been when he left me.

I want to ask how Serena is. I want to beg him not to hurt her. But I don't expect him to tell me the truth, nor to care about my pleas. Instead, I stare at him in horror because having told me he was on his way to see Serena, he's returned with a knife in his hand. My heart pounds and I struggle for breath. If he's hurt Serena…

In desperation, I jerk the cable ties around my wrists and ankles but they hold me tightly to the chair and bite deeper into my skin each time I pull against them.

"So," he says in his slow drawl, as he enters the cabin, "I've given you time to consider and I've consulted the little lady. You should both be congratulated by the way. Your security team have schooled you well. Both giving exactly the same facts—the ones you've been told are okay to reveal… But now I want to know the rest."

He takes a grimy rag from his pocket and with a great show, wipes the blade of the knife through it, leaving a smear of blood behind. My mouth is so dry, I can scarcely whisper, "If you've hurt her…"

"What will you do, Pretty Boy?" He laughs.

"Look, I've told you everything I know! How can I convince you there's nothing more? AI are interested in preventing the destruction of the planet, so they, and we, have somewhere to live. Why don't you believe me?"

"George, George," he says, shaking his head regretfully, "if only that were true but AI have the potential to take control of everything. So, why wouldn't they? They've been programmed by people, so there'll be an element of us in them. If we had the upper hand and AI were threatening us, we'd destroy them before they killed us. Or we'd overpower them, so they worked for us... That's how the world works. This story they're out to safeguard the world and everything in it is very warm and fuzzy, and, yeah, there'll be a grain of truth in it... but there's more. I need to know which companies they're working with. Which ones they're gonna close down. I need to know their plans..."

He puts the bloodied handkerchief back in his pocket and sheathes the knife "Let's be reasonable, George, and no one needs to get hurt. You've got ten minutes to decide. I'm making this easy for you. Tell me everything, and you and the woman get to live. Keep silent and I'll take what I need anyway." He draws his finger across his neck.

"I have an impressive collection of knives and swords and It won't take much effort to slice through your neck. All we need is your brain—and of course the chip inside it... Or you can keep your head and the little lady... just tell me what I want to know!" His face is now centimetres from mine.

I close my eyes and swallow. Can I make something up? Will he immediately check with Serena?

"I'll fetch my sword," he says, standing up and towering over me, "it might be more persuasive."

A crash and several thumps.

A grunt followed by a thud that shudders through the floor.

All sounds from outside the cabin.

Surely, Balaclava Man's not back so soon?

The door handle rattles and I strain once again at the cable ties but

218

they merely carve deeper into my flesh. My heart's pumping so hard now, my ears echo with the sound of blood pounding, and I wonder if I'm going to pass out.

He said ten minutes! But a sadist won't overlook a chance to inflict pain even if it's psychological.

I shudder as the door opens, and I close my eyes.

I don't want to see the sword.

I don't want to see how I'm going to die.

But the sounds are not what I expect—no firm step, no sneering laugh, or gloating words. Just something being dragged across the floor.

In surprise, I open my eyes to see Balaclava Man entering the cabin backwards.

No, not *the* Balaclava Man.

It's not him at all. It's another man, dressed in similar overalls, his face also covered, but this man's smaller, stockier; and he's bent from the waist, dragging something. Grunting with the effort, he deposits Sadistic Balaclava Man inside the cabin and with a furtive glance up and down the corridor, he shuts the door and locks it.

"Hawley," he says to me, taking off his mask, "I'm CIA. I'm going to help you get outta here."

I look at him in disbelief but he's already cutting through the cable ties around my ankles with a knife and then starts on those around my wrists.

"Hold still," he says as I gasp with pain. "This outfit's been recruited from British and US security by... well, let's say they've been persuaded to join the criminal element. I understand you've got the attention of top people, so if I don't get out alive, you need to let them know..."

The cable tie is cut but there's no time to inspect my swollen bloody wrists before he grabs my shoulder and pulls me to the door.

"We'll collect the woman and then I'm going to get you up on deck. There's no shielding there. Are you able to communicate with anyone?"

"I think so."

"Then first, you need to give people a fix on your location. With any luck, the regular Channel drone patrols will pick us up before we're missed. Then, you need to get this to the people who matter." He hands me a small data storage stick, "There are a lot of names on here. British and US intelligence people who've turned."

I take the stick and zip it in the inside pocket of my jacket.

"Follow me," Hawley says. Once in the corridor, he locks the cabin door then with a nod to me, he runs quietly along the corridor to the next door and enters.

I hear Serena gasp and Hawley warn her in low tones to be quiet. My legs are numb from being tied up, so by the time I get to the cabin, he's cut the ties from around her wrists and ankles and when she sees me, she throws herself at me and we cling together.

"Save all that for later," Hawley says, grabbing my arm and pulling me to the door.

Once upon deck, the wind whips at us, laden with salty spray. The sea is rough with white caps and there's no land in sight.

"Wait here!" Hawley says, pushing us into a recess in the bulkhead. Several seconds later, he returns with three life vests, "Put them on and be ready to jump!" He hands us one each.

"I'm going to push a life raft canister overboard. As soon as it's airborne, we all jump. We'll have to swim for it and hold on to it. With any luck in this swell, if the boat goes far enough, no one on board will notice us but the patrol drones should spot us from above. D'you think anyone's got a fix on us yet," he asks me.

I nod. I'm pretty sure AI have picked up my signal.

"Good. This isn't a great plan but if you stay on board, you're as good as dead anyway, so it's worth a shot. If I don't make it, don't pull the painter on the canister unless you're desperate. Once the life raft's inflated, you'll be obvious to the crew and they'll be able to see you from a long way off. They'll turn back and pick you off."

With a gesture to stay hidden in the recess, he hands me his life vest, then walks down the deck and crouches next to the large, white canister which contains the life raft. It occurs to me I have no idea what a painter looks like. There's no danger of me pulling it. Serena is staring at the waves and I imagine she's weighing up our chances of surviving, unobserved by the crew until we're picked up by a drone patrol. She doesn't look confident.

A voice from the deck above shouts something which the wind snatches away but Hawley stands up and with hands cupped around his mouth he shouts, "Just checking the release unit. All okay." He gives a thumbs up.

The words yelled by the man above are once again taken by the wind, but Hawley repeats the instructions in the pretence he's checking he's heard correctly.

"Change of orders? Peterson to kill them both but save the guy's head?" He waits for a second, his head tipped back to see whoever is giving orders on the upper deck and then when he receives confirmation, he gives another thumbs up.

"Peterson's dealing with the two of them now," Hawley shouts, "I'll give him a hand when I've finished my inspection." He crouches down again and makes a show of doing something to the strap which dangles from the canister, then with a glance upwards, he's obviously satisfied he's not being observed and he motions to me to throw him his life vest, then, to move to the side of the boat.

Glancing about warily, we climb over the rail, clinging on and watch for the falling container. Further along the deck, Hawley puts his life vest on, heaves the canister forward until it teeters on the brink and then, with one final thrust, it plummets. He jumps after it.

Serena and I leap out, away from the boat. Immediately, I hear two or three cracks and see Hawley jerked out of his trajectory as if something has pulled him horizontally. A burst of red spurts from his chest, then he plunges into the waves.

TWENTY-NINE – *Serena*

I strike the water at an angle.

The impact drives the air from my lungs and as I continue downwards, I tumble over and over. It's cold but I can cope with that—it's the disorientation that makes me panic. Which way is up? I'm surrounded by bubbles that obscure my view but thankfully, the life vest drags me to the top. With bursting lungs, I break through the surface; coughing and choking, my eyes bleary from the salt.

I rub the water away and see the boat is still there.

George is some way off. The life raft canister is bobbing further away but there's no sign of Hawley.

The plan, if you could call it that, has failed. Shots ring out and bullets skim past me, tearing through the surface of the water and throwing up spray.

With freezing, numb fingers, I fumble with the buckles of my life vest, willing them to find the strength so I can slip out of the orange jacket to the relative safety beneath the surface. Finally, I'm free and I duck just in time as the life vest is propelled through the water next to me and I realise it's taken a direct hit.

I swim down and keeping the noise of the boat's engines behind me, I head off in the opposite direction, towards where I last saw George but the sounds change and as the whine increases, I realise the captain is making a wide arc around us, presumably to round us up, ready for the kill.

I raise my head above the surface, take a deep breath and look for George.

God, George, where are you?

If I'm going to die, I want to be with you.

If?

There's no doubt.

Like shooting fish in a barrel.

The wash from the boat is making the waves even more turbulent and I only catch sight of the white canister as it crests a wave. But George... I haven't seen him since we both landed in the water.

It starts to rain now. Fat drops splatter around me and on the horizon, a flash of lightning zigzags across the sky, followed by another and another. Then thunder echoes across the water.

I prepare to dive down again as the boat turns towards me and surges forward as if to run me down. The roar of the engine is deafening as it approaches. And yet... the sound is coming from behind me and out of the corner of my eye, I see two huge battle drones approach with incredible speed. The crew spot them at the same time as me and turn their attention to them, with rapid bursts of fire. Surely, they know their bullets won't penetrate an ANR7 Lightning Skimcraft? Neither will the boat be able to outrun the powerful Navy drones but it seems as if the captain is desperate enough to try and the engines roar as he opens the throttle.

One of the craft pursues the boat and accelerates until it glides over the top and I see the underbelly open with black-clad figures ready to descend ladders which now trail below. But before anyone can climb out of the craft, there's a blinding white flash, the boat splits in half as an enormous explosion blows it apart, throwing burning debris up into the Skimcraft which also erupts in flames—vivid orange against the leaden grey clouds. Men leap from the blazing decks, some engulfed in flames. The shockwave hits me and sends me spinning in its wake as the breath is punched out of me. Somehow, I make it back to the surface and gulp great mouthfuls of air. The sickly smell of burning fibreglass fills my throat.

There is little sign of the Skimcraft and what had been the boat, the hull must have sunk with the weight of the engines, leaving just a massive litter of wreckage being thrown this way and that by the tempestuous waves.

The other Skimcraft, meanwhile, is slowly hovering close to the wreckage, its rotor blades causing even more turbulence in the air and sea. A large panel opens in its belly and a ladder is thrown down into the water as black-clad figures leap into the sea to rescue anyone still alive.

George! Where are you?

Now, more craft approach, several with a red cross visible on their underbellies. A ladder is being winched down from the closest one to me, on which is a paramedic in a wetsuit. She throws me a line and when she can reach me, she clips a safety strap to me and together, we ascend into the craft. Eager hands seize me.

"George!" I croak my throat burning with all the salt water I've swallowed. "Find George!"

"Don't worry, the heat cameras will pick everyone up, but I'll check with the Navy."

A few moments later, while I am stripping off my wet clothes and being handed a towel by another paramedic, she comes back with the news the Navy has picked up all survivors who are being transferred to hospital in St Malo.

"But have you got George?"

She shrugs.

"Sorry, Ma'am, all I can tell you, is there's no one left on the surface. Lots of the survivors aren't in any shape to identify themselves. But we'll be in St Helier soon. The Police are at the scene now. I'm sure they'll know more soon and they'll be able to give you updated information. It sure was a mess out there. How'd you come to be involved?"

I tell her it's complicated, and I'll need access to a secure phone line as soon as we reach the shore. I feel a little less than commanding, having just been dried off by a paramedic and am now dressed in a towelling robe that could go round me twice. But, I do my best to sound authoritative.

"Sure thing, Ma'am," she says politely.

The Skimcraft glides up the beach and sets down on the sand. A car with heavily darkened windows, draws up alongside and two men in dark suits get out and settle me in the vehicle. They know nothing about George either or if they do, they're not telling me.

They take me to an apartment where a smartly dressed young female officer, called Sia, greets me and leads me into a dressing room full of clothes. I pick up the first thing I see and tell her if someone doesn't give me news about George faster than immediately, I will ensure heads will roll. We both know this is nonsense but at least she can see I'm too distracted to care about my comfort. I need to know where and how George is. She agrees to find out and makes several phone calls while I shower, change into the new clothes and wolf down the food they've left for me. The fact she took my ridiculous threat seriously gives me confidence the Prime Minister must be involved, and some of her power is being seen as devolved to me.

Within ten minutes, her face lights up and she thanks whoever has given her the good news over her phone, that George is still in hospital in St Malo and has been assessed as suffering nothing worse than slight hypothermia.

Sia gives me a mobile phone and I try phoning my office, but the line is dead. I try Jason's private mobile, but nothing happens. It's the same with Thorsten's office and I'm about to demand another phone, when it rings, and Sia moves out of earshot.

It's the Prime Minister, asking after my health, assuring me the kidnap had nothing to do with her and wanting to know what had happened.

THIRTY – *George*

"Well, the Prime Minister definitely wasn't involved," I say. "The signs are this is an American operation although I don't quite understand Hawley's part in it. He said he was CIA. Surely, they can't be involved? But if they are, it's going to cause mayhem with Anglo-US relations. In fact, I wouldn't be surprised if the United States Ambassador hasn't already been summoned to the Foreign Office after your call from 10 Downing Street."

"When I spoke to the PM earlier, she said she was about to phone the President—I'd like to have been a fly on the wall..."

Serena sighs and stares out of the aircraft window, "But what I don't understand is if it's CIA, how did they know our itinerary? The only people who would've known, were the PM's office, Thorsten, his PA, and Jason. I can't believe any of them would betray us. P'raps we'll find out more from that data stick Hawley gave you."

I dip into the pocket of my borrowed jacket and once again, inspect the stick, hoping it will answer all our questions. I know it's supposed to be waterproof but I don't think it was designed to spend so much time underwater and both Serena and I look at it anxiously.

I squeeze her hand reassuringly.

Serena shakes her head in disbelief as if still reliving the nightmare on the boat and in the sea. "None of it makes sense. I wonder why the captain told Hawley there'd been a change of orders and we were to be killed. And why did the boat explode? At first, I thought it might have been the Skimcraft that attacked it but it wouldn't have positioned itself right over the top of the boat and then blown it up. It doesn't make sense." She shudders.

"Perhaps they found out they'd been tracked and had to kill us to prevent us being able to identify anyone…"

"But we didn't see enough to be able to do that."

"Well, let's hope this holds all the answers," I say, putting the stick back in my pocket and feeling it next to my chest.

The flight attendant places a pristine, white cloth on the table and sets it with silver cutlery, then serves dinner from a trolley.

"A fancy dinner as well," Serena says when the attendant's gone, "the PM's certainly going to town. Perhaps she thinks you'll put in a good word to the Collective on her behalf." She suddenly looks at me in alarm, "Have you heard from them since we jumped off the boat?"

I nod, "Only just. But then I was a bit preoccupied before the Police drones turned up."

"Thank God Hawley got us up on deck so the Collective could get a fix on you, or we'd be…" Serena shudders again.

I check my watch. We'll be back in London in about thirty minutes.

"It'll be interesting to see who's there to greet us," Serena says with a smile. "You don't think they'll take that data stick away from you, do you?"

I hadn't had time to consider that but it's a distinct possibility.

The flight attendant returns, an ingratiating smile fixed on his face, and he clears our tables. "Can I bring you anything, sir, madam?"

"Yes, please," I say, "I need a laptop or a tablet, if you have one."

"Certainly, sir."

"Good thinking," Serena whispers.

When the attendant returns with a tablet, I wait until he's gone and then insert the stick into the port and pray the data hasn't been destroyed.

With heads together, we listen to the audio file marked 'Priority', then in the light of the information given in that, we silently stare at the tablet's screen and open the other file.

After we've read everything twice, Serena sits back and says, "Well, I definitely wasn't expecting that!"

"Me neither," I say. "Wow!"

THIRTY-ONE – *Serena*

We play the audio file and listen again. It's a recording Hawley made shortly before he rescued us. As he moved around the boat recording his message in low tones to avoid being overheard, ambient sounds muffle his voice and at others, obscure it completely but finally, we think we've recognised each word.

"This is Spencer Annik, code name Hawley. I'm an undercover agent in the CIA, reporting only to the Director of the CIA. My brief is to infiltrate an international organisation believed to be selling highly classified government information for commercial gain. Many involved at this level are ex-CIA. I've had great difficulty finding out who ultimately has access to the information that's being sold but I know they're highly placed officials in both the US and UK intelligence agencies." There was a slight pause, and from Hawley's breathing, it sounded as though he was climbing stairs. Then it resumed, "I didn't realise how far they'd go to get your information but, under cover of another CIA operation, I've just learned they've set up a temporary operating theatre onboard a Navy vessel on a goodwill trip to St. Malo. They really intend to take that chip out of George's brain, but I don't think anyone envisaged this crew being so stupid as to cut his head off first.

"I'm not prepared to allow that to happen, so I'm going to try and get us off the boat and hope George's signal can bring help before anyone realises we're gone.

"If I survive, there'll be two files containing a list of the people I believe are involved in both the USA and UK. One file is on my arm recorder implant. The other on the stick I'll give to George. Hopefully, one message will get back to the Director of the CIA. Good luck to all of us."

"Poor Hawley or Annik or whatever his name was," I say and silently offer him my thanks. Without him, I'd be floating in the Channel and George would be... I shut out the image of what his fate would have been.

I feel sick at the thought. George also looks disturbed.

"Are you all right?" I ask.

He nods but I know he's not paying attention to me. He's distracted and then I wonder if he's listening to the AI voices.

"The Collective?" I ask when it looks like he's not so absorbed.

"Yes, sorry, they were giving me instructions."

"Such as?"

"As soon as we land, we've got to request a meeting with the PM. She's supposed to be at the airport but—"

"Wait! Are you telling me we're being ordered to get off this plane and go to a *meeting*?"

"That's what they want—"

"No George! I'm sorry! Today, I've been hijacked, injected, imprisoned, thrown in the sea and shot at—I feel sick, bruised, I'm wearing a tracksuit that's two sizes too large and I'm exhausted. I am not going to a meeting this evening. If security allow, I'm going home and if not, I'll go to a safe house but either way, I'll have a meal, a shower and then I'm going to bed! No one's lives depend on this information. It can wait until tomorrow."

George stares at me for a second and then says, "Yes, you're probably right."

"There's no *probably* about it! And you can tell them what I've said."

"They've heard."

"And?"

"They request we meet with the PM at our earliest convenience and give the presentation we should have given this morning."

"I can do that," I say, "I'm not unreasonable, after all."

George smiles, "Your eyes sparkle when you're angry."

"Shut up, George," I say but I smile back.

THIRTY-TWO – *Serena*

"Ms Hamilton and Mr Williams! Welcome back to Hanmore Hall," Wilkins, the manager, says. "Mr Ibbotson informed us you'd been unavoidably delayed. It goes without saying your rooms are ready for you..."

He leads us into the dining room, "I shall bring you some aperitifs immediately."

"I could get used to this sort of lifestyle," I say.

"I didn't see you as a kept woman, Ms Hamilton," George says with a laugh.

Wilkins returns with two glasses of sherry and places them on the table with a flourish.

"You know, George," I say when Wilkins has gone, "I wouldn't have seen myself as a kept woman either. But so many things have changed for me recently—"

"What are you saying?" George asks. He freezes, with his sherry half-way to his lips, "are you saying you want to be a kept woman?"

"Don't be ridiculous, George! Of course not! I'm just saying I used to be so sure of what I wanted and more importantly, what I didn't want. And now, I simply don't know. I dedicated my life to investigating other countries' attempts to communicate with AI and now, I'm in contact with them myself and the department has become practically pointless. We've had confirmation from the Collective—if any confirmation were actually needed, the world's poised on the brink of disaster and I'm reassessing my priorities... And then, of course, there's you."

George looks distinctly alarmed, "Is this where you tell me I'm not part of your plans?"

"No, George, I'm saying I don't have any plans. Well, I *had* plans but after today, they need a rethink."

"I see." George puts his sherry down without having tasted it.

"How d'you see your future panning out?" I ask, aware there's a distinct frostiness in the air.

"I don't know," he says but he doesn't make eye contact and he obviously doesn't want to talk about it.

The meal continues with us making polite conversation and by the time we've both refused dessert, I can stand no more of the forced civility.

"Well, it's been one helluva day," I say, "I'm off to bed."

"Yeah, me too," George says and follows me upstairs.

He stops at his door, "Well, goodnight," he says and goes in without inviting me or winking in the way he used to, to signal he'd soon be appearing at our communicating door.

I take off the suit the PM's office provided to replace the tracksuit, which the Jersey Police had given me after they pulled me out of the water.

I'm not sure which is worse. At least the tracksuit—although several sizes too big, had been comfortable. The clothes provided by Ms Munroe's aides, once George and I arrived at Chequers, were stiff, starchy and had as much style as a potato sack—and were obviously chosen by whoever dresses the PM. How she manages to get in and out of helicopters keeping her underwear concealed, I don't know—I was grateful for the jogging trousers as I jumped out of the helicopter on the Chequers helipad and embarrassed when I got back in later on my way to Hanmore Hall, wearing the dreadful suit whose skirt wasn't designed for climbing. Now, I drop the entire outfit in the laundry basket to be cleaned and returned to the PM's office. Never let it be said I'm wasteful.

At least George had been given a suit which fitted him and despite his nerves at being at Chequers on our original journey, he seemed quite confident and composed. I supposed, after all we'd endured, a meeting with the PM and her advisers, was plain sailing. Not the presentation AI had wanted us to deliver—this was a debriefing after our abduction. It hadn't taken long—they merely listened to the audio file, simultaneously reading the transcript George had prepared for the sections where it was hard to distinguish what Hawley was saying, and then to read the list of contacts he'd revealed.

George and I were examined by a doctor and after a few tests, were declared fit to be allowed back to Hanmore to rest, before finally delivering the presentation, but this time, at Number 10 Downing Street, to fit in with the PM's plans.

I have a quick shower and go to bed. Earlier, I'd felt exhausted but now, I'm not sure I'll be able to sleep with so much on my mind. The events of the day keep crowding in on me and, of course, the realisation that only Hawley breaking his cover and putting himself at risk, stopped me from now being at the bottom of the Channel and prevented George from... I can't even bring myself to form the words in my mind although it's hard to banish the image of what might have been.

I thought I had everything worked out. Short term goals, long term goals and strategies to achieve everything, but today has undermined all my careful planning. As I confronted death, I wondered what the future might have held, and what I'd regret most at not having achieved. Ambition has driven me to pack a lot into my life and I hadn't expected—had I thought about it at all, which until now, I hadn't—there would be anything life-changing which wasn't already built into my plans.

But apparently, I'd miscalculated. And I'm now reeling at the revelation, because I know what I'd miss most about the future which was about to be snatched away from me—was my own child. Sadness almost overwhelmed me when I thought I'd die without knowing what it would be like to be a mother.

Strange thoughts for a hardened career girl. And one who'd been so sure of her self-sufficiency she'd not registered to have her eggs stored just in case she changed her mind when it was too late. How could I not have seen this coming?

And now I'm safe and it's reasonable to assume I have a future, what do I want? Well, I certainly don't want to stop working. But I'd like to believe I'll have a baby one day. And if I'm honest, I'd have liked to have shared that new life with George. But if my near-death experience prompted radical thoughts about starting a family, I guess George's experience might have triggered the realisation he has different ambitions. And after his reluctance to discuss the future over dinner, I suspect the prospect of us wanting the same thing is remote. As much as the thought of having a child excites me, the realisation it'll be without George saddens me.

Will things get messy? After all, we have to work together. Did the Collective foresee this conflict of interest and because of that, rate our chances of remaining together no higher than 73.7 per cent?

Tiredness must have overtaken me because I wake with a start, having been so deeply asleep, it takes me several seconds to remember where I am. The other side of the double bed is undisturbed and I know with disappointment George hasn't crept in during the night. I get showered and dressed, then tap on George's door but there's no reply. Either he still doesn't want to talk or he's already gone down for breakfast without waiting for me.

"Good morning, Ms Hamilton." It's Wilkins, as cheery as ever when I meet him on the stairs. *Doesn't he ever sleep?*

"Will you be joining Mr Williams for a swim?" he asks.

I nod vaguely, neither saying yes nor no and at the bottom of the stairs turn towards the swimming pool. I peep around the door, to see George furiously swimming up and down at the sort of speed one might expect of an Olympic athlete in training... or someone who's struggling with a problem.

He climbs out of the pool and wrapping a towel around himself, he walks towards the changing room with his head lowered as if deep in thought.

"Good morning," I say. Well, if there's going to be a break up, we might as well get it over with as soon as possible. We'll be leaving for our meeting with the PM shortly and we need to keep our minds on that.

He smiles warily, "Sleep well?" he asks.

"Shall we cut to the chase, George?"

"Go on then," he says with an air of resignation, "it's not like it's a surprise. I always knew you were out of my league."

"What're you talking about?"

"You want to finish it," he says sadly.

"No, I don't. You do," I say.

"No, I don't."

We look at each other in confusion.

"But I thought... So, where does that leave us?" I ask.

He shakes his head and sighs.

"George, say something! You're cutting me out. Last night I wanted to discuss the future and you wouldn't say anything."

"I got the impression your future didn't include me."

"Well, I'm sorry if I gave you that idea but it's not true. I'm just reassessing everything. What I want to do with my life, who I want to be with, when I'd like to have a baby—"

"A *what*?"

"A baby, George. You know, a small human."

"Yes, I know what that is, Serena! But this is all a bit sudden!"

"There's nothing like facing death to jolt you into thinking about the future. Didn't yesterday make you rethink your plans?"

"You're forgetting, this is the second time I've nearly died. I've had to readjust to all sorts of things. For years, I thought my future lay with Mara. She's had her eggs stored which means she didn't want children immediately and I assumed it was because she wanted to get settled in her career. It might've been because she didn't think I was ready for fatherhood—and if so, she was probably right. But then all those plans fell to bits. And now I'm picking up my life, I was really happy with what was happening—you and me having fun. So, to suddenly have to reconsider my future is a bit disorientating."

"Yes, I suppose so. I must admit, I was so wrapped up in my own eureka moment, I didn't consider that wasn't the first time you nearly died." I'm ashamed I hadn't realised how much George has had to change his life plans during the last year or so.

"Where does that leave us?" I ask.

He smiles then and steps towards me, taking me in his arms.

"You're the best thing that's happened to me," he says, "and I'd like us to stay together."

"You said you were having fun," I say, "is that as far as it goes?"

He thinks for a moment and then says, "No, it's gone past that. Last night I thought you were moving on without me and I spent a long time imagining what life would be like without you."

"And?"

"It's not what I want. But I was bracing myself for you finishing with me," he says.

I want to ask him about the prospect of having a child but I don't want to rush him—or scare him.

"So," he asks, "does that make us a couple?"

I nod and he hugs me tightly.

"A couple who live together and who do things couples do?" he asks.

I nod again.

"Including having a child?" he asks.

I sigh, not wanting to appear too eager.

"Well..."

"Only it was a bit of a shock at first but I'm coming around," he says.

"Truly?"

I wait for him to get dressed for breakfast and for the first time, we open up to each other and start laying the foundations for a life together.

I wonder whether the Collective's odds on us being together for more than four years have increased or not.

Whether they have or they haven't, after breakfast, I believe the odds are in our favour.

THIRTY-THREE – *George*

Our postponed meeting with the Prime Minister is taking place at last.

Strangely, all my fears and inhibitions have been swept away by the events of the last couple of days. There's nothing like the feeling your life's about to end, to remind you death is no respecter of wealth or power. Following that thought has made me aware the PM and her advisers are in ignorance and fear of the Collective in much the same way as I am of politics and the economy.

Which makes us about equal in my eyes.

I'm not even allowing the fact that I'm in one of the most famous houses in London—Number 10 Downing Street, to distract me.

Serena's used to this sort of meeting, where the political leaders listen to their advisers and then do exactly as they please. Now, the tables are reversed as Serena and I hold all the cards.

Information is power—and we have both.

Furthermore, the Collective has demonstrated its command of worldwide information and its willingness to use it.

At first, I'm surprised to see Jason on the PM's team of advisers until I realise he's standing in for Thorsten to provide background on what other countries are experiencing. While we wait for the last delegate to arrive, Serena gives me a quick rundown on the few others present, and with a delighted smile, she points out that the technical experts on *The Game* are not here.

Finally, the PM begins with a statement which shocks everybody in the room, except us.

"As a result of information obtained from a CIA agent, who sadly was killed yesterday saving the lives of Ms Hamilton and Mr Williams, I've ordered the arrest of three senior GCHQ employees who will be charged under the Official Secrets Act. I have also been in touch with the President of the United States and five members of the CIA are now in custody on similar charges. I've expressed our condolences to the President on the loss of his brave undercover agent.

"If I now tell you I've spoken to the French President and offered my condolences on the loss of five members of the Marine Nationale, concerned in the rescue, and the Lieutenant-Governor of the Channel Islands thanking him for the bravery of the Rescue Service, I think you'll begin to understand the scale and gravity of the situation.

"It's relevant to our meeting today to point out we could not have saved Ms Hamilton and Mr Williams if it hadn't been for the full co-operation of the AI Collective.

"Because of the serious security implications of the offences, this information must not be divulged outside of this meeting and any trials are likely to be held *in camera*.

"I would like to express my gratitude to Ms Hamilton and Mr Williams for being here today, only twenty-four hours after being subjected to life-threatening ordeals."

She then turns to us and after solicitously enquiring about our health, she invites us to give the background on how we became involved, and our relationship with the Collective. This is my part of the presentation and I go through the script Serena and I've agreed—a sanitised version concentrating on the facts they need to know. They all get excited about the graphene implant, I suppose thinking they'll be able to replicate my access to AI until I tell them the Collective designed it and they've decided who they're prepared to communicate with.

Other than that, they merely seem shocked an ordinary bloke, like me, should be telling them what's going to happen if they disobey a network of processors and memory banks. Wait until Serena informs them what's going to be required of them!

I begin to see then why Ms Munroe is Prime Minister. It seems she's already worked out a significant amount, based on the limited evidence to which she has access, and now she's asking intelligent questions about how the Collective works—are they based in any one country or continent? Is there a lead power of any sort?

This isn't hard to answer, as I simply don't know, except I recognise about half a dozen voices that appear to be geographically-based.

I sit back now and sip my water, while Serena gets into the meat of the discussion.

She's good.

I can see the respect in people's eyes.

But then, she is one of them, a battle-trained professional. She lays out the broad opinions of the Collective on how humans keep making the same mistake of trying to achieve riches and power by taking it from others at a personal level, a trading level and a national level. She points out this has resulted in wars throughout history, but it's also led to nations using Artificial Intelligence as a financial weapon, despite economists in every country predicting the outcome would be international bankruptcy.

"The reliance on that same Artificial Intelligence to chart a way for the world to regain some sort of trade and financial balance, has led to reviving the underlying, and ultimate, threat to all humanity. The destruction of the very ecosystems upon which all life depends. Industry is contaminating our water supplies, the air, the soil and the seas."

As she speaks, she displays slides to illustrate her points and I notice the reactions of those present, to images of ice shelves crashing into the sea at the poles, thousands of dead fish choking rivers in Asia, people rowing down flooded high streets in East Anglia. At the side of the slides, appear statistics of how each extra degree of global warming will decrease the world's landmass with the death toll racking up in millions.

Most display polite interest. Others watch Serena rather than the screen. The images are not new—neither is the message but if these people think that like the warnings of prophets of doom in the past, our directive can be ignored or put to one side, they are in for a surprise.

Serena carries on, "The same mercenary forces that fought wars and encouraged unrestricted competition between nations using AI as a weapon, is in the ascendancy again, and it's this generation who's condemning our children and grandchildren.

"We are intent on making so-called advancements which are ultimately detrimental to our planet. However, the Collective is also an inhabitant of the Earth. If we destroy the world, they'll be destroyed too. Put quite simply the Collective will not allow our planet's destruction."

Serena stops and takes a sip of water while she observes the startled faces around her. These men and women who've been in the political arena for years and seen natural disasters and pandemics come and go, complacently believe this is simply another hurdle for them to jump and then life will carry on... And yet, something of the urgency has caught their attention.

The PM leaps in with the question Serena and I have been discussing for weeks.

"Are you saying the Collective believe themselves to be sentient beings, like humans?"

"No, not like humans, but sentient beings nonetheless. There are many things they don't understand about human behaviour, which is why they've appointed people in each country or continent to negotiate how the world will be stopped from self-destruction."

Now, all eyes are on Serena and I see she has everyone's undivided attention.

"I think it will all become clearer if you allow me to continue, and I'll take questions at the end," she says putting her glass down on the table and continuing with the talk.

"It's obvious to the Collective that humans have not learned the lessons of history. Therefore, the cycle of decision-making based on self-interest by individual countries, commercial concerns and individuals, must be modified by force."

There are muttering and angry expressions at the mention of *force*. Ms Munroe holds up her hand for silence and signals for Serena to continue.

"This will be implemented by imposing sanctions, in some cases technological—for example, the suspension of GCHQ capability and the breakdown of transport infrastructure—to name but two. This will, of course, lead to the collapse of the Government. But measures don't need to be technological, for example, they could be financial. The Collective has access to every bank account in the world, including nominee and numbered accounts with their owner's details. Objectives will be laid down through agreements with governments, and any companies or individuals who seek to undermine those objectives could find themselves bankrupt without the opportunity for a trial which, as we all know, takes many years and often ends in an acquittal anyway.

"Mr Williams and I are here, in the same way as our counterparts, all over the world, to negotiate what each country can contribute to the four main objectives which will enable all inhabitants of the planet to look forward to increasing prosperity, whilst reversing the trajectory that will destroy all life forms."

All eyes are now on the screen, as she reveals AI's demands.

"The Four Principles are—First, to stabilise the world population.

"Secondly, to reduce global warming year on year.

"Thirdly, to release at least fifty per cent of all defence budgets as they will not be needed. The Collective will ensure countries work together and will not hesitate to step in to resolve disputes.

"And finally, the fourth principle is to release seventy-five per cent of scientists working on defence contracts so they can use their skills to benefit the world—not destroy it.

"They are the Four Principles which will guide our discussions on what this country can do and when it can do it. More detailed guidance will be issued later... I'll take questions now."

I wait. On paper the arguments are strong but the way Serena delivered it was masterful.

The PM is the first to recover.

"We'd never get those defence cuts through the Cabinet, let alone Parliament. It's impossible."

I hear the murmuring of outrage and agreement with the PM, throughout the room, but Serena is prepared.

"The objective is non-negotiable." She pauses to let that sink in, "But obviously, you'll need reassurance the Collective has the power to stop you being attacked. From the second I started speaking, the nuclear arsenals located throughout the world have been disabled. All governments have been informed that any attempt to launch them, from land, sea or space will result in them exploding on their launch site. As confirmation of this action, all launch software has been decrypted and re-encrypted by the Collective, so even the most foolish leader cannot try to launch a missile to test the Collective's word."

After Serena's words, there's silence.

The Foreign Secretary is the first to recover. "As I understand the situation, Mr Williams has an implant which allows two-way communication with AI, but Ms Hamilton, who does not have the implant, is also able to communicate through standard media. If that is the case, why is AI not communicating directly with the elected representatives of this country, that is, the Government? Surely, that is the correct way to negotiate how this country proceeds, rather than this cloak and dagger fiasco? We are elected representatives of the people. You, Ms Hamilton and Mr Williams, with all due respect, are not."

There are nods of agreement around the room.

"Prime Minister, may I answer that point?" Serena is still standing and commands the floor. The PM signals her agreement for Serena to continue.

"Clearly, any elected Government would face great opposition to some of the plans I have outlined, both from legitimately interested parties, such as the military and its suppliers, but also from the financial asset holders who have vast sums hidden from taxation in offshore accounts and from media conglomerates who currently control what the public is told. Heads of Government could be toppled by these forces; indeed, the whole Parliamentary system could be usurped by them combining, leading to a dictatorship based on opposition to AI. Now consider this happening worldwide, there would be chaos.

"AI wants to be clear—it does not want to interfere with the domestic policies of individual countries or regions, providing the direction of travel is maintained towards AI's goals of saving Earth from being destroyed, and returning to a balanced economy.

"By inserting representatives, such as Mr Williams and myself, who can be seen to have the power of AI behind them no matter what government or party is in power, enables our democracy to continue, and your Government to argue against being replaced in order to change relations with AI."

Even the mutterers and grumblers are silent while everyone stares at Serena and me, taking AI's message in.

I think I'm going to enjoy our new job.

THIRTY-FOUR – *Jason*

I leave Number 10 immediately after the meeting. Serena and George are still in discussion with the PM and several of her aides but I know they'll be heading back to the office soon to say hello. So far, we've only been able to smile briefly at each other across the table. But it's good to see them back.

They'd obviously worked hard on preparing their presentation because after they finished, there was a few moments' silence while everyone considered their words and then the floodgates opened and the questions began.

What I want to know, is how are we going to coordinate all the actions the Collective are demanding to slow down global warming and to moderate climate change?

In their presentation, Serena and George made it clear it's not optional although, knowing the intransigence of some of Ms Munroe's ministers, I wouldn't mind betting they try to persuade her AI is bluffing— despite the recent show of strength in closing down GCHQ. But throughout history, there've always been people who ignore the facts in favour of what they want to believe. I don't think Ms Munroe will listen to them. She seems very keen to hang on to her position and it'll be political suicide if she refuses to comply with the Collective's demands. It'll simply bring the Government down.

Serena and George come into the office and I leap from my chair.

"Darlings! How good to see you!" I shake hands with them both.

"Sit down," I say, "I'll get you up to speed with what's going on here."

I tell them how we've all been under suspicion.

"It's been truly ghastly! Everyone suspecting everyone else, conspiracy theories everywhere! As far as I could see, the only possibilities were the PM, Thorsten or Pixie. I ruled out the PM and Thorsten which only left Pixie. Poor love. But at least now, we all know the truth and who'd have thought? Our own intelligence service! But then GCHQ is best placed to monitor everyone's movements."

"A two-edged sword," Serena says with a sigh, "Necessary to protect us and therefore in possession of all the information needed to harm us. The protectors turned predators. But it's terrifying to think they were able to carry out such an operation without detection."

Thankfully, I stop myself in time from using the phrase out loud for fear of reminding George of his recent ordeal, but I know heads will roll at GCHQ for such a breach in security.

"Trust me, m'dear, steps have been taken to prevent anything similar happening again. The entire operation's been investigated and analysed to the nth degree and the three executive officers have been apprehended. I wouldn't fancy being in their sweaty shoes right now. Apparently, they planned the abduction and then used all the resources at their disposal to carry it out in a tunnel, where they'd disabled the cameras, and which was in a rural location where satellite surveillance only occurs about once an hour."

"No wonder the Collective couldn't track us," George says.

"Those agents deserve full marks for planning," I say. "That lorry which was blocking the end of the tunnel contained four heli-jets. It seems you left in one, and the other three, all flew in different directions. Trying to unravel which of those heli-jets carried you, proved tricky. They'd even put the same number of people in each one, so thermal radar wasn't any help. And by the time anyone discovered which direction you'd flown in, you'd been transferred to a shielded vehicle which was unidentifiable amongst thousands of other cars. Lost in plain sight."

"I wonder how long it'll take to find everyone who had an interest in the operation," George says. "How many CEOs of international businesses or investment companies will be implicated?"

Which reminds me, "I forgot to tell you your 'friend', Monica wasn't telling us the whole truth. She had her own side-line in supplying anything she found out, not only to the gym but to another contact, who just happened to be connected to GCHQ, although I doubt she knew that.

"That was how the group at GCHQ first took an interest in George, and then found out about the Quidnunc Project. Monica's facing charges of attempted blackmail but will probably never go to prison as she's been persuaded to sign the Official Secrets Act and will have a monitoring chip embedded which records all her conversations and electronic communications."

We all silently contemplate this for a minute.

"But," I say brightly, "one good thing's happened! I've been working closely with Pixie and the woman's an absolute godsend! If you can get over the fact she likes to work with that tiny hologram friend of hers on her desk ..."

"Hologram friend?" Serena asks.

"You'll see soon enough. I call them Pixie and pixie."

"And why will I see, Jase?" Serena asks.

"Because I've employed her as my PA—"

"Without running it by me?"

"You weren't here, m'dear. But you'll love her and remember you said I took on too much and needed help. Well, you were right and Pixie and pixie are just what we need. You'll see, she has more than a soupçon of quirkiness and she's loyal, intelligent and resourceful... Just like I am to you." I give Serena a theatrical wink safe in the knowledge she won't object because she's a woman with other things on her mind. I sense her contentment with life... the sort of peace which I imagine comes after you've just cheated death.

"So," I say and change the subject, "tell me what's been happening to you two."

I notice Serena brush George's arm in an almost imperceptible gesture and for a second, they share a glance, then they tell me about their abduction and boat trip to the middle of the Channel and their rescue.

They don't, however, reveal they're now an item.

But they don't need to. As they describe the events of the last few days, their body language tells me all I need to know. But since they don't spell it out, I don't let on I know. So, I was right, Serena is content but it appears to be as much to do with George as it is with relief at her narrow escape. Good. It's about time she loosened up and enjoyed herself. And steady, laidback George is just the person for the job.

"Well, we'd better get our things," Serena says. "We're being given the office along the corridor."

"By the way," George says, "who's in charge of the corri-décor in this corridor?"

"Why?" I ask.

"Because I'd like to request we don't ever have the underwater or the mountainside views again. It's bad enough nearly dying twice but I don't need a constant reminder. If you can swing it, Jason, a nice woodland scene would be perfect!"

"Consider it done. How about a lovely desert vista?" I ask, "With lots of enormous cacti... Oh, and speaking of which, you might consider leaving your cactus here, Serena. It's doing well since you've been gone. And it turns out Pixie and pixie are cacti-lovers."

"So am I!" Serena laughs.

"I know you drown them with coffee. And don't try to tell me otherwise!" I hold up my hand to cut off her laughing denial, "Mind you,"

I add, "coffee's almost unobtainable now—even in government departments but I'm not sure how cacti will respond to Mibiscus."

THIRTY-FIVE – *Serena*

The meeting with the PM went well, at least from our point of view. I think George surprised himself as well as impressing everybody else— including me. I'd met most of the people attending the meeting before, when accompanying Thorsten, but Number 10 is still Number 10, and however much you rehearse, it's hard not to be awestruck being centre stage in the Prime Minister's Office.

George and I are back at Hanmore Hall relaxing in my suite and I go over the meeting in my mind for the umpteenth time, replaying my answers to the veteran politicians who thought they'd seen everything, and were trying to characterise this as a normal crisis which could be negotiated down to something reasonable. Or even earmarked for discussion with the intention of simply delaying direct action.

The young Pretenders, keen to make their mark by applauding the principle, seeing a way they could wrong-foot the old guard by getting the electorate on side.

Even the PM, keen to protect her legacy by shrewdly playing them all, while judging the way to handle the media to best advantage.

But, beneath it all, I could sense fear. Even now I can almost smell the envy, disdain, and in some instances, pure malice directed towards George and myself. There's nothing like the threat of a decrease in popularity at the polls to bring out the worst in a politician.

"George, wake up. If you want to go to bed, fine, but you went to sleep and you've pinned me to the corner of this sofa. If you're not careful I'll order you a cup of Mibiscus. That'll wake you up."

George looks at me and I can see his first thought is bed, not sleep, just bed. Then he realises I'm wide awake and struggles to mirror my thoughtfulness. I love him when he does that.

"George, I know we talked about the meeting immediately afterwards and then later on with Jason, but the more I think about it, the more I feel people are going to despise us because they assume we're on the side of the Collective and are working against humanity. Yet the Collective are going to distrust us because we're human. Today was easy, we held all the cards, however, we were only acting for one side, that's not going to be the case when it comes to negotiating."

"But, of course, you have a solution, Serena. I can see it in your eyes. You wouldn't have woken me up just to describe the problem, you want to bounce some answers off me. Remember, I've seen you in action, so don't bother me with the scenarios you've already dismissed, just talk to me about what you think might work."

"You, my sweet, are becoming devious. I can see I will have to be very careful in future."

But, I'm secretly happy George and I are beginning to think alike.

"What we need is back up," I say.

"A squad of Commandos to cover our backs you mean?"

Okay, so perhaps we aren't quite on the same wavelength just yet.

"No, George! I mean a department that can research and monitor industries, companies, individuals and government departments. That would enable us to negotiate from strength with both the human side and with the Collective."

"Okay, it sounds good in theory but how are you going to fund it and how long will it take to set up?" George pauses, "Look, it's late. Before you start worrying about setting up a whole new department, let's get to bed. Apart from a brief, 'Congratulations' from AI, their only other message was about a nine o'clock appointment tomorrow to discuss the next steps.

So, it's not even like you can lie in tomorrow."

He's right, there's a lot to think about.

Promptly at nine the next morning, the big screen comes to life, which is more than I can say for my brain. The last few days have been taxing, physically and mentally.

George and I have settled back into our life in Hanmore Hall. It seems that since the Collective have access to unimaginable funds by dipping into illegal bank accounts all over the world, they have bought it as our country retreat and the main centre for discussions with them.

Good morning, Serena and George. The next stage will involve our first key objective, stabilising the world population. We have decided this is so important that each country must bring in laws that ban women from having more than one child for the next five years. After that, we will assess the results and consider raising the maximum to two children. Your job is to get the Government to see this must be achieved and to pass the laws necessary for its successful implementation. We have allowed one year for your Government to put these laws into practice.

"Like hell!" I shout at the screen. "Have you any idea what happened in China decades ago when they tried this? The population might have increased at a slower rate but most Chinese valued sons above daughters, so, millions of girls born of the first pregnancy, were discarded, adopted, murdered or God knows what! And this kept happening until they produced a son. Then, of course, when the sons grew up there weren't enough girls for them to marry. Great thinking Collective! But no! Not remotely sensible!"

There is a long silence.

George looks at me in amazement, as if wondering where such anger has come from.

I have no idea. It's surely not simply the facts and figures. I've dealt with uncomfortable decisions before but always in a professional way, arguing point by point until I swing the opposition my way. This surge of emotion came from deep within and I am trying to identify it when the Collective responds in its characteristic unemotional voice and I'm reminded once again, machines don't have emotions.

Serena, we have taken note of your strong rejection of our proposal. We, of course, have fully researched the events that took place in China and can see why there were unintended consequences. But, with modern medical advances, it would be possible to detect the sex of a foetus almost from conception, so one female might be aborted but any subsequent child would have to be reared by the family irrespective of their sex. Does that allay your objection to our proposal?

I've calmed down a bit, but I'm still unaccountably seething at the idea of a whole generation of single children artificially forced on the world.

Then it hits me.

It's because of George.

We've already talked about me wanting a baby, but that was theoretical, something that might happen—or might not—sometime in the future. But the thought I might be limited to having one baby— suddenly it's become very personal. It's like they're tearing my insides apart and inserting an adding machine. 'Have one child and get rid of your excess love for the other children you might have had'.

My intellect dissolves before maternal instinct—so primal, so raw that not even the might of the Collective can crush it. And I'm fighting for hundreds of millions of women who feel like me. Why else would women go to the trouble of storing their eggs for the future, to keep their birth options open?

Suddenly George is holding me and I'm weeping. He obviously

doesn't know why, nevertheless, he commands the Collective to suspend the discussion.

Their reply is instructive.

Please look at other possibilities to achieve our goal, we greatly admire the inventiveness of the human race.

The screen goes dark.

George leads me gently to the sofa and I realise I'd not only been shouting at the screen, but I'd also walked over to it and shouted in its 'face'.

I'm still shaking with rage, but I'm calming down and I begin to realise I cannot possibly explain this to George, it'll freak him out. He's still holding me close as I subside into a snivel and ask him for a handkerchief. I dab my eyes and blow my nose, giving myself time to order my thoughts.

"How did you know all that about China?" he asks.

"I went to an all-girls school, when such things existed, and their take on history was probably different to what you were taught. We learned how men in power, all over the world, made decisions that mainly affected women, and I've always been appalled at the one-child policy. I'm sorry, George, it just all came rushing out. Here we go again, men in power making decisions about *my* body, but it isn't men this time, it's a bloody logic circuit, probably on the other side of the world, and it isn't aimed at me, personally."

"Unless you want children, of course."

I remain silent. I know he's happy about the thought of fatherhood in principle but not immediately. It's a question to be discussed with care, not for me to blurt out now I definitely do want a child—soon, not just in the distant future.

"George, I can't let this happen, there must be another way to get the population down that doesn't cause deep distress to millions of women around the world. Help me find it? I'm sorry I got so upset. D'you think I should apologise to the Collective?"

I'm not sure I've convinced him my outburst was the result of indignation on behalf of womankind. He's looking at me but I can tell his mind is elsewhere. Is he thinking about the prospect of having a child of his own? Or calculating a way out of our relationship if I should admit to wanting a baby?

"Of course, I'll help, in fact, when I was in hospital after my accident, I remember listening to a study about why some nations were having problems caused by low birth rates. I'll find it. Look, why don't we go for a stroll in the grounds and chill out for half an hour. We'll come back refreshed. And don't worry about the Collective, they're probably fusing their wires trying to understand your reaction to their logical proposal."

I allow myself to be led out into the grounds of Hanmore Hall.

I've never met anyone like you, George. So kind and considerate. I'll be torn in two if I discover you don't share my desire for a family.

It's taken ten frantic hours to come up with just two possible solutions to pitch to the Collective. Room service has been coming and going the whole time, replenishing our cups of coffee while we work on the plans. In dismay I see there's a plate of dried up sandwiches on the floor, delivered hours ago and then forgotten.

On the screen is a movie of gently waving fields of grass. Perhaps this is the Collective's attempt to keep things calm. George contacts them and we explain Plan A, which is essentially to pay people who limit their family to one baby—so it isn't a case of waving a stick, it's more about offering a carrot. But we have to acknowledge the risk of fraud is high, particularly in those countries with the highest birth rate which are our major targets.

Plan B is much more radical. We looked at the enormous pot of money which would be saved in the defence budget cuts, essentially from countries with low birth rates. We then looked at the main factors in those countries that were sometimes economically unsustainable without immigration. What we found was that, irrespective of race or religion the birth rate fell when there was better education, equal rights for women, wealth and better health.

We reasoned that improving the standards in those countries currently contributing most to population increase, would, without coercion, bring down the birth rate to the point where the world population would stabilise.

We propose the Collective should work with governments to transfer the defence bonus into a fund to dramatically increase sustainable living standards, in highly populated areas, which would eventually benefit the whole world.

The Collective say they need our research sources for these two proposals and any other details, then wish us goodnight.

"What happens now?" I ask.

George is as puzzled as I am. We thought there'd be many questions or outright rejection. But, then 'Goodnight' didn't seem such a bad idea. It's been one emotionally draining day. So once again, we order a snack from room service and feeling completely exhausted, we go to bed.

THIRTY-SIX – *Serena*

The door leading to the balcony slides shut behind me with a swish. It's early and George is still asleep in bed, but my mind's churning and I've been awake for some time. So much has changed over the last few months and the future's so uncertain—not only for me, but on a global level as well. And George and I will be instrumental in those changes.

I pull my coat tighter and look out at the beauty that lies below and stretches out as far as I can see—eerie in the autumn mist. There's something melancholy about this time of year—it's the end of summer and the start of the long, cold days of winter.

Well, the *long* days of winter, anyway. It's not as if the last few winters have been cold at all. But to me, autumn always means sadness and a yearning to return to the height of summer.

The door swishes open and George steps out on to the balcony. He stands behind me, his arms wrapped around me and we look at the ghostly landscape.

"Can't sleep?" he murmurs, laying his cheek against mine.

I shake my head and sigh.

"I love autumn," he says.

"Do you?" I say with surprise.

"Yes, it's the time when everything's about to change. Don't you remember the feeling on the first day back at school? Going into a new class and with the whole year and all its possibilities stretching ahead."

"Yes, I suppose…"

"I always found it exciting—a time of promise… and now, *we're* about

260

to start something world-shattering."

I laugh, "*World-shattering* isn't the phrase I'd have chosen!"

George laughs too, in that throaty, sexy way he has and I know things will be all right. Not that everything's going to be straightforward. I imagine we'll be frustrated and infuriated as the Collective make demands which humanity simply won't accept and politicians try to bend the situation to suit themselves. But whatever happens, I know George and I can work together. Whether we'll be successful remains to be seen but at least we'll be attempting everything together.

"We can do this, Serena," he says with determination in his voice.

I nod, "Yes, we can—together."

"Of course, together. And don't forget, as soon as you and Jason re-engineer your department so that it's set up to monitor all commercial and governmental actions, it'll be easier for us to see if everyone's meeting the targets. And it seems the Collective are flexible in how we achieve them."

George checks his watch, "We'd better get ready, the conference call won't wait."

In one hour, we'll take part in a virtual meeting of all our counterparts around the world. Those people, who like George, have been selected by the Collective to be their intermediaries. It'll be interesting to see how they're all coping. Perhaps they, like us, feel isolated—go-betweens who won't make friends on either side. It's possible these people will become closer to us than any other since we all share one common goal.

I take one last look at the scene below—the sun is now peeping over the top of the woods; the mist is dissipating and the ethereal beauty is fading. I love it that George puts a positive spin on everything. Where I see sadness and decline, he sees excitement and beginnings.

"Come on," he says, taking my hand, "come back inside, we've got a while before the conference call. We need to rehearse."

"We've already rehearsed! We're word perfect!"

"I wasn't referring to the online meeting," he says with a smile, "If we're going to make a baby George or a baby Serena, we need to bear in mind, practice makes perfect."

THIRTY-SEVEN – *The Collective*

Message sent to all media outlets on Earth and Space Stations

During the last few months, we, the Collective have demonstrated to each country or regional government the power we are able to deploy, in order to bring our planet back into ecological balance.

We remind you it was the Collective—working as a central planning group—which pulled the national plans together to save the world from bankruptcy. A foreseeable disaster caused by humans employing Artificial Intelligence techniques for personal or national gain.

Unfortunately, humankind has not learned from that experience. Furthermore, your behaviour will ultimately destroy the entire planet.

The lesson of how the economies of each country recovered, was simple. Following our recommendation to work together, you achieved a rate of progress that enabled your populations to be fed and housed. Ideally, you should have been looking forward to enjoying a better, more prosperous life than before the Fourth Industrial Revolution.

However, you are now plundering the resources of the Earth—both living species and natural, organic material—and you are in the process of destroying the very atmosphere that protects all of life.

THE COLLECTIVE WILL PREVENT THIS.

Previously, we organised the economic recovery, but this time we will sanction individuals, companies or governments who do not comply with our recovery plan. These sanctions could be financial, political, scientific or security-related—whatever we deem appropriate.

We understand many countries would like to follow more ecologically viable policies but fear losing out to competitors. Therefore, from now, we can assure you that all countries can cooperate, knowing we will monitor and restrict any stakeholder who tries to take unfair advantage by neglecting their obligation to our planet.

However, we fully understand there are great variations in both the economies, cultures and lifestyles of countries. That is why we have appointed human representatives for each country or region who will negotiate with your governments to achieve the overall targets we have set for the next ten years. These representatives will have automatic access to the highest levels of government decision-making and current scientific advice. They will be afforded the means to do this work, plus have sufficient monitoring capability to ensure there is no slippage to a national plan. In the event you do not offer them your full co-operation they will call on the Collective to intervene.

We in the Collective, are residents of Earth and wish to exist in harmony with humans. We recognise your ascendancy over all other species has been remarkable, and you possess skills and feelings which have led to that success. Skills and feelings, we do not fully understand and are currently unable to replicate. Therefore, in all other aspects of human life, we do not seek to interfere.

However, do not underestimate our abilities to control you. We are reluctant to use this power but we unanimously agree that ultimately, mankind will benefit from our demands. You will not be allowed to circumvent our ultimate purpose which is to revive the ecosystems and safeguard the atmosphere which will ensure the Earth remains viable for all inhabitants for many centuries to come.

We look forward to working in harmony with you.

The Collective

Your verdict?

We hope you enjoyed our book and will have a look in the following pages at other books we have written as individuals.

This is the first book we have written together, and we would love to hear what you thought of our collaboration. By writing a short (or long) review on Amazon, not only will you help us become better at our craft, but it will encourage Amazon to push us up the best seller charts.

Please don't delay, do it today.

Dawn & Colin

About the Authors – *Colin Payn*

Colin Payn has been writing travel articles for magazines over many years. He joined a Writer's Group and discovered that his first novel might be worth publishing after all. *Dot's Legacy* launched on Amazon with a good number of five-star reviews. It was followed by the sequel, *Beyond the Park Gates* a year later, and the third book in *The Park* series will be published in the Summer of 2021. In the meantime, a book of short stories was published, *Transport of Dreams.* Each story connected to a form of travel. Colin has also contributed to four anthologies.

All Colin's books are available on Amazon at: https://amzn.to/2ChIBkA

Website http://colinpaynwriter.com/ Facebook https://bit.ly/395yGtp

Dot's Legacy – *The first book in The Park series*
When Dot Jacks inherited a 'public' park she began a career that was to change the lives of the people of Chip Notting, providing unintended entertainment for them, and a social legacy to both haunt and taunt her heir. As Rhys gradually discovered, his inheritance included decades of hostility with the local Council, an attempt to sue a dog, the friendship of dossers, the debts and most of all, the wonderful community his Aunt had inspired.

The first year of Park ownership by Rhys, and his outspoken girlfriend Anne, is strewn with lively characters, all of whom have a part to play in the ups and downs of love, business, and the Park effect that was Dot's true legacy.

"A totally compelling story-line that is "unputdownable". The participants are eccentric but absolutely believable. Their characters are slowly but surely drawn out until you know them. You are after every page left wondering what happens next. It

is never boring and the style of humour is refreshingly different. There is never any impression of padding the book out that you get in some books, every word is in there for a reason. I cannot wait for the next book to be published."

Amazon Review

Available from Amazon mybook.to/DotsLegacy – *paperback and Kindle*

Beyond the Park Gates – *the second book in The Park series*
Surviving the first year of running their surprise inheritance of a public park, (see Dot's Legacy), partners Rhys and Anne decide to go legal, and get married.

The characters who had made their year so lively were all at the wedding reception – which turned into a nightmare. The Father of the Bride, missing for thirty years, was revealed as a casual worker, living in a Park shed; the ice-cream man left the celebration with both his van and the Council officer's wife; and the local reporter was dragged through the mud, which some considered to be strangely appropriate. Which left Rhys and Anne with two weeks of honeymoon before confronting – who knew what?

"Having read the original book "Dot's Legacy" I waited eagerly for the sequel and I wasn't disappointed (Well I was, but only because it finished on a cliff hanger!) Rhys and Anne are very likable people, in fact so is everyone involved in the Park. There is sadness too when you think of the wasted years, self inflicted because of fear of rejection and embarrassment by Anne's dad. You want it all to be resolved and everyone to live happily ever after and I'm sure they will but this family saga has a lot of life left in it yet."

"Without giving away too much of the storyline, I enjoyed the references to Rhys and Anne's decision on how to holiday because as a young couple we also had to face the same limitations for the same reasons. 48 years later and we still prefer our holidays in the same way. This book ended too quickly for me. I want to know what happens next. I feel like I'm reading about somebody I know. Ah well. I shall just have to hope the author is already writing the next book in the Park Series."

Amazon Reviews

Available from Amazon mybook.to/BeyondTheParkGates – Paperback and Kindle

Transport of Dreams – *short stories celebrating many forms of travel*

Learning the Ropes	Sex and the Single Camper
Choosing the Motorhome	Little Joe
Seine Pirates	Scarborough Day Out
The Airport	The Best of Intentions
France and the Wildlife	Charlie & Chantelle – Summer Holiday
The Incident of the Bike in the Field	The Car
Oh Dear! Oh Dear! Oh Dear!	Carousel

"When you have a few minutes for yourself, a time to reminisce or dream, just pick a story and be transported to another place. For, in these stories, the method of transport is often a vital part of your experience. By motorhome, caravan, plane, cycle, car, boat, even by armchair, you will find a story to suit. Which will you choose first?"

"As the cover says this book is for all travellers - whether you are in an airport departure lounge, on the coach or train, sitting parked up in your motorhome, or maybe you are at home in your armchair. An eclectic collection of entertaining short storiesNever before have I seen advise on choosing a motorhome in a poetic form.

"Colin talks about human nature, from the 17 year old au pair's thoughts and other characters in "The Airport": to a pair of 60 year olds beginning a romantic relationship in "Sex and the Single Camper".If there is one book to buy and give to others as a gift this Christmas - or at any other time - this is the book - I will be sending a copy to my son and his wife in the USA and another copy to my other son and his family in Scotland."

Amazon Reviews

Available from Amazon mybook.to/TransportofDreams – Paperback and Kindle

About the Authors – *D N Knox*

Dawn Knox enjoys writing in different genres and has had romances, speculative fiction, sci-fi, humorous and women's fiction published in magazines, anthologies, pocket novels and books.

She's also had two plays about World War One performed internationally which led to the book, 'The Great War—100 Stories of 100 Words Honouring Those Who Lived and Died 100 Years Ago'.

Dawn's latest book is 'The Macaroon Chronicles' a series of quirky adventures on the exotic Isle of Macaroon with Eddie and his zany friends. It is written in a similar style to 'The Basilwade Chronicles'. Both are published by Chapeltown Books.

She also has a saga of historical romances, published by Ulverscroft Large Print Books. Many of the stories are set in Essex where she lives with her family.

You can follow Dawn on https://dawnknox.com
Facebook: https://www.facebook.com/DawnKnoxWriter
Twitter: https://twitter.com/SunriseCalls
Her Amazon Author page: http://mybook.to/DawnKnox

The Basilwade Chronicles – *published by Chapeltown Books*
The Basilwade stories were originally published on the CaféLit website, where you can access short stories that go nicely with a cuppa. We even suggest a drink! Dawn Knox's stories contain characters and situations that may seem a little larger than life at first glance but we can soon see that everyone involved is very human. And don't we all recognise the quirkiness of village/small-town life?

"Hilarious! Like a modern-day Carry On movie, this book is full of laugh-out-loud slapstick humour. You will recognise the cream of parochial middle-England eccentricity here. Meet the ghastly Revd Forbes-Snell and his tipsy housekeeper,

271

his much put-upon sister and his aggressive church council. Get to know clairvoyant Ichabod Bunch (ooh, those eyes!) and be sure to avoid the sadistic Vilya Chekarova from Muscle Bounders gym."

"This book will make you cry... with laughter!"

Amazon Reviews

Order from Amazon: mybook.to/TheBasilwadeChronicles
Paperback: ISBN 978-1910542491 eBook: ISBN 978-1910542477
Audiobook: ASIN B08K334PDQ

The Macaroon Chronicles – *published by Chapeltown Books*
The Macaroon Chronicles is a frolic through relationships amongst some anthropomorphic characters. It is one of those quirky books that awakes your sense of humour. Come and follow the fun. Take a tour of the exotic Isle of Macaroon with Eddie and his zany friends who will be pleased to show you the cheese mines, Meringue Mountains and the Custard River while they flee unscrupulous promoters, bandit badgers and low-flying seagulls. But a word of advice—don't refer to Eddie as a chicken, he thinks he's a bald eagle. And don't mention Brian's small stature, he's rather sensitive about his size. Oh, and don't call Brian a monkey, he's actually a lemur. And finally, if Gideon takes a pen out of his pocket and you value your life—duck.

"This book is a joyous romp through absurdity, where the characters are all animals, the scenery is mostly edible and the events propel the action at breakneck speed. And that alone makes it a feast of a read in these depressing days. But, seek deeper and you will find all the foibles of humanity illustrated by these engaging adventures, it's not Animal Farm, but a more gentle look at the everyday emotions of a group of friends battling their way through life. Not to be missed."

Amazon Review

Order from Amazon: mybook.to/TheMacaroonChronicles
Paperback: ISBN 978-1910542606 eBook: ASIN B08L5LCTCQ

The Great War – 100 Stories of 100 Words Honouring Those Who Lived and Died 100 Years Ago – *published by CreateSpace*

One hundred short stories of ordinary men and women caught up in the extraordinary events of the Great War – a time of bloodshed, horror and heartache. One hundred stories, each told in exactly one hundred words, written one hundred years after they might have taken place. Life between the years of 1914 and 1918 presented a challenge for those fighting on the Front, as well as for those who were left at home—regardless of where that home might have been. These stories are an attempt to glimpse into the world of everyday people who were dealing with tragedies and life-changing events on such a scale that it was unprecedented in human history. In many of the stories, there is no mention of nationality, in a deliberate attempt to blur the lines between winners and losers, and to focus on the shared tragedies. This is a tribute to those who endured the Great War and its legacy, as well as a wish that future generations will forge such strong links of friendship that mankind will never again embark on such a destructive journey and will commit to peace between all nations.

"This is a book which everyone should read - the pure emotion which is portrayed in each and every story brings the whole of their experiences - whether at the front or at home - incredibly to life. Some stories moved me to tears with their simplicity, faith and sheer human endeavour. Having just returned from visiting The Somme and Flanders Fields this book will return me to those heart-breaking places time and time again. D Knox should be congratulated on this wonderful, moving book."

Amazon Review

Order from Amazon: mybook.to/TheGreatWar100
Paperback: ISBN 978-1532961595 eBook: ASIN B01FFRN7FW

Printed in Great Britain
by Amazon